A DAY LATE AND A
BULLET SHORT

A DAY LATE AND A BULLET SHORT

BULLETS TRILOGY BOOK ONE

NICHOLAS OSBORN

WOLFPACK
PUBLISHING
— EST 2013 —

A Day Late and a Bullet Short
Paperback Edition
Copyright © 2024 by Nicholas Osborn

Wolfpack Publishing
1707 E. Diana Street
Tampa, Florida 33610

www.wolfpackpublishing.com

Editing by My Brother's Editor

Paperback ISBN 979-8-89567-083-5
Ebook ISBN 979-8-89567-082-8
LCCN 2024947006

A DAY LATE AND A BULLET SHORT

CHAPTER 1

"*Help!*" A cry came from deep within the trees.

Neon light bled into the night sky through a murky fog as the silhouette of a strange man stumbled through the horizon. While he struggled to walk toward the blue glow cast out into the darkness, he saw salvation few had been able to find in such a place. He'd finally made it close enough to see a large sign responsible for his misplaced hope hung above an old, tattered building that read—Pine Box Bar.

The bar's neon sign buzzed monotonously in the air against a backdrop of woods that made it difficult to see more than a few feet ahead. It was just cold enough to see every exhaled breath, most of all the frantic plumes escaping the man as he continued to walk out into the open street. He moved with trembling knees and shallow breaths as though he could collapse at any moment.

Just as he gained the courage to holler for anyone

close enough to hear, he clutched at his stomach and fell to his knees. The music coming from the bar was faint, but it meant people were there, or at least that's what he was telling himself. He only had to hope it wouldn't drown out his pleas from so far away. With a final ragged breath filling his lungs, he managed to let out just one more word. It was the same word he had repeated over and over again without end, only it was quieter now than he'd ever wished, but it was all he had left.

"*Help*," he muttered again with a raspy whisper before collapsing to the ground with his hands covered in blood.

Just as he fell, a second silhouette broke through the fog that had settled in low to the ground for the evening. It was a woman. Her stride was confident and her long hair draped down her back as though it was reaching for the earth beneath her feet. It took just a few steps before she was staring down at the man gasping for breath. She looked down at him with an unnerving presence as his hand reached upward, begging for mercy where he'd found none yet. Instead of a helping hand to lift him from his misery, the woman extended her arm slowly to reveal a small black revolver grasped in her fingers, nearly hidden by the cover of night. In the blink of an eye, a bright flash blasted from the muzzle, and the man fell lifeless to the concrete. The shot went unnoticed, drowned out by the music of the bar just as he had feared. Without a moment's hesitation, the woman continued on her way.

The clicking sound from the heels of her roughened leather boots went unnoticed as she made her way up the handful of wooden steps leading to the entrance of the bar. When she burst through the double doors, the noise of mundane chatter and blaring music screeched to a complete stop. Everyone looked in her direction, but quickly returned to their vices. With their drunken stupor most likely to blame, no one inside had any idea what had just transpired out in the darkness.

The clatter of pool balls and overly loud conversations mixed with a haze of cigarette smoke filled the air, surrounding the ragtag group of men hovering inside. It was a place found off almost every back road in small-town America, unapologetic in its simplicity, but desperately in need of a serious remodel that no one would ever pony up the cash for.

"What'd ya want?" the lone bartender called out, breaking the silence and queuing up the music to play back again.

"Point 'em out." The woman's voice was as cold as the air outside as she propped herself against the countertop, taking care to put her back to the wall. She allowed her eyes to scan the room just briefly before turning back to the man behind the bar. His belly hung over his waistline and what little hair he did have was slicked back, held only by what looked like a day's worth of built-up sweat.

"Lady, I don't even know who the hell you are. Look around, lots of people come through here asking for only God knows what. That's not my job," the bartender spoke through his frayed mustache, twisting his fist into a glass with a rag. "I *can* get you a drink if you're gonna be hovering over my bar like that though."

"Won't do any good."

She counted six plus the bartender and oddly enough, no other women besides her. The questions in her mind were already starting to pile up, but she had to keep her focus if she hoped to get anything worthwhile out of all this. She was here for a reason and wouldn't allow herself to be distracted, not after she'd come so far.

"Maybe you can start by telling me who you are looking for?" the bartender questioned while toiling away at his work.

"It ain't who," the woman said out of the side of her mouth with an encroaching attitude. "It's what."

The music continued to blast, but no one in the bar was moving anymore. Everyone's attention was focused on her. It was clear the situation had taken a turn for the worst, and the woman carried herself as though she was the cause. A smirk crossed her face as she glanced out of the corner of her eyes to make sure no one was trying to pull a fast one before it was too late.

"Take it easy now, assholes," she quipped. "I'll get to you real soon, promise."

"We just don't want any trouble," the bartender replied for them, gesturing defenseless with his hands raised into the air for whatever good it may do him.

"Sure you don't," she said, rolling her eyes back over to the mustached man behind the bar. "I'm after a family heirloom, have been almost all my life. So, before you go rattling off any more rehearsed questions, I'll tell you what I already know and save you some time. I know it isn't here, and I know you are about to tell me you have no idea where it's at. What you can do though, is point one of those fat sausage fingers of yours right at one of the damned drunks behind me so I can go ahead and get to work."

"They'll kill us both," he whispered.

"I doubt that."

The woman turned her attention to the threatened men in the bar who had abandoned any intention of blending in. They were all facing her, bracing themselves for things to get out of hand. She'd put more than a few regular barfly-type bullies in their place before, but these guys weren't just anyone. They were Pinkertons, hired agents built on a legacy earned in violence and bloodshed. Luckily, it wasn't her first time dealing with their type either.

The bartender, on the other hand, was completely out of his league. He cowered down as far as his worn-out knees would allow him, unsure of what was about to happen next but all too certain he didn't want to be involved.

"Since you've all just been standing around like a bunch of jackasses waiting for me to waltz in, that must mean you need something from me." The mysterious woman was growing more serious by the second and letting her demeanor show it. "So, here's what I'll do. I'm gonna put a bullet or two in each one of you, but I'll leave one of you alive. Then, I'm just gonna hope that one person lucky enough to be able to suck air in his lungs can use it to answer every single one of my questions. Because if not, I can damn sure promise only those fiery pits of what you call hell will be waiting."

A steel guitar crying out from the jukebox in the corner faded from one song to the next. They all stood motionless amid the harsh smell of cigarette smoke still blanketing the area as they listened to a new song crank up.

Before anyone could answer, one of the men started to laugh. His shoulders jerked up and down as he chuckled at first before bursting into a boisterous laugh that echoed through the bar. He slapped his leg a few times and looked toward the men at the pool tables when they joined in on the fun. Before the mysterious woman knew it, everyone but the bartender was having a laugh at her expense.

"Who is this bitch kidding?" The man's words were forced through his laugh before he managed to find a more serious tone. "Well sweetheart, you can walk in here and talk all the shit you want, but you got one thing wrong. We sure as shit don't need you."

It was after these words were uttered that the surrounding men in the bar began to take notice of exactly who they were instigating. The woman who had burst through the doors moments before carried a presence that could only be described as unsettling. At first glance, she wasn't particularly large or imposing, but she wasn't someone to be underestimated. The keener of the men did more than just feel her presence, they saw her for who she was. They saw her bruised and bloodied knuckles, her worn boots with reddish stains which weren't caused by mud, and most importantly, the piercing look in her eye that went right through anyone unfortunate enough to draw her gaze. The men who did see this began to think twice on what was about to happen.

But the stupid one just didn't know any better.

While he continued his almost incoherent tirade, tossing one pointless insult after another and looking around for any reaction he could latch onto, it also gave the woman a moment to reflect on those who stood before her.

The Pinkerton men she was getting ready to face down may have tried to look like barflies, but they were betrayed by the arms they carried. Only one cradled a short-barreled rifle built for the fight ahead and a polymer pistol clipped to his hip; he was likely the one who fancied himself the sharpshooter of the bunch. The others carried interchangeable steel hand-guns, shotguns, or for one of the men who clearly had other issues—a combination of the two. It seemed the longer the woman studied the group, the more weapons she saw on them.

None of that changed the fact it was six armed men and one bartender that she was staring down. Numbers never lied to her, and they certainly weren't about to start now. These were odds the woman would take every single time. If only she could get the dumb one to shut up.

"You hear me, you son of a bitch?" He spoke up a bit more this time, leaning forward and looking as though he was ready to get in her face.

"You actually run these jackoffs?" she said finally, turning her stare to the annoying one. "I bet you're the one I need to speak to a bit more privately. Aren't you?"

He finally paused to think. He knew his next words should be chosen wisely, but unfortunately for him, he lacked the wisdom needed to choose correctly.

"You ain't going to do shit—"

Pop.

The pesky man's threat was cut short by the cracking sound of a bullet striking right between his eyes. He mumbled nonsensically for only a second longer before a drop of blood appeared on his forehead and streaked down the bridge of his nose, then down his right cheek.

It wasn't the startling sound of the gunshot from the woman leaned against the wall that put everything in motion, setting the bar into complete chaos. For just a few excruciatingly long seconds, everyone stood in uncertain silence. Unfortunately for the men still left alive, that wouldn't last forever, because it was the sound of the dumb one's now lifeless body thumping to the dirty floor that did the trick.

Two more gunshots rang out immediately. Opposing muzzle blasts and residue spewing into the smoke-ridden air of the old bar resulted in one ricocheted bullet striking the wall next to the woman, and the other causing one man at the pool table to slump over before he could even lift his pistol. The woman had already downed two just as the fight started, but the bursts of two rapid shots from the sharpshooter threatened to change all of that.

The woman ducked behind the bar to her right as two shots went blazing just above her head. Only a second later, two more struck just inches from where she had just sat. Before she could think, two more shots whizzed by over the bar. The gun hand was covering for the others. She waited until another two rounds sunk into the bar then broke cover and started working from right to left. The next few seconds happened as just a blur.

A flipped table signaled her first target. Gripping her 1911 pistol in both hands close to her chest, she popped out from behind cover, pushed her gun out, and fired the first round, just as a man tried to steal a peek from behind the table. Before his body could sink to the ground, she had put two more bullets into the stomach of another who had hesitated in the firefight a few seconds too long. He grabbed at his gut frantically as if he was trying to hold his blood inside himself and fell in seconds. She got just one more shot off, but before she could pull the trigger again, a burning sensation jolted through her left arm and caused her to wince in pain. She ignored it completely and fired three more rounds at the shooter in the corner who was doing his best to keep her pinned down.

Squatting for just long enough to eject the magazine in her pistol and jam a new one in, she noticed the bartender lying face down behind the bar next to her. He was terrified. Blood ran down her arm where she had been struck, but she paid it no attention. She pushed her index finger to her lips and winked at the bartender instead.

As bullets kept flying by, a loud boom rocked through the building overhead and forced the woman to fall lower for cover. Then, another blasted into the bar. One of the men had broken out the shotgun, and that meant her time was running out even faster. She laid on the floor and caught a view at an angle through a reflection in the one bottle that hadn't been blown to pieces yet, only to see the man with a shotgun moving for cover behind a table across the room. She moved quickly, firing three bullets into his gut before he released his grip on the 12-gauge pump and let it fall to the ground. His moans carried throughout the rafters of the old bar almost as loudly as the sounds of his abandoned shotgun.

"That's five you know," she yelled out to the sharpshooter still tucked behind cover in the corner. "You ready to talk now?"

"Sure," he yelled back, ignoring his buddy's dying pleas for help. "Step on out from behind that bar and we'll talk all night long. Just you and me, like we can't get enough of each other."

"I told you I'd leave one of you assholes."

"You go ahead and throw that gun down and come out then," he said. "I'm all that's left, and I know all about that heirloom you were just going on about. Probably more than you, even."

Moments later, a 1911 pistol was tossed out from behind the bar. It hit the ground hard and slid across the floor until it slammed to a stop under a scratched up wooden table that had gained a few new dings in the firefight. The unmistakably unique black pearl handles that glistened in the neon as it slid, revealing the outline of a rose etched into both sides. The woman's voice followed quickly behind; she was still yelling over the ringing in her ears even though the place had fallen silent in the ceasefire.

"I'm coming out now. You do the same."

The man gently leaned out from behind cover, but kept his firearm trained right on the bar ahead. "Is this the part where I answer all of your goddamn questions?"

"You tell me where the Eternal Flame is, I walk my happy ass out those doors. Simple as that."

"I didn't really hear a question in there."

"Do you want to walk out those doors yourself, or do you want to get carted out in a bag in about an hour? How's that?"

The sharpshooter didn't seem too eager to sacrifice himself in the fight, but he knew the deal. He was only as good as the information he could give to her and that wasn't much. The woman stepped out from behind the bar and the two locked gazes. Instead of firing a round off at her, he paused to get a glimpse just a moment longer. There was a desperation in her eyes that made him linger.

It was all the time in the world for her.

The woman effortlessly drew the same small revolver she used outside the bar from behind her back, then squeezed the trigger. She squeezed it again and again and again. She didn't stop until a dry fire round click of the hammer coming down with no effect for the second time snapped her out of it.

Just as quick as it had started, the fight was over.

The gun hand fell over dead in the corner he had holed himself up in. The rest were either dead alongside him, or on their way soon with ragged breaths and halfhearted cries. The woman glanced around the room, reloaded the revolver she held one bullet at a time, and returned to find the old man bartender still face down mumbling to himself. She used her boot to flip him onto his back and stared down at him, striking nothing but fear into his heart, yet offering him a chance at redemption all the same.

"I said I'd leave one alive. Looks like you're the only one left," she told him. "Name's Rose. I want you to tell me what you heard your fine patrons here talking about tonight. Every damn bit of it."

The bartender lay motionless on the floor and tried in vain to get his voice to work. At first it was a raspy whisper, but all Rose had to do was turn her head and feign hard of hearing for that to change.

"Ranger...Davy," he finally let out in between quick gasps for air. "Works out in Daingerfield. They said he knows something about something. They were after him."

"That wasn't so hard now—was it?"

The man nodded and looked away finally. Every bit as mysteriously as she'd entered the rundown bar, Rose turned to leave, spinning her hair around behind her as she did. Just when she thought she could turn her back, the bartender suddenly yanked up a double barrel sawed-off shotgun he'd been holding onto for dear life during the shootout and aimed it at her.

Rose spun, drawing her small revolver once more to send multiple shots flying out of the two-inch-long barrel. Each bullet sunk deeply into the bartender's chest causing deep red blood to pour through his white shirt and puddle into the ground next to him. His final act in life was to squeeze off a blast of his shotgun into the ceiling of his own establishment. He went lifeless as the debris from the ceiling crumbled and fell down onto him.

"There's always one," she mumbled. "Made a damn liar out of me too."

With everyone in the bar dead, the building riddled with bullet holes and her next destination in mind at last, she turned and walked out of the doors back into the cold night air to slide into the driver's seat of an oversized SUV. The vehicle was probably too big for her by most standards, but now wasn't the time to be picky. Its thundering motor fired right up, and she made her way past the neon glow of the bar, headed east. Her arm was burning now more than ever, but she still chose not to look at it—either out of pride or apprehension—to see just how bad the gunshot was.

Blackened silhouettes of trees reaching toward the stars lined the road ahead as bugs swirled and danced in the headlights. There was a calming familiarity, a placated sense of purpose that fell over her as she stared out across the landscape. As she pulled out of the bar leaving so much death behind her, she looked toward a future that could only be achieved by what she was about to finally hold for herself. It wouldn't just fix her life; it would fix everything—and she'd do just about anything for it.

The sign leaving town said Daingerfield | 311 mi. and Rose cruised right past it without a second thought. Tonight, she was closer than ever to putting to rest a problem that had plagued her family for generations.

CHAPTER 2

Daingerfield State Park Ranger David "Davy" Patton was only just getting familiar with his thirties, but he'd already reached a dire crossroads in his life.

He was unsure of what could come next, or even what should come next if he was being honest with himself, but Daingerfield had been his fifth park in as many years, and he could feel yet another transfer deep in his bones. Until then, all he could do was linger inside the woods he'd always yearned to find something more in. If every cloud really did have a silver lining, Davy's was the simple fact that being a park ranger gave him a chance to pass on the stories that made him who he was. Sitting at the front of an amphitheater with only a handful of listeners scattered throughout the rows of hard concrete seating, Ranger Davy basked in the warm sunlight touching down between the pines that towered above and tossed his cares aside once more.

"There are some who would go down a path of sin, who are wrought with malcontent and determined to prove something out of it, all while saying to hell with the consequences. This will never lead to much of any worth, but for the few willing to suffer through to the end, every so often it can lead the way to something often mistaken for the same—wealth," Davy said. "That was the choice of the outlaw known as Hank Heck in the late 1800s."

Davy wore a full beard and had for quite a while. It matched his lengthy dark brown hair with an occasional red tint in just the right light. This was paired with eyes that always had dark circles tucked away behind a scratched pair of old sunglasses, and a uniform that was neither efficient nor aesthetic, even with the all too memorable park ranger hat resting on top of his head every day. He knew he could be spotted as a park ranger from a hundred yards out and that was just fine for him.

It wasn't the uniform he had a problem with when it came to being a park ranger, it was the boredom.

He wiped gently at a line of sweat that sat above his brow with his forearm, overlooking the generally mundane faces who stared back at him waiting to be entertained—or for him to stop talking—whichever came first. He had seen these same bored faces, time and time again. They had become an unfortunate reflection of himself, but they would almost always leave his park with a smile, just as he did when he'd first heard the story he was about to share.

"He was mean and dangerous, but he was also ambitious. Mr. Heck was the kind of man who could get by no matter where he was, and more often than not—he did a lot more than just get by," Davy continued.

As the gentle breeze brought leaves from oaks and sweetgums down around them, signaling a change coming soon, the park ranger lowered his tone to build anticipation, glancing around to see if it worked.

"Hank Heck was many things, but most knew him only as a killer, a swindler, and a forsaken product of the dying Wild West. It was the kind of reputation that burdened him just about everywhere he went."

It was a story he'd known most of his life and he'd been sharing it twice a week for the past year in Daingerfield State Park, ever since he had been transferred in from Martin Creek Lake. Somehow, every time he told the story, he always found a new way to be interested in it himself. Today was no different.

"Before he became the feared outlaw Hank Heck, known all 'round as one not to be crossed, he was once just a man from Fort Worth, a man no different than anyone else hard pressed for luck at the time. He would make his way from meal to meal with small-time robberies and shenanigans until youthful ambitions pushed him to take on trains and stagecoaches, where the chances of striking it rich were just a little better. After a few years, he discovered that not only had he done just that time and time again, but he also happened to be pretty dang good at it too. Since he was better than anyone he had faced down, or even heard of, it didn't take long for Hank Heck to find himself an ego.

"The life of crime on the run wasn't for every-one…" the ranger trailed off for just a bit to

take a breath and sneak a look around, "but it was for him. He outlived and outgunned just about everyone he faced down and managed to make more than quite a bit of money in his swindles too."

The ranger took notice that a few more faces had joined the group to listen to his tale, as was usually the case. It would continue on like this most days and despite the occasional insistent teenage heckler looking for a quick laugh, the people were usually more interested than not in what he had to say. Meanwhile, Park Ranger Davy went on without paying too much attention to any one face staring blankly back at him.

"While Mr. Heck was still learning the ropes to the life of an outlaw, he managed to get himself shot once or twice, believe it or not," the park ranger continued. "You won't find this in any history books, but one bullet wound he snagged in the shoulder actually forced Hank Heck into the hands of the Caddo Nation from the East Texas area before their forced displace-ment. These particular Nations used the Sabine River to trade and often took advantage of travelers stop-ping at the port down south near Port Arthur. They brought Hank Heck back to health—for a price, of course. After living with them for months and trav-eling back up the Sabine with them, Mr. Heck found his time with the Natives had influenced him more than he thought would ever be possible. As it would turn out, this was mostly because of a woman he met.

"Their connection was brief, yet transformative all

the same. So much so, Hank Heck for the first time came to understand the truth that there was more in the world than just a life of crime as an outlaw. Though he would leave their home, the woman who had caught his undivided attention gave him a way to come back to her with a map she called the Eternal Flame. It wasn't just any map though; this map was a family heirloom that had been passed down in her family between loved ones for as long as their history knew. It was a promise." The ranger gave a brief pause here to let it sink in for those who had become invested in his tale.

The connection between the outlaw and the Caddo woman was probably his favorite part of the story because it had the dramatic, sometimes cheesy flair his favorite old westerns always seemed to romanticize in just the right way. If Davy was anything, he was a sucker for the classics.

"A few months after returning to stealing everything he could lay his hands on, he had come across more opportunities than he could imagine and more money than he knew what to do with. The growing west was full of roaring opportunities at the time and riches were being made in every corner. He exploited and took advantage of just about every single one of them; then he cheated, stole, and even killed when nothing else worked to get the rest. It went on like this for years and neither a bullet nor the law ever caught up to him. Until one day, almost out of nowhere, he faced an even worse problem. It was a problem he almost certainly didn't expect to ever confront in his lifetime," said the park ranger.

"The outlaw Hank Heck was so good at what he did, he ensnared himself a problem that all of us could really only dream to have," Davy continued. "He had too much money to carry."

A few smiles and even a laugh from the people in front of him told the ranger he had their ears at last. Rather than draw the tale out with details that only he would really appreciate—like the time Hank was arrested and only stayed in jail for half an hour before he was out again after escaping through the chimney of the jailhouse and robbing the local bank before the sun had come up—so he went right to the problem at hand.

"All of the cash, gold, jewelry, trinkets, and treasures, plus more than a few precarious deeds, including land, homes, and even one to a general store just outside of Fort Worth, started to quite literally weigh him down. He got larger saddlebags for his horse, then he got more horses, but it quickly grew to be much more than even a team could handle. He moved to a horse pulled wagon, then got himself a few of the stagecoaches he had robbed so often, but his wealth only grew more and more." The park ranger himself was getting into the story even more. "So this time, he had to get a little more creative, because he of all people knew you couldn't trust just any old hand for hire to help him carry what he'd amassed. Everything he'd stolen seemed as though it could fill an entire town square and it wasn't long before Hank Heck couldn't stand the thought of losing a single piece of it. That would be a risk he would never take. He was becoming obsessed, and he wasn't ready to stop just yet, not while he was still in his prime.

"When it was simply too much to carry with him everywhere he went, the outlaw tried his best to find a secret hiding spot," Davy explained carefully. "He searched for a place where he could dig a hole big enough to bury everything he couldn't use. Then he did it again, and again, and again, never placing all he had in one spot. This actually worked for a few months, until one day he came back to one of his secret spots only to find an empty hole in the ground. Though he was smart enough not to put all his worth in the same hole, he knew burying it wasn't ever going to work in the long run, as there would always be others who would come along looking for their piece of the pie."

Davy never really thought this would be where his life as a park ranger would take him. He always dreamed it would be one long adventure; that was far from the case though. He loved the land around him, but he knew there was more out there somewhere. Davy was determined to find it, and while today was as good as any day to request yet another transfer to a different park to do just that, the breeze that circulated through the area was reason enough to stay a little while longer on such a warm day. He paused his story momentarily once more to pull a dinged up one-liter water bottle out of the pack next to his feet for a quick drink. He was getting to the good part now and figured he might as well let the people linger on it just a bit more before he left.

"So, he decided to try his luck in town," said the

ranger as he screwed the lid back onto the bottle and jammed it back into his pack without looking. "Mr. Heck had robbed his fair share of banks in his day, to say the least, and the irony of him needing them now a place to stash his earnings wasn't lost on him. He created a fake name and dressed up in the finest clothing of his wardrobe—taken from a man who directed one too many cuss words at him while he robbed a train one day—and strode into a private Fort Worth bank named Tidball, Van Zandt and Company to give his best shot at depositing nearly his entire fortune."

"Can anyone guess how it turned out for him?" The ranger asked this question both to liven the mood and prevent his wandering mind from going too far. One hand shot up in the air before he knew any better.

"They killed him," her voice rang out coldly, and the amphitheater suddenly found itself

in a more solemn mood.

"Not quite, but I can see how you might think that," the park ranger responded hesitantly to the strange intrusion, trying his best not to be caught off guard. "The bank actually informed the mysterious man who went by Mr. Harold Hadfield, or H.H. for short, that the amount of his deposit was far greater than the privatized bank could personally guarantee. He was asked by a wealthy banker who sat across from him behind an ornate wooden desk dressed in a striped suit far nicer than anything he'd ever seen, to try elsewhere, perhaps at a larger bank who could help accommodate wealth his size."

He stole a few seconds to scan the small crowd of

people, searching for the woman who had been so eager to answer and found her sitting toward the back of the crowd, staring right at him. He didn't know what to make of her, but he knew he wasn't thinking about where he'd be transferring to next anymore.

"It was a rejection he honestly didn't see coming. But when the outlaw Hank Heck saw the powers that be at work in such an immovable way, he concocted one last brilliant scheme," Davy said, pushing onward to the conclusion of his tale. "A solution that would last lifetimes beyond his own."

"At the time, land to homestead wasn't exactly difficult to come by and Mr. Heck realized that he would eventually need to own a place of his own, so he didn't have to rely on those like the smug man sitting across from him at the bank. He would instead rely on what those kinds of men obeyed, and what men like himself had always broken. He would find a place to purchase legally for himself where he could be left to his own devices, large enough to store his treasures out of sight, and far enough away from town where no one would bother to come looking. So, he traveled back to East Texas," the ranger said as he gestured around him broadly. "He purchased a ranch with a few hundred acres from a family desperate to leave the frontier behind them and join the booming city life, and he wasted no time moving in either."

Looking down at his clasped hands, the park ranger finally let out a smile before saying, "And he brought someone with him."

"You see, that was the entire point of his newest plan," Davy continued. "Along with the woman who had stolen his own heart, the two would make a home of their new land growing crops and raising livestock until eventually, they decided on even raising a few kids. Their life on the ranch together was one that Mr. Heck never knew he could have and even better, it was protected by law, along with everything on it or buried beneath it.

"The outlaw wasn't one to settle down, however. He was made for a life of crime on the run, and that's what he did, even while giving the woman he loved so much of the life she'd always wanted. He would leave for days, sometimes weeks at a time, always returning home with a huge smile and even more money, jewelry, and whatever else he could get his hands on to throw on top of the horde of wealth he'd already gathered. It went on like this for years, and while their five kids never really knew what their father was up to when he left the ranch—she knew all too well. She knew that there was no one who could stop him, but she also knew that he would always come home to them. Until one day, he stumbled home for the last time."

The park ranger was nearing the end of his tale and it was as bittersweet as it ever was, like the fleeting feeling of a dream you never want to wake up from. Maybe it was worse this time because of what he planned next, he even felt silly for thinking it, but it was there, nonetheless. Soon, the crowd would disperse and everyone would go back to their activities in the park, and Davy would head down to HQ to let Daingerfield State Park Chief Ranger Tom Wayne know what was on his mind. Before that happened, he

would do his best to leave those listening with something unexpected to ponder and maybe even a dream
or two to chase.

"You see, the woman knew exactly who the outlaw
she'd married really was," Davy finally said. "It was a
long-lasting relationship born of a mutual understanding. But, when he struggled through the front door
after walking for God knows how many miles back
from the Big Thicket, all while trying to plug the bullet
hole in his stomach with only his hands, she knew the
time had finally come and arrangements had to be
made. Even if Hank Heck wouldn't, she would be
certain to put their family before anything else."

The Texas sun was shining a bit brighter through
the tall pines and the gentle breeze had slowed to a
crawl as Davy began to close his story.

"Before she cleaned her husband up or dressed his
wounds, before she got him a drink of water, or called
for her children to come help, she asked him the only
question that needed to be asked—what should she do
with all the money?" The ranger spoke intently, not
wasting any time, and definitely still avoiding eye
contact with that woman in the crowd. "Hank Heck's
response wasn't what she expected. He told her first
that he was sorry. He told her that he regretted
spending his life chasing a treasure he never found
instead of treasuring what was in front of him, and he
told her to do what he never could, raise their family.

"Even Mr. Heck himself knew the wealth they had
acquired was more than any of them could spend in a
lifetime, so anything that was left was to be hidden on
their land with only one way to find it—the Eternal

Flame family heirloom. A map that would always bring them home and a key that would always unlock their future."

Following just a brief pause, he began to speak softly at first as he finally attempted to reel everyone in before the story came to an end.

"Rumors say that over the years since Hank Heck's death, the map of the Eternal Flame had been split into pieces to protect its secrecy by the family it once belonged to. The pieces are said to be found where its fire burns brightest."

Ranger Davy finally stood up from his seat, which was really just an overturned log he'd wiped clean with his bare hand and slung his pack over his shoulders just as he'd done a million times before. The people listening seemed to follow his lead judging from the shuffling sounds as they began gathering their things to leave as well. A sound of rustling backpacks and casual whispered conversation began to swell just as the ranger gave one last comment, making sure he was loud enough for everyone to hear him.

"Some of those pieces may still be hidden right here in Daingerfield. No one has ever found anything, so keep an eye out."

A couple of the people still getting ready to leave the amphitheater laughed halfheartedly, but most paid no attention and continued on with their day, dispersing back into the wilderness of the park to continue on with their lives. Except for one person who sat still in their seat, refusing to move even a single muscle. The ranger did his best to pretend not to notice. Chills went down his spine just from thinking about her.

Forcing himself to make his way to HQ so that he could break the news to chief ranger Tom Wayne about his plans to look for a new park, Davy left the amphitheater for the last time. He was trying his best to ignore the feeling of someone watching every step he took when he found a familiar path—the Rustling Leaves Trail. It stretched out in front of him, winding through the pine trees and around the lake as if it was naturally occurring, lit only briefly where the sunlight could break through the shade from above. Exploring the parks never lost its luster for Davy. It was the same today as it was when he was a child with grand dreams of embarking on an adventure that would put his own name in the history books. He felt himself relax a bit more as he crunched pine needles and leaves beneath each step, thinking back to his naive notions as a child almost made him second-guess what he was about to do.

Whether he was lost in his youthful hopes and ambitions, the thought of moving to another park, or the fear of the woman's stare back at the amphitheater, the mile-long hike back to HQ gave him more time than he would've liked to consider where he was at in life. Usually, he could easily lose himself in his favorite stories like the outlaw Hank Heck, but it was one of those days where a story just wouldn't do. His pace rose and fell with the hills of the park and he finally let himself fall into the familiar rhythm of hiking to avoid letting his thoughts spiral.

Just as he did, he heard a sharp cracking sound

before a jolt of paint rocketed up through his right leg, past his knee, and jarred his hip.

"Son of a—" Davy let out louder than he meant to.

He'd stepped right into a hole that swallowed almost his entire leg, nearly breaking it in the process and knocking the breath out of him. It wasn't like him to be careless on the trail, but then again, he'd walked this trail every day and this particular hole had never been there before. Frustrated, Davy looked down to see the six-inch-round cavity that stretched deep down into the earth.

"Damn armadillos," Davy said.

With his leg trapped, he felt a growing heat begin to creep up his boot and into his leg. At first he mistook it for a burning pain caused by his fall, but it soon turned far more intense than he'd realized. Before he knew what was going on, he was scrambling as fast as he could in a blind panic to crawl out of the hole he found himself in. There was no one around to hear his gasps at the searing heat clawing at his leg or see his mad dash out of the ground. For that, he was thankful.

The blackened ground where he'd just fallen through looked as though it had been a campfire just minutes before. Soot and ash came billowing up before a faint red glow began to seep from below. It was as if something melted its way deep down into the dirt. Davy thought he may have knocked himself out during the fall because his eyes were clearly playing tricks on him. The burning red glow began to pulsate from within the hole and Davy couldn't help himself but to peer inside.

The next few seconds saw his arm buried up to his shoulder as he dug aimlessly in the hole in the ground. The red glow was fading from sight, but the heat was almost enough to burn his skin. Sweat poured into his eyes as he squinted and dug around even harder. Dirt packed beneath his nails and he started to flail his arm in fear that he would lose whatever was down there. Finally, his fingers wrapped around something smooth.

Davy yanked his arm upward and when his hand had finally been freed, he saw a spherical object locked in his grasp. It looked manmade, only not of his time. Intricate patterns decorated its sides which would've been easier to distinguish when it was blazing hot. As it cooled in the humid East Texas breeze, Davy knew that had he found it moments before, it would've charred the skin right off his fingers. He was far from an expert, but it didn't take much to see that what he found was some kind of ancient artifact which looked like it belonged in a museum.

"And now our sufferings would come to an end after the long and weary march over hard trails," Davy whispered as his eyes fixated on the artifact he'd discovered.

The words he uttered were not his own, but the irony when they were first strung together by the explorer Álvarez Núñez Cabeza de Vaca during the Narváez expedition of 1527 was there all the same.

CHAPTER 3

Despite uncovering what he could only hope was the answer to his problems in life, all that park ranger Davy could truly bring himself to focus on was the way that woman back at the park looked right through him.

He tried his best to put her face behind him and focus on what he had dug up on the trail, but it was as if he could feel her presence following him wherever he went. With a glance over at the passenger seat, he made sure the artifact was still tucked away inside his backpack. For reasons he couldn't yet explain, finding it had convinced him to stave off a transfer for at least a few more days. It had already paid off too, as Chief Ranger Wayne thought it necessary to send him to Austin with the artifact in tow for the Nations Heritage & Culture Preservation center to inspect it. All things considered, he didn't mind the task too much, since thinking of that woman had him reconsidering going back at all.

The sun had started to set around him as he drove, casting out an orange glow through the trees that was easy to admire. His trusty old Ford pickup looked like it had belonged to a few too many owners despite being in his family since its first day off the lot in the 1980s. It was mostly red to the naked eye, but the rust and chipped white pin striping gave it a certain undeniable charm, especially against a sunset like the one he was driving into. Ranger Davy turned the clamoring truck off the highway leaving Daingerfield State Park and onto a county road that would stretch out for nearly ten miles into the piney woods leading home. His plans for the evening were not unlike what he was doing at work. While he knew he wanted something more at this point in his life, he would also be the first to admit this evening would consist of one of various frozen meals, a shower, then a movie that turns into a reluctant second movie before crashing on the couch.

He worked hard for what he had in life, but he couldn't help but feel a lonesome sense of discontentment growing in everything he did now that he had settled into his mid-thirties. Sometimes he felt like a ghost habitually wandering the woods rather than someone living in them. What if there was a giant box of gold, someone other than himself he could care about, and a whole bunch of land just waiting on the other side of the state if he only could brave himself long enough to at least look? These types of senseless questions cost him more sleep than he ever cared to admit, but somehow tonight, they didn't feel quite so impossible.

It wasn't long after he'd gone inside that darkness

had set in at his home out in the woods, and the stars at long last revealed themselves dotted across the night sky. The ranger had settled into what would surely be a night just like any other as he thought about the task ahead of him. When he showed Chief Ranger Wayne the artifact he'd found, there almost wasn't any discussion at all. He was told to deliver it to the Nations Heritage & Culture Preservation group where it would most likely then be placed in a museum or university, but he didn't even want to hold it for himself. It struck Davy as odd at the time, and even more so now while he reflected on it. However, Davy also didn't mention in Chief Ranger Wayne's office back at HQ that he was still holding out hope that if he was lucky enough, the artifact would lead to something else even more interesting. His heart thumped at the prospect alone.

He double checked his bag before zipping it closed, then reached into a pocket beside his bed stand and pulled out a 9mm pistol tucked inside a worn black leather holster. He dropped the magazine, checking to make sure it was still loaded then gently checked the chamber, confirming the round was still ready to go. He popped the magazine back in, stuffed the pistol back into the holster and dropped it into the bag. After he gathered his belongings and folded his clothes for the next day, the park ranger walked out to the front porch.

The ringing sounds of cicadas blasted through the air as soon as he opened the door. It was just the soundtrack he was looking for. He listened with a smile on his face as he made his way over to his old rocking chair, the perfect place to look out over the patch of land he called home and think about the day ahead.

Delivering historical artifacts wasn't typically part of the job, but he'd be lying if he said he wasn't interested in the opportunity more than just a little bit. As much as he enjoyed interacting with the guests at the park and watching over one of the most scenic places in the state, the chance to play even a small role in the discovery of a new piece of history made him anxious to get started. He allowed himself to wonder about the possibilities of maybe even having his name in *The Bee*, a local newspaper, once he got back from delivering it.

Just as he remembered he was still holding a glass bottle still half full of a local beer he had recently taken a liking to, he saw a shadow move in his peripherals. He darted his eyes to the left and waited to adjust to the darkness.

Just as he figured, it seemed to be nothing.

The more his eyes focused, the more he was able to make out the shifting of trees in the distance. A chilled wind was picking up from the north; it was the same wind that picked up every evening to sweep into his home around this time. It was so predictable he had made it part of his nightly routine to open the windows and cool the house while he slept. Tonight, there was a different chill in the air though.

There it was again.

This time he stood up quickly and shoved the creaking rocking chair backward as he jerked himself up onto his feet. The sound of the wood screeching against the porch was easily loud enough to be heard from beyond the front yard, but the ranger didn't care. Just at the edge of the wood line in the distance, Davy could make out the silhouette of someone standing behind a tree. They were peering back at him without moving. The second his eyes could make it out, he reacted unexpectedly.

"Who the hell are you!"

The silhouette disappeared further into the woods immediately after he shouted, but the ranger was already at a dead sprint in the same direction. His pistol was in hand just in case, and he ran as fast as his legs would carry him toward the woods.

Flashes of the woman from the park earlier that day

and the way her eyes pierced him raced through his head as he put one foot in front of the other.

A few seconds ticked by as Davy ran ahead, focusing on the woods in front of him and scanning from side to side hoping to catch any movement that would betray who he was after. While staring out across the familiar trees of his homestead, he couldn't help but think back to all the times he had gone out to the middle of these very woods as a kid to tuck a plinking rifle into his shoulder and take down something worth eating for dinner. Sweat beaded on his forehead and streaked down his face. Somehow, it calmed his nerves though. As his body continued the desperate search for the stranger in the night, lost in the woods of his childhood, his mind drifted to his first hunt with his father.

It was a cold morning that had them waking up a few hours before the sun. This didn't bother him at the time as he was mostly just concerned with not drawing the harassment of his dad for walking too loudly or carrying his 30-30 lever action rifle in the wrong manner. He could still remember the feeling of the wet morning grass that soaked his boots, how it made his socks slightly damp and the entire hunt incredibly uncomfortable. These small details stuck out more in his head than the actual hunt, but even so, killing his first doe that morning was something he would never forget. His dad pointed it out from inside the blind as it emerged cautiously out of the wood line, and a very young Davy held his breath from that point until it was time to squeeze the trigger. But the doe never stood still, it took off at a dead run instead. Davy shot it while it sprinted across the pasture, against the advice of his dad who'd nudged him to wait. The doe never saw it coming at that speed and fell to the ground lifeless without pause. His dad had cheered with sudden surprise when he watched what happened, but Davy didn't quite understand the significance of the shot at the time.

Even so, it was this morning so long ago when Davy developed a philosophy that had stuck with him his entire life—whether he wanted it to or not. He could never place an accurate shot on a still target, but when it moved, somehow he could feel it and place a bullet more accurately than just about anyone out there. It came in handy more times than not as a hunter and hurt him like hell when he made his way to a practice range, but tonight, back in the same woods, this philosophy would undoubtedly serve him well. If only he could find whoever it was.

"You better show yourself, you damn bastard!"

Silence suffocated him. Cicadas and other noisy wildlife at this time had seemingly been scared off by his yelling as there surprisingly wasn't a sound around. The ranger couldn't hear the footsteps of anyone escaping, so he thought for sure someone was hunkered down somewhere nearby. He searched through the trees that he'd known for just about his entire life to find someone who shouldn't be there. After an hour, he continued to turn up empty-handed. He moved to the backyard to check the barn, the woodshed, and even the abandoned pens, but never found anyone. With his head down and his firearm tucked back in the holster clipped on the inside of his jeans, the ranger made his way back to the front porch unsure if he felt safe in his own home.

For a reason he didn't understand, the words of his Dad chimed in his head. *"You don't ever run,"* he would say. *"Life's gonna throw all sorts of shit in your face, so you might as well get used to putting your head down and gettin' through it."* His words weren't encouraging when Davy first heard them during their early morning hunting trips, but they stuck with him. Tonight, the memories only made him feel lonelier than he already was, even though he hated to admit it. The old handful of acres his family called home wasn't the same since he'd been left to tend it himself. There were ghosts everywhere he looked, and he felt he'd started to become one himself, and admittedly nights alone like this sure didn't help those feelings.

The sounds of his boots hitting the old wooden

boards on his porch were usually music to his ears when he made it home, but tonight it was haunting. The thought of someone wandering his property while he slept at night made his skin crawl. There was nothing he could do about it now though. He had to turn his mind to the task at hand.

Thrills weren't always what he was after in this career. A life out on the trails was all he thought he'd ever really want, but the history that every park held so closely had always drawn him. No different than the land he lived on now that his own dad purchased to be handed down to each new generation. An old Native American artifact important enough to send him away to Austin had to have a story behind it that was worth knowing. Plus, it wasn't like anyone was waiting on him here back at home.

The way Davy figured, this whole thing was an unexpected adventure, so he might as well enjoy it as best he could.

CHAPTER 4

Waking up to the same silence that carried you off to sleep hours before would simply never have the same solace as a bustling house. The routine he'd been stuck in just wasn't meant to be for any man. Davy wasn't afraid to acknowledge it, but he also couldn't do much to change it. Mornings just never really sat right with him.

Davy propped his head up from the couch he'd fallen asleep on and stood up with an unnatural ease just seconds after opening his eyes. It was a habit he had formed as a child that just stuck all the way into adulthood. He wasn't one to waste time in bed. Never one to use an alarm when he did wake up, he simply found it more useful to start his day as soon as he had the chance. In his mind, he had been there for hours, what would he gain from forcing a few more minutes?

It took longer this morning to get ready since his routine needed to include a few extra steps. The first of which, obviously, was ensuring he still did in fact possess the valuable artifact and it would be ready for safe travel. He gathered his bags, making certain not to forget the one holding the artifact, and loaded them into the back seat of his old truck before making his way quietly back into the house. It was cooler out than usual, and the fog had set in heavily, blocking out any visibility for more than a few feet. Humidity certainly wasn't hard to find in this part of Texas. The sun hadn't burned the dawn's clouds off just yet, but the gray light offered just enough to get the day started. Paying no attention to the feelings that ached him on mornings like these, he tended to the chores that were needed before getting dressed for his trip.

His park ranger uniform of green ripstop pants and a khaki short sleeve button down was the same every day, and his trusty wide-brimmed ranger hat always fit like a charm. But this time, a holster was strapped to his belt with a .38 Special revolver tucked neatly inside his waistband, just in case. The ranger completed his attire with an outdoorsman's vest that covered the pistol resting against his lower back.

The drive to Austin was pushing five hours from his home outside Daingerfield, so getting on the road early would certainly help his day go a bit smoother. His old Ford would appreciate it too. As Davy turned off the secluded county road that led to his old ranch home and got up to speed on the highway, he glanced over at his bag and checked for about the hundredth time the artifact was still packed away unharmed.

It was curiosity that compelled him. It wasn't the money he could get for the artifact or as much as he would appreciate it, the recognition for its discovery; it was the thought of who had it before the state and its teams of relentless researchers would keep it locked away from who it belonged to for the rest of time. He tried to imagine what it had been used for without allowing his thoughts to spiral about how it had burned its way so deep into the earth where he'd found it.

This wasn't because he was afraid of what he'd find out, it was because he was afraid he already knew.

It was a long drive that gave him plenty of time to think himself out of it though. Luckily, it didn't take long for him to fall into the rhythm of road noise and succumb to wherever his mind decided to take him next. The ranger was almost three hours into the drive when he had to pull over for gas. The pine trees had wistfully faded away into open pastures where oaks dotted the landscape, but soon, there would be only concrete as far as the eye can see. That was the only part Davy wasn't looking forward to. Pulling into one of the many open gas pumps on a corner store set in motion a near-unconscious chain of actions for the ranger. Having driven that same old Ford for years now, Ranger Davy had become all too familiar with the motions of filling the tank with gas again and again. Nothing was particularly out of the ordinary until he clicked the handle back and looked around.

There she was. Staring at him again.

Ranger Davy almost fell right on his ass. It took him a second to recover and when he was able to get his eyes focused again, she was nowhere to be seen.

"The hell was that about," he questioned aloud for no one around to hear.

Davy really was starting to feel like he'd just about lost his mind. After the night he just had that sent him scrambling through the brush nervous as hell, he was becoming more and more certain that his mind was playing tricks on him. There wasn't even time to grab a candy bar and a Coke from the store, much less investigate his crazed visions and paranoid projections. The excitement of something meaningful happening to him was making this out to be more than it was. That's all it was.

Just when he was able to get back on the highway and force the old Ford truck—very much against its will—up to speed, the sound of his phone ringing suddenly caused him to jerk in surprise.

"Where is the doggone thing," he said with a tinge of annoyance in his voice as he searched the seat next to him with his hand, keeping his eyes fixed on the road ahead. With a quick flick of his thumb, he answered the call without even seeing who it was.

"Ranger Davy," he said as if he'd done it a million times before.

"No time for pleasantries today, buddy," the voice over the phone said. It was probably the only friend he had back at the Daingerfield State Park and the one who sent him to Austin to begin with, Chief Ranger Wayne.

The man pretty much exclusively talked about the lake and always had ever since they'd first met. It ended up making him the perfect candidate for the chief ranger position. In fact, the first time they shook hands was when Davy had been called over to deal with a guest trying to empty their black water tank from their RV in the lake before anyone would notice. Unfortunately for them, Tom was also there. He had yelled at them so much his face was bright red by the time Davy finally made it over to them to try and defuse the situation. Tom's passion for his job was refreshing most of the time, but today he had something else on his mind.

"No kidding, it's been one of those days," Davy told him. "Do you know what the heck this thing is yet?"

"Would it have made a difference if you did know?"

"Well, I mean, at the very least I think it would be helpful to know what I'm doing, not just where I'm going."

"You really haven't figured it out yet?" Chief Ranger Wayne sounded taken back. "Everywhere around that park has been the digging ground for enthusiasts, wannabes, and college undergraduates for decades. It's the same people you bullshit with every day, telling that old Treasure Island make-believe story?"

"That ain't *all* bullshit," Davy cut in quickly. "I figured this was just some old piece of history that didn't belong buried in the mud by a lake for outdoor tourists. I'm not complaining. I told you I was looking to do something more, and this is fine by me, but have you heard anything?"

"They said it's invaluable, Davy."

"Things in museums are usually worth quite a bit

of money. I'm talking about the way it burned through the ground though. I've never seen anything like it."

A few seconds of silence hung between them before it was broken. "That's why I'm calling now," said Tom. "No one believes it's real."

The ranger sat still in his noisy truck flying down the highway, trying his best to think of how he could prove what happened. The only problem was, he couldn't.

"There's a rumor floating around about a bunch of people dying in the last few weeks and it's got everyone wondering if it's somehow connected to what you're carrying right now," explained Tom. "No one would even entertain the idea that what you said could have actually happened. I think they're scared."

"Scared? And what do you mean, connected? Like someone's after this damn thing?" The woman's face flashed in Davy's mind one more time before he shook his head to focus on what his friend, and boss, was trying to tell him.

"I don't know. Just be careful, please." Tom's voice on the other end of the phone sounded concerned.

"I always am. And Tom, I appreciate the head's up."

That wasn't the call he was expecting. Sometimes it really did pay off to have friends in higher up the chain. The Ford truck he drove continued clattering down the highway, making people stare the ranger down every time they got a chance to go around him. All he could bring himself to do was wonder about what Tom was trying to warn him about, though. Their impatient and frustrated looks had never bothered him, and they especially didn't now that he had heavier things on his mind.

In becoming lost in his thoughts, Davy realized he hadn't taken a moment to notice the change of scenery as he drove. There weren't many pine trees to be had like back home, but getting closer to Austin had an unmistakable and quintessential Texas landscape charm. If you make it past the development and construction, get far enough from the highways, and just take a moment to see what it has to offer, there is a horizon unlike any other. Davy tried his best to find the time to appreciate it.

Turning the corner onto a road that wasn't a highway for the first time in a hundred miles was a nice change of pace for the ranger. The artifact was closer than ever to its destination at the Nations Heritage & Culture Preservation research facility on the outskirts of Austin where it belonged. The nonprofit organization was involved in many govern-ment-based initiatives that handed out local contracts. It wasn't a group Davy had any experience with, but he'd worked with countless others that were more than likely identical, so his nerves had thankfully settled a bit the closer he got. He knew these were mostly just good people looking to do their small bit of good in the world by lending a hand—and their exper-tise—where it could be difficult to come by.

When he pulled up to the research facility, he found a long gravel driveway that led to an inconspic-uous gray metal building with a handful of empty parking spots bunched up at the front door. Ranger Davy reached for the bag with the artifact packed neatly inside. He went ahead and took the time to check once more that it was still there to avoid any chance of making a fool of himself. The backpack holding the reason for his trip today was all black with a brown leather patch featuring a twisted looking symbol he didn't recognize. It had been given to him for this particular trip and it seemed to suit the purpose just fine for what it was. He slung it over his right shoulder but paused for a second. He pulled down the mirror and checked his reflection with an awkward smile, making sure there wasn't anything stuck in his teeth in case there were pictures to be taken, and flipped the visor back up with a loud *thunk*.

"You got this," he said to himself as he hopped out and slammed the door of his truck behind him.

Despite all the words of warning from those around him and even his own anxious anticipation, the trip had been smooth sailing all throughout. Things were actually looking up. One of the local barbecue places even popped into ranger Davy's mind just for a moment. Today's adventure would prove to be an easy one as well as great for his career, and he didn't consider that a bad thing by any means. He strode up to the glass door covered in tint so dark you couldn't see inside and swung it open confidently, wide enough for him to walk right in with his hat untouched.

That's when he saw the receptionist gagged and bound to a chair with rope. There was terror in her eyes that only widened when she saw him.

He saw deep red bloody handprints that had been smeared against the door leading to the back. A pool of blood that someone had been dragged through stained the floor leading behind the counter. Suddenly, he'd found himself inside of a terrible nightmare where the only thing he could think to do was get out alive while he still could. That's all the park ranger would see before he felt a sharp pain jolt through the back of his neck. His vision went white and his body collapsed to the ground with a hard thud.

Davy struggled in vain against losing consciousness as long as he could, but the fight was over before it had even begun.

CHAPTER 5

The black nothingness of unconsciousness could only be broken by very few things in the world. Smoke filling a room making it harder to breathe, the smell of flames singeing both hair and skin beyond any recognition, and the burning sensation coursing through the body could each do the trick on their own. Together though, it was just plain ol' torture.

These were the feelings that brought ranger Davy out of his hazy stupor. He had no idea which he felt first, or which was the most difficult to endure, but he did know this wasn't supposed to be happening. He had tunnel vision and felt deaf, was unable to move his arms or legs, and couldn't speak. The terror started in the pit of his stomach. It welled up inside him with an unimaginable and paralyzing sense of dread.

Clearly, he had his work cut out for him. He just needed to think. His vision cleared just slightly, and he saw two men standing just ahead of him, hovering tightly over a bright light that he was unable to make out just yet. The only thing he could figure out was that he didn't have much time for thinking. The two in front of him were large and imposing, dressed in black garb with noticeably thick, heavy leather boots. Their jackets fell below their knees with no discernible markings and their faces were shrouded in a black cloth mask, making them almost impossible to recognize. Davy was more immediately concerned with what one of them was holding, however. The burning smell that has brought him back to life and the deep burning in his belly that made dizzy with pain suddenly made a lot more sense.

"Mmm," was all he could get out from behind the duct tape pressed tightly against his face. "Mmmhmm."

The two people in front of him were coming closer to him now and the fear of what was about to happen lodged in his throat. The blinding pain still coming from his stomach told him this wasn't going to end well. As they each drew closer, pointing the branding iron directly at him, all Davy could do was tense his body and plead through the tape while trying to get as much information as he could before he'd most likely pass out. He did his best, but once the hot metal burned its way into his flesh for the second time on his stomach—in the exact same spot as before—his eyes clenched shut and he writhed in pain. There were no sounds coming from those doing this to him, no reactions to his muted screams, no remorse to be found.

The only thing he saw that was worth remembering was the shape of the brand, and considering the pain he felt in his belly, he knew it may be one he'd never forget. It was the same shape that was on the bag he carried to this place of nightmares holding the artifact; three thin bars of a letter "E" combined with what resembled an ornate letter "J" jutting out from its side. Try as he might to commit the brand to memory, it would only be seconds later against all the will he could muster, he lost consciousness once again.

There was no telling how long he lay in that closet before his eyes shot open once more. Judging from how he felt though, it had been more than long enough to try and force his own escape. He wriggled his hands back and forth, trying to get a feel for the rope that was used to tie his hands so tightly. It didn't give much. There was just a hair's worth of room, so he got to work loosening it as best he could, moving with undetectable motions and fearing every audible scrape the roughened rope made going back and forth against his skin.

"Are we really going back in there?"

Davy's arms locked in place as his body immediately went rigid and the room fell silent. This wasn't something he was trained for by any means but judging from his pounding heart rate and tunnel vision still closing in, fight or flight was setting in and he was going to have to make a decision one way or another.

"We just need to find the damn thing. It's supposed to be here, but he isn't giving us anything useful! I'm telling you right now, we're wasting our time with him."

"What the hell would you do then?" a second voice chimed in, this one far less aggressive.

"Kill him, grab everything, and throw it in the truck, then get the hell out of here. You're gonna be the one who gets caught doing this stupid shit because I can guaran-goddamn-tee you I won't be sticking around to see how all this turns out."

"We're Pinkertons; that's not what we do." The second voice asked with a chilling sincerity found within his voice, "We have a job to do here and we're going to finish it. You want to tell Damian you just didn't feel like doing it?"

Davy sat wide-eyed in the closet, still bound and gagged, listening to his fate still being determined just a few feet away behind the door. He recognized the Pinkerton name and knew it didn't mean anything good for him, but the name Damian didn't mean anything to him. What if they really did have the wrong guy? His fear was turning to anger in one hell of a hurry.

"You don't actually buy all of that never sleeping shit, do you? It's just a load of bullshit. Tell me you know it's all bullshit."

"You shouldn't be here if that's what you believe," the other one replied.

"The only thing I really believe is we need that damn money. And that's all I believe too, you son of a bitch. You can keep the rest of all that ass kissing, but none of it will make a difference if we're dead or locked up. We gotta move quick and we gotta do it now."

"He wouldn't be pleased if we left it like this."

"What are you getting at?"

"I'm saying this may be our only chance, and we don't want to be the ones who botched it. And I also don't want to be known as the person who was *with* the one who botched it. So, get your shit together."

It would seem that one of them finally made a point worth considering because everything got quiet for a minute or two. Davy had worked through about a quarter of an inch of his bindings already and was actually feeling the progress. Soon, his hands would be free, but what would have to come next seemed unconscionable.

He was going to have to fight his way out.

"I really don't see how the guy keeps attracting people like you," said one of them, now closer to the door that separated them from Davy.

The door creaked open slower than Davy would have liked and the two men made their way in. He knew it wasn't going to end well, but he had to try something. They both stood in front of him side by side and stared into Davy's eyes for a few awkward seconds.

"You've got one more chance to go home alive," the larger man finally spoke up. From the sound of his voice, Davy knew he was the one who wanted to kill him and leave, so he took the man for his word. "If you don't give us what we want, that burn on your stomach is going to feel like fuckin' butterflies compared to what we've got next."

"All you need to do is tell us where the artifact is," the other one said. The man dressed in black was calm, but for a reason that Davy couldn't explain, he was much more terrified of him. "We know you had it when you came inside. Tell us where it is and we walk out that door and out of your life."

The smaller one reached a gloved hand out and started pulling at the gag wrapped around Davy's face to let him speak. With a few uncomfortable tugs it went loose and fell to the floor. The park ranger took a deep breath as soon as he could, and without showing the men in front of him, never stopped working the binding around his wrists looser and looser. He was getting close to freeing his hands. If only he could just buy a little more time.

The steaming piece of iron was still lying on the floor in front of him, its red glow becoming fainter as it cooled. A distinct smell of his own singed flesh and hair lingered in the small closet that made Davy's nose curl at each breath. While the brand would have looked like it belonged on the hide of cattle to some, to the ranger, it was the mark of a hellish trial. As soon as could catch his breath amid distraught heaves, he finally spoke.

"It's in my bag, I swear," he said.

"You think you're funny, asshole? That was the first place we looked. Try again."

"It was on me when I came in, it's gotta be just outside that door," Davy argued while using his head to motion toward where he believed the entrance to the building was. "I swear."

The smaller man turned to look at his partner.

"Did you check the bag?"

"I thought you checked it?"

"Goddammit. Go find it, we have to be sure."

"You do it. I'll deal with this problem."

The smaller man didn't move a muscle, say a word, or even afford a passing glance at his partner who had so obviously forgotten his place. The awkward seconds ticked by and the over-eager Pinkerton grunt soon got the hint. Despite their back and forth, he turned and left the room to check for the park ranger's bag as he had been told. Unfortunately, the other man stood in place without moving and waited in silence. Davy's wrist could almost fit through the hole in the bindings now. He moved and twisted his hands and arms fiercely, keeping his shoulders dead still to not give himself away. It was working. He only needed a few more minutes and the fight would be on.

Thump.

"What the fuck," the one still standing in front of Davy let out at the sound. "Don't fucking move," he told Davy before he walked out of the closet.

With a forceful, jerking motion that just about ripped all the skin from Davy's hands, he

slipped free of the rope bindings as soon as the man left. He reached down and frantically tried to undo the bindings at his ankles through the violent shaking in his hands. Fear and adrenaline were settling in. When he moved, he felt the terrible stinging on his stomach. The burns were so bad he couldn't even bring himself to look at them. Instead, he pushed the pain from his mind and focused on escaping. The knots at his feet were tight and he knew time was running out. He yanked on the rope at every spot he could find and nothing was giving way. Panic rose into his chest as his blood flooded through his extremities and into his fingers and toes in a rush that was starting to make him feel dizzy.

Then suddenly, as if it had been so obviously easy all along, the rope went loose with just

the right tug and his legs were free. A wave of relief washed over the ranger. He got to his feet and immediately looked around the closet for a weapon. The only thing he could find in the closet full of bottles of chemicals and supplies was an old wooden handled broom. He grabbed it from the corner of the room, held it out to his side at an angle, and kicked down at it as hard as he could. A loud cracking sound filled the air and he was left holding a broken piece of the handle extended out to a sharp point. It would have to do. He took a deep breath and before exhaling, stepped out of the closet, ready to fight.

The hallway he walked into was empty. To his left there were offices and a pair of

restrooms, and to his right, the hallway extended out into a larger opening. Assuming this was the way to the exit, he stumbled a bit from disorienting pain coursing through his body but started walking toward the desk. He held the broken broom handle in one hand and braced himself against the wall with the other, still refusing to look down to see the burns on his stomach that stung horribly with every step.

Pap. Pap. This time the sounds were muffled. but Davy knew he'd somehow found his

way into a gunfight, the only problem was that he was armed with a wooden broom handle instead of a gun.

Pap. Pap.

Two more shots. Davy was all out of panic, but he had plenty of adrenaline surging through him. His fight-or-flight feelings response was buzzing, but he'd already made his choice. Davy was fighting for his life come hell or high water. The gunshots stopped as soon as they started, so after giving it a few fleeting moments, Davy decided to press on. He hobbled down the hallway until he was ready to make a last-ditch push for the exit. With his body tensed and the wooden handle raised in the air, Davy then turned to look out into the lobby and froze right where he stood.

It was her. The same woman from the park, the one he couldn't get out of his head,

the one who just about scared him senseless only from looking at her. Now, he struggled to think of a time when had been so thankful to see anyone. He didn't know how to react.

Davy was speechless, but Rose wasn't.

"Where is it? Where the *fuck* is it!?"

Davy lifted a finger and pointed at the ground just in front of Rose without saying a word. The lifeless body of what was left of a familiar man—the one who was mercilessly jabbing him with a hot branding iron just minutes before was lying face down on the floor, bleeding out from his wounds with a death grip on the same backpack he'd walked in with earlier.

Rose was holding the bag like her own life depended on it within a matter of seconds. She ignored Davy completely, consumed with what was inside until she pulled her arm out with a palpable wave of relief washing across her face as she did. The ranger had no idea who she was or what she wanted.

He could only hope to slip away to save his life while Rose took the discovery that could've changed it forever. Unfortunately for Davy, she read his mind.

With the lost artifact in one hand and her revolver pointed right at the park ranger in the other, Rose once more stared a hole through Davy before finally speaking up.

"You told a story back at the park," she said. "That story isn't yours to tell."

Davy lifted his hands and surrendered his wooden stake. Rose waited until the sounds of its awkward clunking against the tile flooring came to a stop before speaking again.

"You're coming with me."

CHAPTER 6

"Y ou killed them. You left them dead in that building back there and we didn't even call anyone."

"I saved your life," Rose said. "There's that too, just saying."

"You *killed* them."

They were driving somewhere. Ranger Davy just didn't have the mental fortitude to ask where, and at this point, he honestly just didn't care. Trauma and shock had gotten to him. He stared out the window in a daze and tried to gather his thoughts. He'd been captured, held against his will, tortured, and for what? His eyes darted over to his bag that sat between them and in that moment, he remembered exactly what it was all for. His suspicions about what he'd stumbled on at the Daingerfield park had proven to be true. Chief Ranger Wayne's words of warning during the phone call before he made it to Austin echoed in his thoughts. There was something larger than any of them at play here and Davy had just gotten roped into it. Whether he wanted to or not.

"You're gonna kill me next, aren't you?" he blurted out, turning his lost gaze over to focus on the woman driving next to him.

"The hell?"

"Why didn't you just do it back there to leave me with the rest of them? Am I some kind of sick hostage of yours now or something?"

"They were actually torturing you, and you're mad at me? First, you should be thanking me. Second, no, you aren't my damn hostage. That's ridiculous. And third, I already told you why you're not dead."

"I've been telling that damn story for years. It's not even real!"

Neither said anything for a few minutes. The unwanted silence allowed them to sink into their thoughts and try to digest everything that had just happened. Davy studied the woman sitting next to him. She looked like she hadn't gotten a full night's sleep in weeks and he couldn't help but to wonder why. Her long black hair pushed behind her shoulders didn't do much to hide the bags under her eyes, and the clothes she wore seemed to be hanging on by their last thread in some places. The pistol she had was clearly tucked in front of her stomach, protruding as she sat where it was easily within reach. She looked tough, like she had been through hardships he wouldn't know anything about, but there was still something about her eyes that made him think differently.

He soon realized he had no idea where they were

or where they were going. He'd jumped into the SUV of a murderous stranger who was obviously stalking him without asking a single question. Of course, he was held at gunpoint when he did, but now they were fleeing a crime scene. He was most likely days away from getting fired from a job he most certainly didn't want to lose entirely, despite how he felt just one day ago. It was all just too much.

"Fuck!" the ranger let out unexpectedly, pushing his face into his hands. A flood of emotions ran through him, so many he couldn't pinpoint one from the other, but also because the only thing he could really feel was the stinging of fresh burns on his stomach. He had been branded in the middle of his torture and he was feeling all of it.

"We'll get you all fixed up," Rose told him as if she knew what he was thinking yet again. "We're going to a safe place where we can lay low for a bit. I'm not going to hurt you, okay? I'm sorry for earlier, but just so you know, I'm the one who should be thanking you. My name's Rose, by the way."

"Davy," the ranger answered solemnly.

Rose glanced over at the park ranger still in shock next to her judging by the sound of his breathing. His shirt, from what she could tell, was probably a nice one before it had been ripped open and burned to pieces. She could make out only a small piece of his bright red and scabbed flesh between his arms covering his stomach. It looked bad and must've felt worse. His face looked like he hadn't bathed in a month. He was a broad man, and his usually kempt hygiene had now been turned into a disheveled mess from the day he'd endured. Being tortured had a way of doing that.

"I was there when you first found it out in Daingerfield," Rose said.

"Yeah, I know, trust me I saw you. I went to bed with nightmares from thinking about whether or not you followed me home with that crazed look in your eye."

"Oh come on, stop being dramatic."

"*Dramatic*? Well I wasn't the one sneaking around in the dang woods trying to catch a peek in the middle of the night," Davy rattled on. "I mean seriously, that's some *out there* shit. You had me running around like a jackass."

A loud chuckle escaped Rose before she could stop it from going any further. She covered her mouth with one hand and looked over at Davy. "That's so specific, almost sounds like you meant it," she tried to say in between laughing. "Trust me, you aren't worth that kinda trouble."

Ranger Davy took a moment to contemplate what she was saying. If it wasn't Rose, who the hell was out on his property last night? He tried to stop his mind from racing to figure out who the shadow figure he chased for hours had really been. He felt a new fear begin to grow in his belly. How many people were after this artifact?

"Well, I must be worth some trouble," he finally spoke up. "You sure went through a lot to come find me, then even more to save me. Can't help but connect the dots y'know?"

"We aren't doing this right now."

"Well what the hell are we doing then? I have been sitting here with a son a bitchin' brand still smoking on my stomach, asking myself that question over and over again," Davy said, getting more worked up the longer he talked.

"I've been after that artifact you were carrying around so carelessly for as long as I can remember," Rose told him. "My mother did the same, in her own way. You have no idea what it means."

"That part we can agree on."

"I came to Daingerfield because there were rumors about the story you were telling. I figured it was another dead end, no different from who knows how many others that me and my family have been falling for the last few decades," Rose explained. "But I went to check it out anyway, and I found you. Turns out, it was exactly what I had always hoped it would be."

Davy knew he should choose his next words wisely, but it was harder than ever to think straight with the searing pain still throbbing in his stomach. "And what was that?"

"Our past and our future. Our Eternal Flame."

"I wish that made more sense. I really do."

"When we get to where we are going, I will explain as much as I can," Rose told him as she glanced over to him once again, noticing him wincing in pain. "After we get you up and running up first. You look like shit."

"Yeah, thanks."

The next hour of the car ride went by in total silence. Road noise hummed along in the background as Rose's thoughts drifted from one worry to the next.

She allowed herself a moment to think back to her childhood on the reservation in Oklahoma. She thought of her family that passed down the skills she used even today and the experiences she had with them that helped to mold her into the woman she became. Her heart dropped at these thoughts, but she forced herself to focus on the bright side, starting with the park ranger who was sitting next to her. After what they had found in Daingerfield—and what he seemed to know about her family—for the first time in a long time, she had a sense of hope that removed the longing and regret that had swirled inside her for so long.

Rose may have been lost in what she needed to do next, but Davy was still just trying his best to not think about the severe burns that forced their way into every second. Despite this, he was considering his options given the situation he'd found himself in, ultimately hoping he could come up with an explanation that wouldn't end up with him losing everything he had worked so hard for. This wasn't at all what was supposed to happen when he left his home this morning. Until he could come up with a better plan, he knew he'd be forced to see it through though. If his opportunity to snatch the artifact and make his way to authorities came up, he'd have to be ready for it. Until then, he'd have to trust Rose not to kill him.

They were driving further from anyone or anything than they had been before since the trip started. Davy forced the thoughts of Rose being a violent stranger out of his mind as best he could. He looked over at her and the two made eye contact for just a brief second for a fleeting moment, but it was just enough to change everything that he was thinking about her.

Before it got too awkward, he broke the silence with a question that should have been asked much earlier. "Can you tell me where we're going?"

"A secluded place, far from prying eyes and anyone who might be following. It's a small place on the other side of Deadwood. We can tend to your burn there," Rose said. "I'll need some time to put together some medicine, but it shouldn't take long."

It would take over an hour before the black SUV turned onto a dirt road only speckled with occasional bits of gravel that were once potholes. It curved through the woods and brush like it had been there all along, taking Rose and Davy to who knows where and not doing it in any kind of a hurry. The rolling hills covered in thick trees would have been a welcome sight to see for Davy if only his stomach hadn't been burned beyond recognition. It was getting harder for him to focus on anything else.

Luckily, the silence was cut short when they came into a dirt road giving way to a dead end with a driveway sprouting off it. Not much further down the hill was an unsuspecting tannish brick house that looked as if no one had been home in a year or two. Overgrown grass with old furniture scattered in the yard gave it an abandoned feeling, but the chickens wandering the yard gave pause to such suspicions.

"Home sweet home?" Davy asked, only half-jokingly.

"Not even close, but it will have to do until you feel ready to continue on."

"Who said I was going with you? I may be hurt, but I'm not desperate just yet."

"That decision's yours to make."

"Well whatever happens, regardless of what I said earlier, I really am glad you shot those assholes who did this to me."

Rose didn't answer him, but she did offer a quick smile in return which told Davy everything he needed to know about who exactly he had found himself with. As they pulled right up to the front of the house, the ranger began to brace himself to move again. He knew there wasn't any other choice, but his body was already fighting his urges, begging him to remain seated through a violent burning sensation flaring up. With a quick jerking motion, the door to the SUV swung open and Davy forced himself out, half stepping and half falling, but determined to get inside. In his peripherals, Rose's long black hair swayed with her walk as she moved quicker than him, getting ahead to open the door and watch him make his way to her. He stumbled in line just behind her and grunted.

The door to the brick house opened with a loud creaking sound and smelled of deteriorated moth balls. Inside was an empty living room except for a desk with an office chair on caster wheels tucked into the corner. The kitchen was bare, with no table or groceries, and every wall was painted a plain white with nothing hung up, adorned only by an occasional brown stain that had made its way into the wall only to be ignored entirely. It was an unexpected sight for Davy. He was eager to not waste any time in starting to ask some of his many, many questions, but then thought again.

"Yeah, this makes sense," he let out.

The place reminded Davy of an office, but he just couldn't force himself to care about where he was at the moment. He needed to find some water and more importantly—he needed to lie down. With only the strength to accomplish one of those tasks, he went into the closest bedroom and fell onto the carpeted floor on his back.

Three hours later he opened his eyes in a panic.

Davy sat up way too fast and felt his entire abdomen scream in pain. With a guttural groan, he fell back to the floor. Within seconds, the door to the room pushed open, and Rose came walking in with a bag in her hands. She kneeled next to him and started working without saying a word. As she tended to his wounds, Davy stared at the ceiling and thought about how this had happened to him. A cloud of blame began to form above him as he considered his desperation to shake up his own life before he'd dug up the artifact. What had happened to him could be nothing more than a self-fulfilling prophecy of his own creation.

Rose worked for quite some time before she began to bandage his stomach all the way up to his chest. She wrapped a partially stained roll of gauze as many times as it would stretch around him and fastened it tightly into place. The silence between the two had reached deafening proportions until Rose was the one to break it.

"My entire life has led me to today. I'm going to tell you everything I know, so I'd like you to listen to me for a little while longer. Then I'm gonna ask you a question."

Davy propped himself up on his elbows as best he could and nodded. Rose acknowledged his agreement with a smile and continued speaking.

"The story I heard you tell those guests at the park."

"The one you said wasn't mine to tell?"

"That's right," Rose answered. "Because it's mine. At the very least, it's my family's."

"I don't think I'm following."

"Let me explain. The artifact you were delivering is actually a map—the map of the Eternal Flame. It's been passed down by the same family from one generation to the next, all while their story was lost into so many of the history books not written by us. Now, it's an irreplaceable family heirloom. Most people don't even know anything like this even exists, and if I'm being honest, I've even had my own doubts."

Rose explained in a calm voice, like it was something she had rehearsed by telling the story a hundred times over. As she talked, Davy felt his pain begin to fade and allowed himself to follow her every word. He had to admit Rose was easy to listen to, even though he could never say such a thing to her face.

Before he'd realized it, Rose was holding the artifact that had already upended his life so much. The object was, at first glance, a simple stone sphere. The details showed something much more intricate, however. Two carved halves cut at the center rotated around a hollowed-out cylindrical core, each with delicate etchings that crisscrossed all over the surface. Rose spun it in her hands and admired it closely. It looked as though it was missing the top and bottom to complete the surface's ancient artwork.

"My ancestors were Caddo," Rose continued. "Before we were all either killed off or forced from our homes and onto reservations, a woman named Angelina in your tongue used this heirloom to protect her family in a way no one has ever seen before. For some people, this artifact is the key to our past, but for others like me…" Rose trailed off, looking down at her hands and the artifact that was finally hers at long last. "It's the precious guarantee of a future."

"Like you?"

"Don't you see? The woman who fell for the outlaw in your story, she's my kin, Davy."

Her last sentence hung in Davy's ears for a second before he could react. He wanted to laugh purely from the preposterous statement he'd just heard, but he damn sure knew better than to do that. The story of the treasure of Hank Heck was only something he shared with his dad the few times they were together in his life. Public parks were one of the only places he would actually go where they could do something other than work together. Those memories had stuck with Davy through the years.

"My story? You really mean the one about the old west outlaw and his piles of gold that got too heavy to carry? You can't be serious. That's what all of this is really about? I made most of that story up years ago before I came to work at Daingerfield. Boy Scouts and camping families love to think they might come across some of the lost treasure while they're at the park, so I've used it everywhere I worked. It's just for fun, Rose."

"There are many different versions of what is all the same story," she said. "You have to tell me, where did you first hear it for yourself?"

"What do you mean?"

"The last person to tell the story you know died over fifty years ago. I know because it was my grand-mother who told it. There's no possible way for you to know those kinds of details. I couldn't believe it when I heard you in Daingerfield, but there you were. You knew where Angelina met the man she fell for, where he got shot, and even what she did after he died. You knew about the lost pieces of the map of the Eternal Flame. My own mom would have never said these things to me, yet here you are with all that knowledge and more."

"Fifty years ago? The story about the treasure is something my dad and I heard at the park together. I was about nine years old and he took me to Tyler State Park for the day to see the Whispering Pines trail. We listened to an old woman tell us a story about a trea-sure locked away behind an Eternal Flame. She said that we could find pieces of a lost treasure map in the park and if we found all of them, we'd be rich. We spent the rest of the day searching every corner of the park for a piece of that made-up map. We didn't find shit of course, but I did find out a lot how much I loved being at the parks. As I got older, I started to tell the same story to others, hoping to inspire some other kid to love the parks and what they offered. I had some notes of my own to add to the story of course though," he admitted.

"The woman's name you and your dad listened to was Larue, wasn't it?"

"How the hell could you know that?"

"Because what I've been telling you is the truth. Larue was my grandmother who died more than fifty years ago."

"Then how did I hear her when I was a kid, Rose? Was she a fuckin' ghost?"

"I know it's a lot to take in."

"You're being serious, aren't you? Oh god, this whole thing is just a damn fever dream. It can't be real. There's no way any of this is real."

"What you heard was all true, Davy," Rose tried to reassure him. "I knew when I heard you telling the story back at the park that something bigger than either of us was happening, and that I wasn't alone in this anymore."

"So the map of the Eternal Flame is real?" Davy was dumbfounded.

"Yes," Rose confirmed bluntly. "The map is real and it's here right now—with us."

"And an old outlaw's treasure is still hidden somewhere out there and that's why I got tortured and branded?"

"That's one way to look at it."

Davy wouldn't have ever believed what was happening to him in any lifetime. Rose wasn't providing any evidence to support her case—much less convince him to go on some Godforsaken treasure hunt—but her body language, her sincerity, and her determination made him think something deeper really was at play here. "I saw you sitting in the crowd when I told the story. I know you listened to all of it. How could I trust you? How do I know you aren't just making all this up to bait me along?"

"You don't know, not for sure," Rose said, looking right into his eyes. "But wouldn't you like a chance to find out for yourself?"

Davy had no clue how to respond to such a question. How could he tell her it was exactly what he was looking for without throwing the life he'd built for himself all away?

"Just hear me out. You could return to your life in shambles as it is now. You are probably already fired on top of being at the top of the suspect list for everything that happened today, and I do mean everything. You could return to face those consequences, and maybe you are shielded from them with your status as a park ranger, but maybe you aren't. Or you could avoid all of that..." Rose trailed off, giving Davy a second to absorb what she was trying to tell him. "You could return to your life a celebrated hero, with the map of the Eternal Flame, a lost ancient artifact in your possession and your name credited for a historic discovery unlike anything the modern world has seen in a very, very long time. Not to mention the places we'll go in order to find it."

"Why me? I don't understand."

"Because I need you," Rose said. "You were given

this knowledge when I wasn't for a reason. I've been doing this for so long, failing for so long all by myself, that I forgot what fate's interference felt like. When I heard the story of my ancestors being passed down by you, of all people, I knew we would have to do this together."

Davy looked down once again at the object in Rose's hand as she moved it around while she spoke. It definitely didn't look as special as she was claiming it to be. How could it possibly be a map? And how could he possibly know that she was truly the living descendant of the Native woman who fell for the outlaw? Davy looked into Rose's eyes to see if he could find any lies in what she was telling him, her face was stern and serious. It was the face of someone who had risked everything and finally found even the slightest bit of hope. He couldn't deny her, and he knew that almost immediately. It was a feeling he couldn't shake.

The park ranger couldn't think of anything to say, he was growing tired of being at a loss for words, but here he was again. He looked at Rose and tried to mask the urge that crept up in his belly to believe what he was hearing. He was almost being persuaded.

"I told you I'd ask you a question when I was done explaining everything," Rose said. "Will you help me complete the map of the Eternal Flame and find the treasure it protects?"

CHAPTER 7

The wreckage left behind at the Nations Heritage & Culture Preservation facility was one worthy of headlines at the Chronicle, along with just about every other local paper that was willing to make the drive. So much so, there was a line of reporters and other camera-holding fanatics stretching down the road leading up to the driveway. It was a crime scene that drew about as much attention as anyone could imagine in such a place.

Broken glass, destroyed furniture, and the carnage of dead bodies strewn throughout the lobby and hallway inside the building made it difficult to understand what had actually happened. Chaos had found its way into the nonprofit organization and there was no shortage of people standing out in the humid heat of the morning sun trying to decipher any details they could.

Local police lined the border, holding back spectators of the violence while detectives calmly made their way through what was left after evidence had been documented and sent away. There were a few other emergency personnel at the scene including paramedic and forensics specialists who were trying to help in any way they knew how. There weren't any smiles or typical jokes passed back and forth between the people working the scene. Even though most had known each other for years and worked several other scenes before, the circumstances that surrounded this one created a solemn atmosphere.

The lobby inside the Nations Heritage & Culture Preservation facility caught the worst of the damage. It was the room that held the most bodies, so it was also crowded with the most personnel. The swarming back and forth buzzing of professionals trying to get through their tasks almost made it too difficult to see the man who was approaching the scene.

"Just take a look around. We've got multiple homicides and about as many other charges as you could think of," one of the detectives said to his partner inside the lobby area.

"Think they all died right here?"

"Well, I know they're all dead. We'll get the answers as to where and why soon enough," the detective answered. "And hopefully a lead on who was twisted enough to pull something like this off."

"I'd tell you who did it," a booming voice from off in the distance interjected. "But then I'd have to kill you both."

The detective and his partner hovering over the scene noticed the approaching man far too late into their discussion. They both tried to hide their surprise by his sudden appearance, but for reasons that weren't the same. When the detective didn't say anything to him immediately, his partner naively decided it was his queue to speak up.

"Sir, you can't be here, this is a crime scene under investigation, you need to—"

"Shut the hell up," the detective cut in.

The imposing figure standing next to the two men studying a bloody stain smeared across the floor was undeniably intimidating. His aggressive demeanor was unnerving, and the awkward silence that fell after he spoke only made it more so. He wore cowboy black boots made of exotic leather and had a wristwatch to match, tucked neatly within his tailored sleeve. His shiny black hair was slicked back without a single strand out of place, but his trimmed goatee was graying, and it afforded him a sense of respectability that was only earned with age. In his eyes, however, was something much more threatening.

"Don't you know who you're lookin' at, dumbass?" the detective whispered quietly, trying to avoid eye contact as best he could. "Just look around. No one says anything because they know the deal. He can stay as long as he needs."

The partner answered with an honest question but didn't try nearly hard enough to hide his voice. "Who the hell is this guy?"

"His name is…"

"You can both call me boss," the man answered for both of them. "Now, tell me, what the hell happened here?"

They froze in silence and tried to not dig their

grave any deeper than they already had. The crime scene was already bad enough as it was. The detective had met this man before and it didn't exactly go well for him the first time. His name was Damian De León, and he was what most would call a businessman, but the detective had learned all too well that he was something else entirely. He was ruthlessly drunk on power and simply didn't have the word boundaries in his vocabulary. His arrival at this crime scene undoubtedly meant worse things were sure to come. Looking around at the dead bodies outlined into the ground and overall destruction that had found its way into the facility, the detective shuddered to think what could possibly get worse from here.

"Sir, I honestly am not even sure where to begin with what the hell actually happened here. So far, we've got multiple homicides, breaking and entering, burglary, and countless other charges we're looking at here," the detective told De León, hoping to distract him from his partner's transgression.

"I have eyes, Detective," Damian answered.

"Excuse me then, sir, what is it that we can do for you?"

"You've done quite enough boys," Damian said before turning his back to them and walking away.

The two cops chose to do the same, leaving the crime scene to make themselves useful elsewhere. Damian De León had seen everything he needed and knew what had to be done next. There were few in the world who could pull off the kind of killing he'd seen inside. That made his job easier than most would expect. As he strode confidently away from the bloodshed behind him and toward the rows of reporters and small crowds outside, he reached into his pocket and pulled out his phone.

"Yes, it's her. She's beginning to cause problems, the kind we can't afford to risk."

There was a pause in the phone call while Damian stood motionless. "You need to get it through your head. She's getting closer, I'm telling you. I can feel it."

The silence returned for just another brief moment, giving Damian enough time to habitually check his wristwatch. He couldn't wait much longer, but he knew he'd have to. With a glance back at the building before shaking his head and lifting the phone back to his ear in frustration, Damian made his demands known. It was a mess he didn't expect, but it wouldn't deter him from what mattered most.

"You need to get down here, now. Find out what happened and where she's going next, and don't fucking lose her this time," he said to the Stranger with a mischievous tone in his voice. "You hear me? Don't fuck this up. She's finally gonna take us right where we want to be."

CHAPTER 8

When he finally woke up to feel the gentle warmth of the morning sun against his skin, Davy at first didn't remember anything of the day before. He stretched in bed with a yawn, blissfully unaware of his own torture, the deaths he saw back at the nonprofit facility, and most of all, the dangerous path that now laid before him.

When he tried to sit up, it all came rushing back to him.

The park ranger felt a violent surge of pain flare up in his gut that made him groan, and a flood of unwelcome memories assailed his mind. The house he was in was unfamiliar and it did little to set his nerves at ease. The bedding smelled like it hadn't been washed in months. It was stale and stiff, but he tried to be thankful because it could have been worse and he was all too aware of that fact. His painful moans must have alerted Rose, before he was able to even try to stand, she cracked open the door slowly and walked inside.

At first, she didn't say a word. She was wearing the same clothes she wore the day before and it looked like she hadn't slept a wink all night. In her hands was a steaming bowl filled with something that made her walk more gently so as to not spill it. She sat down at his bed and pushed the bowl toward him. After a few loud sips, she decided to speak up.

"Here, drink this."

"Thank you," he answered. "For everything."

"Don't thank me just yet, you don't get to lie around all day doing nothing. We're leaving before the sun hits high noon."

Davy took a moment to think about what she said before answering, knowing still that he could be in a more dangerous position than he realized. He'd have to play his cards right if he wanted to survive unscathed. His silence seemed to say everything to Rose though.

"You are welcome to stand up and walk right out of here and find your own way home anytime you want," Rose said, making an attempt to ease some of his worries. "But you have to know there could be so much more for you if you help me with this."

"I actually don't know that yet," the ranger assured her. "I have no idea who you are."

"There are worse things that could happen to you," she said. "Now, pull back those covers, let me see the brand those assholes put on you."

With a careful tug at the blankets laid across his stomach, Davy revealed the seared skin that was just as red as the day before, only scabbed and raw now. He tried his best not to look directly at it. The burning pain was more than enough to tell him how bad it really was. There was only a slight resemblance of the letter "E" combined with a swirled "J" scorched into his stomach, but it was enough to make Rose's eyes flash in a moment of horror.

"It will heal as long as we stop infection from brewing," Rose said as she reached out her hand to gently inspect the wound, hiding her reaction to the symbol that had been burned into her in its own way.

"It better. The only bright spot is at least those assholes who did this to me are dead."

"Some of them are dead," she corrected him. "There are a lot more where they came from and they aren't going to stop until they have this." Rose reached into her jacket pocket and pulled out the artifact that had put them through so much already.

The small sphere made of stone looked insignificant, but it had turned Davy's life upside down in a matter of hours. Judging from what Rose had said about her entire family searching for so long, he knew this was much larger than he could have ever guessed.

As Rose spun the once-lost family heirloom in her hand, admiring it more with each turn, Davy noticed some of the more intricate details he hadn't had the time to see before. The map of the Eternal Flame, as Rose called it, was made up of two parts that spun individually around a cylindrical core with holes at either end. There were patterns carved into each half, indistinguishable to Davy, but clearly crucial to following wherever it may lead.

"The map," he said as he began to remember their conversation from the night before.

"After a few lifetimes of searching for it, you and I are going to find out where it will take us. And we'll make history by the time we're done. The story you told back at the park may have been full of half-truths and exaggerations, but you knew the map of the Eternal Flame and how it had been followed home so many times before. Even though the name Hank Heck was just about one of the worst things I've ever heard..." Rose joked in an effort to lighten the mood just a bit.

"Hey," Davy reacted. "I thought it was a cool name, much better than the name that old woman—I mean your grandmother—used a long time ago at the park. I just livened it up a bit."

"Do you remember the name you heard from her?"

"Henry Hunter."

Rose glared back at him for longer than what was probably necessary before it slowly slipped into a smirk. "Still better than Hank Heck."

"All right, I get it," Davy acknowledged.

"Henry Hunter was a man, a white man, who robbed and cheated his way through life in the late 1800s just before my people were hunted down and forced off their land by other white men. He became wealthy beyond comprehension, traveling from one all too vulnerable town to the next, leaving most he confronted either robbed blind or dead. He didn't ask for much of each town. He took everything from them though, and with it, he built a legacy. One that he knew would last long after he was dead, because the white man who robbed and cheated his way through life eventually met a girl, a girl who looked like me named Angelina, and he fell in love with her," Rose explained.

"No shit?" Davy let out unexpectedly.

"The world at the time wasn't kind to the couple though," Rose continued as she ignored his outburst. "It was the only thing Henry couldn't buy. So they left, and took with them everything he had ever stolen, alongside all of their children. The legacy he spent his life building wasn't just a horde of gold or more cash than a dozen horses could carry at a time. There was something more, something that couldn't be put into words."

"What do you mean?"

"I don't know, that was never told to me," Rose admitted to him. "We're going to find out though."

Silence found its way into the room. The ranger thought of the story he had told so many times before. He was looking right at the woman who continued the legacy of the woman who was the endearing heart of his story. Even if he did believe it, what could he say in the face of someone like that?

"I really don't have a clue how I am supposed to help you," Davy confessed.

"I know, but you're gonna it all the same."

Davy passed the empty bowl back to Rose and summoned as much strength as he could find to sit up in bed. He pushed the covers back and shook his head to clear himself of the pain he was starting to feel again. With a quick swing of his legs, he was upright with his feet dangling off the side of the bed, the skin on his abdomen tighter than ever and howling in pain.

"How do I know I can trust you?"

"You don't," Rose responded as coldly as ever. "But if I were in your shoes, I'd trust the person who saved me from getting tortured a *hell* of a lot more than the people who were doing all the damn torturing."

"You don't have to be so warm and welcoming all the time, you know, I get it."

With another audible groan, Davy was on his feet and eye level with Rose. He saw a pistol strapped to her hip, but he also noticed her knuckles. They looked like she had done more than her fair share of brawling over the years. She clearly wasn't someone to shy away from a fight and it was at that exact moment that Davy abandoned any thoughts of fighting his own way out of this situation. He would either have to do what she's asking and help her on this wild treasure hunt—or sneak away without her knowing. Something told him the latter might be more difficult than fighting.

"When are we leaving?"

"When you can get dressed and get in the car," she said immediately.

"Fair enough. Where we headed?"

"I'll tell you on the way, it'll be a long enough drive, trust me." With that, Rose turned and walked out the door she had come in, shutting it behind her to give Davy enough privacy to get dressed on his own. It was something he dreaded, as every muscle in his torso ached horribly. He knew putting on a shirt was the least of his worries, but he had to face it all the same.

"Don't ever run." The important words resonated in Davy once more.

Rose stood just outside the door in the hallway and listened to the pained grunts coming from inside the room as Davy put his clothes back on. Deciding it would be best to wait in the car, she left him to his own troubles. She'd end up waiting outside in the black SUV they arrived in for almost an hour before the ranger came limping out of the front door to the house. When he stepped out, he winced at the bright sun that went right into his eyes. His hand was draped across his stomach as if it would help him to not feel the pain of the brand emblazoned into his skin. Rose watched silently as he moved across the grassy yard to the vehicle.

Davy slid into the vehicle without saying a word and stared straight ahead. He was wearing a button down not too different from the one that had been burned through, albeit without the park ranger patches and just a little darker shade of brown. Rose started the vehicle and backed it down the driveway, mirroring Davy's quietness with her own. The drive was long and after over an hour, Davy still didn't know where they were going. It wouldn't be until the town of Burkeville that he would get the first bit of insight wherever they were driving to. It was a sign that said Port Arthur I 90 miles.

"We're going where they met, from the story?"

"You sure figured that out in a hurry. We're following the Sabine River south," Rose said when they drove past the sign. "It'll eventually get us to Port Arthur, our first stop in completing the map thanks to what you said back in Daingerfield."

"Going to where it all began isn't a bad place to get started," Davy said. "You really were paying attention."

"Like my life depended on it. The artifact has two halves that must be brought together to complete the map, those two pieces are all we need. They were the pieces carried by Henry and Angelina, the pieces meant to always bring them back together again. Only after aligning the two halves will we be able to find the treasure hidden where my ancestors called home."

Davy let himself think about what she was telling him and more importantly, what exactly he was getting himself into. What he knew of the old west myth is what he had learned when he was nine years old, apparently from someone who wasn't even part of this world anymore, so he wasn't feeling all too confident about his prospects here. Rose was following his story like it was scripture, though.

"How do you know all of this?"

"The same way you know anything that happened to your own family before you were brought into this world. It was told to me."

"By your mom?" Davy wasn't sure if the question was appropriate, but he went for it.

"That's right," Rose said before pausing. "And a few others."

Silence fell back between them. Rose's thoughts drifted from Davy's understandable struggles to the opportunity that now laid before them both. Despite the fact that Davy couldn't yet understand the weight of the journey, Rose felt it with every fiber of her being. Though it was difficult to admit even to herself, she did need Davy's help, and it was going to take some convincing to ensure she could count on him when the time came.

Davy's thoughts, however, returned to the towering pines back home in Daingerfield. Just thinking about the sounds they made swaying in the breeze, and the smell of the woods when all the pine needles filled the ground, brought him inexplicable comfort—especially during times like this. He was starting to kick himself for ever wanting to leave such a place. Doubt was beginning to creep in that he would ever see those pines blocking the sunlight above again.

Road noise swelled in the SUV as they sped down the highway southbound toward the oceanfront town of Port Arthur, right on the edge of Jefferson County. It wasn't a place Davy had been before. After all he'd been through already, he honestly didn't mind the chance to travel across Texas and see the natural beauty he knew it had in spades. He tried his best to think of the silver lining in every situation, and considering the day he had, it was admittedly as diffi-cult a task as he'd ever undertaken. But not everything had to be so terrible. It was this overly positive outlook that had carried him through some of the most trying times in his life and he wasn't about to lose it now.

"Is there anything else you can tell me about the map? Or maybe what the heck we're doing when we get to Port Arthur?"

Rose didn't acknowledge him at first. She drove with both hands on the leather wrapped steering wheel and kept her eyes locked on the road ahead.

"I told you we are after the missing pieces of the map. They're a piece of who my ancestors used to be, a token that only they could find direction in. What we're missing from the map of the Eternal Flame will not only hold the door to a lost treasure open for us, it'll make sure it won't hit us in the ass on our way out."

"I'll pretend like I know what you mean for the sake of my next question. The guys that are after us, the ones who are after the same treasure, and who did all of this to me," Davy said, looking down and motioning toward the brand in his stomach. "I can't help but worry they won't stop just because you killed a couple of them. After what they did back in Austin, I don't want to leave it to chance. My gun was in the bag with the artifact and if it's all right with you, I'd like to go on ahead and have that back before we get into whatever is about to happen next. It's only fair."

Rose sat forward in the driver's seat and reached behind her to pull out a small black revolver. It was heavy from the five rounds it carried in the cylinder. Rose shoved the gun over to Davy and glanced out of the corners of her eyes at him.

"This all right?"

"Wait. What happened to mine?"

"There weren't any guns in there when I found the bag. This is all I've got."

"We'll damn," Davy remarked. "Better than nothing I guess." He flipped out the cylinder of the revolver and spun it, listening to its rapid clicks speed up before coming to a slow stop. With a flick of his wrist, he slammed the cylinder back shut and then pushed the gun down into the front pocket.

The shock of the situation was setting in on Davy's body. Everything hurt, some places more than others, but all of it at once was taking its toll. He pulled his park ranger hat down over his face and allowed himself to close his eyes just for a moment. Davy knew better than to sleep at a time like this. He knew Rose could be taking him anywhere, even if she did just give him a gun. He needed to be ready for anything, but he also could barely keep his eyes open even with the fullest of intentions to stay awake.

It would be hours later when he opened his eyes again, still curled into the passenger seat, using only his sweaty folded arm as an uncomfortable pillow. The sun had only just decided to set for the afternoon as its light shifted through radiant colors seemingly on a whim.

He woke to the sound of waves crashing against a sea wall and a salty burn wafting into his nostrils. It all made for a picturesque moment that he would normally be happy to find the time to appreciate, but this time was far from normal. It was a view he didn't expect, seeing the enormity of the coastal ocean stretched out before him, listening to the water and feeling the breeze that swept in from the gulf. It was a tranquil feeling that he wasn't familiar with.

"Wake up, Davy," Rose said, forcing him out of his much-needed moment of reflection. "It's time to get started."

CHAPTER 9

A gainst the dwindling light of sunset, there was no one around to see a mysterious Stranger walk right up to the front doors of the Nations Heritage & Culture Preservation building and let himself in.

The Stranger was young, tall, and gangly, dressed in all black from his boots to his wide-topped cowboy hat. He was biting down on a half-smoked cigar as he strode into the building's lobby area. The cloud of smoke just barely escaped his crooked mouth with each puff that caused the end of the cigar to light up, revealing a square-jawed face with short stubble and tired, shadowy eyes.

He made his way through the remains of the crime scene that had been picked apart and cleaned profusely by law enforcement. There wasn't much left behind for him to see, but it was more than enough for someone who knew what to look for. The stainless wood-handled six shooter holstered at his hip gave the impression that the Stranger was someone who knew just what to look for. The lobby of the destroyed facility still had shards of broken glass that crunched beneath the worn soles of his boots. There were scrub marks on the walls and floors that most likely had been stained by blood in the violence that found its way inside.

The Stranger walked more delicately than his stature would suggest, brushing past tables and letting his hand drag across their surface, unafraid of leaving anything behind that might give the wrong person an idea he was there. A thin trail of smoke leaked from his nostrils, lingering in the air until he breathed in again. He reached up casually gripping the cigar between a couple of fingers before spatting some of the flakes of tobacco out. He readjusted the cigar and stuck it back into the corner of his lips, biting down on it as he did. His black mud-splattered cowboy hat was pulled down low just above his eyes, making it even harder to read his face. He wasn't one that took kindly to being around a lot of people, he preferred to work in silence and by himself.

As he walked over to the last room in the building —a broom closet that looked like it had hardly been touched by the police—he stopped and glared at it.

"Damn amateurs," he finally whispered under his breath.

The door was cracked open slightly, just enough for the Stranger to give it a slight push and watch it swing open. What he found inside the room caught him off guard.

Burned into the floor tile was an outline of a

symbol he was all too familiar with. It was a brand. There was a second person at large here, and they had been marked purposefully with a family symbol that didn't mean anything good for those who came face-to-face with it. The fact that it was used here was news to him, and probably Damian De León too. The Stranger knelt gently to the ground, inspecting the burn that was almost certainly missed by everyone who had come through after the incident. It was just barely noticeable, but to someone who knew what it was, it meant everything.

The brand was hundreds of years old and featured an "E" connected to a letter "J," an unmistakable mark from the De León family throughout history and used by Damian today in flame only against those who would oppose him. Though it may have been spiritual in origin, whoever was on the receiving end these days at his hand was likely either dead or lucky to have their life. It was more than a sign; it was an affliction of righteous vengeance.

"Espíritu de Jesús," the Stranger whispered to himself.

When he left the broom closet, he made one last pass through the lobby to confirm his sneaking suspicions. He had seen just about all he needed to see in this place. Sounds of his boots hitting the floor trailed off through the building as he left with his cell phone in hand. Standing outside in the parking lot beneath the stars beginning to dot the sky, the Stranger looked up into the night and listened to the phone ring. He stood motionless in the dark, silhouetted only by the cowboy hat he wore and the phone pressed to his ear.

The call rang three times before it was answered without a word on the other end.

"They're headed south," the Stranger said, followed by a quick response. "Yes. We're after more than one now."

He looked down with a new pain surfacing in his eyes that hadn't been there before. In his hand was an old photograph. It was difficult to distinguish in the dark, but the Stranger knew what the picture was through the stains and torn edges. It was a young woman, her eyes squinted and her mouth pursed with curled lips. Her black hair went straight down behind her back with a band that held it away from her face. She had the look of an age-old wisdom that betrayed her youth.

"A black SUV, got it."

There was a brief pause as the Stranger listened to his directions.

"I can be in Port Arthur by morning," he answered. "I won't be stopping tonight."

Against the dull moonlight finally beginning to make itself known, the Stranger looked at the woman in the picture. The burning in his gut was fueled by her stare, keeping him up at night and fighting during the day. When he'd had enough, he flipped over the old photograph in his hand. As he listened to the threats and ramblings of the man on the other end of the line, he stared at the same scribbled letters he'd read more than a hundred times before. There was only a single word written on the back of the dated picture, it had faded slightly, but was still recognizable in just the right light.

"Understood," he answered. "Better get yourself ready, it's almost time."

He closed the call and pushed the phone into the pocket of his faded denim jeans, keeping the picture in his hand as he did. He took one more glance at it and allowed himself to take a deep breath of the cool night air. What little moonlight was able to make it through the trees in the area cast shadows that looked like people watching him in the distance, waiting for something to happen. It only added to a claustrophobic feeling outside of the Nations Heritage & Culture Preservation facility that would have set most on edge.

Standing alone in the parking lot left to his own thoughts for just a few seconds, he felt only anger. He was driven by it, and rather than falling victim to directionless rage, he was instead able to channel it into a mission. Although it had dragged on for as long as he could remember, his mission was finally reaching a boiling point that couldn't be avoided. He took one last glance at the old photograph in his hand before setting off once again.

On the back of the picture, written haphazardly in the center was the word that held the Strangers attention—Rose.

CHAPTER 10

It was almost dark out when Rose and Davy pulled up next to Sabine Pass, a stone's throw away from the Gulf of Mexico if you had the arm for it.

They had passed an old lighthouse only a mile or two ago once known as the Sabine Pass Light, and as they passed by, Davy could only be distracted by thoughts of the stories it held in its rounded walls. It stood tall in the distance, a faded stone structure with one small window halfway up and several legs jutting out from the side for additional support. There was what looked like an iron cage on top that had been rusted over for some time. The once trusted beacon looked as though it was built to never be destroyed by the passing of time. Its green overgrowth that had crept up the tower gave it a decrepit look that could only be realized through the years.

He didn't know enough to have any expectations about what was going to happen next, but he did know the old Sabine Pass Light would be a good place to retreat to if they needed it.

Their drive didn't continue much further after passing the lighthouse. The ocean was swallowed in encroaching darkness getting larger and larger by the second in the horizon, and before too long, the two had pulled up to a shoreline where stars hung over its black waters. They both climbed out of the SUV and listened to the waves crash in the blackness that extended out across the ocean. It was a threatening natural force that they stood in front of, and it had a way of humbling all your hopes and dreams of the world.

The Sabine Pass was likely once quite a sight to behold. Things had changed for the area in the new world with all of its overreaching demands, however, as Rose and Davy saw mostly industrial equipment bleeding into the shores and land marked for even more commercial development behind them. It had turned into a place of modern industrialist necessity rather than one of picturesque beauty.

"Henry got shot for the first time back there at that lighthouse, you know," Davy finally spoke up. "I usually leave that part out of the story. Not everyone wants to hear about the outlaw who rides up at night when nobody is awake, leaving anyone nearby full of bullets with empty pockets. The old west was a place without mercy, where not everything had to make sense, but who wants to listen to that? Besides, the most important part is how he met a certain woman afterward."

Rose didn't say anything. She looked out across the

ocean and watched in silence, letting the sounds of the waves guide her thoughts until she could adjust her vision to the night. This was the end of the line for her people when they followed the Sabine River. She thought of what her family had gone through to bring her to this point. Her grandmother's sacrifice. Her Mother's lifetime that was spent cozying up to narcissists trying to find an artifact that would only tell her to find yet another artifact. A clue to find a clue.

A wave of regret and fear washed over her that matched the ferocity of the ocean she dared to face. It was difficult not to think about the possibility of her family being incapable of leaving the endless path to nowhere. After all, the map of the Eternal Flame was designed with the failsafe to do exactly that. One clue leading to another clue could continue on and on for her entire life just as it did before. Rose's thoughts drifted to the park ranger who would be her only hope of finally tracking it all down once and for all. Finally, she decided to answer him.

"She told you this, the woman at the park when you were a child?"

"Your long dead grandmother? Yes, she did."

"What else did she say? Do you remember anything?"

"Only that a flame was sparked in the waters here. That's why I go right to them meeting when I tell the story, that's what stood out to me most. This is the place they fell for each other."

The stars scattered across the night sky above them offered a welcome distraction from the darkness that hung in just about every other direction, punctuating the ranger's last sentence. Oceanic sounds now carried loudly through Sabine Pass, making it difficult to hear each other speak, but the smell of seawater was something Davy welcomed. It was different, so much more unusual than the scent of pine trees and lake water he had grown accustomed to.

The two stood in silence for longer than either anticipated until Rose finally turned slowly to face the park ranger she'd arrived with. She's been so focused on getting to this point in her life that she'd never imagined being here with someone by her side, much less someone like Davy. For reasons she couldn't explain, the treasure she was chasing didn't seem so far away now.

"I can't believe it really is here," Rose said. "It was difficult to know if I could trust what you were telling me. Somehow, it's comforting to know you were meant to be here, knowing what you know."

"Wait, what?" Davy asked, visibly caught off guard by what she had said.

"The flame sparked in the waters, her half of the artifact that was lost years ago in the same place where she found the one she loved, don't you get it? The first missing piece to the map of the Eternal Flame is out there," she said. "It has to be."

"I'm glad you feel like you can trust a complete stranger like me. I really am, but we don't actually know if any of that is true," Davy explained. "How do we even try to search for something that was just tossed in the ocean decades before we were even born? Where do we even try to start?"

As Rose listened to the park ranger's naive doubts,

she instinctively felt for the artifact in the bag slung over her shoulder. Her hand brushed against the canvas lining until she recognized the weight of the map of the Eternal Flame and suddenly recoiled sharply out of nowhere.

"What just happened?"

"Damn thing is scalding hot!" Rose hollered while shaking her hand from the pain.

Her reaction startled Davy who quickly made for the bag to get it off. She slipped the strap over her head and tossed it to the ground as each of them kneeled to get a closer look. Davy extended his hand to see if he could feel any heat. He expected it to be cool to the touch, but that isn't what he felt at all. The map of the Eternal Flame was living up to its name. It was almost hot enough to burn his hand just from being a few inches away, as if someone had just pulled it from smoldering coals and it hadn't had time yet to cool. He jerked his hand back and looked up to make eye contact with Rose. The look that she gave him was one that he would remember forever.

"The map is doing that thing again," Davy said with alarm in his voice. "It's getting hotter."

"That means we are too."

A loud thump saw the artifact burn right through the bag in Davy's hands and fall into the sand at their feet. He and Rose both scrambled to try and pick it up, searing their hands in the process. Its deep red glow was slowly swallowed by the melting sand, sinking at first just a few inches down before the earth seemed to give way, letting it fall more than two feet deeper. The light cast from its hole in the sand struck Davy as familiar. It was the same thing that happened back at Daingerfield State Park.

Rose suddenly gave up on fumbling for the artifact at the same moment the memories of Daingerfield returned to Davy. Their eyes met, illuminated beneath by the artifact buzzing with heat like filaments dancing in a bulb. Their stare wasn't at first intentional, but something changed as they analyzed one another's reaction, something that shouldn't have been spoken of. Just as easily as their eyes locked, they distracted themselves with the task at hand.

"This happened back at Daingerfield," Davy said. "Had to pull it out of the ground myself."

"I know, I was there."

Davy tried his best not to dwell on the fact that he knew he'd felt like someone had been following him that day. His doubts on the prospects of finding anything close to what they were after had already set in, however, giving his thoughts nowhere else to go.

"Look, Rose, I know the story I told got us here and all, but I really don't know what comes next. Being out here with you, and with this," Davy gestured in front of him, his back to the ocean as Rose stared intently at him, "I don't know where to even start looking for this missing piece of the map."

Davy looked for any reaction from the woman in front of him, ignoring the artifact still smoldering in the sand. Rose was staring with black eyes piercing right through him like only she knew how to do. When she did choose to speak up, what she said immediately changed everything.

"We're gonna start right there," she said, pointing

off into the distance, revealing that she hadn't given Davy even a passing glance, but was instead focusing on something particularly curious out in the ocean behind him in the distance.

There was a single crashing wave that quickly attracted both of their attention—only fifty yards out into the distance—glowing in a striking blue color. It was only happening in one spot, illuminating the passing of each wave with neon blue lightning repeating over and over again like a beacon just beneath the water. Rose had never seen anything like it, and judging from her response, Davy knew it had stolen her attention entirely.

"We've gotta stop wasting time," Rose said. "Come on, let's go."

He watched as Rose stayed true to what she said as she hurriedly walked down to the edge of the water, kicking her clunky leather boots off as she went. The ranger followed closely behind her, trying to catch up —both literally and figuratively.

"Wait, Rose," Davy spoke up, trying to manage expectations. "What the heck is going on?"

"I'm going after it," Rose said as if it was the most obvious thing in the world while continuing to strip down. "You can't follow me out. I need you here to get me out of the water if I need it. I don't know what I'm getting into here."

"It's just a bunch of *algae*!" Davy called out to her in fear. "That's all you're going to find."

Standing right at the edge of the water with the Sabine Pass washing out into the Gulf of Mexico at her back, Rose looked at Davy with a twisted face.

"You're fucking with me," she said while trying her best—yet failing miserably—to stifle a laugh which just about obliterated all the tension that had found its way onto the shores with them.

"I am one hundred percent not fucking with you," he answered bluntly. "I've seen those same waves in Galveston before and I didn't believe it then either. Not many people know about them, and even less are lucky enough to see one for themselves, but it's a real thing. I swear. It's bioluminescent algae that's just reacting to the waves out there. It can't be the spark we're looking for, there's no way."

Rose turned to look back at the wave that flashed and flickered in the distance like a siren made only for her eyes to see. It called her name with each strike of blue that shot through the passing waves. She could hear it over and over again, urging her out into the water, begging her to swim. Anxious concern mixed with a slight sense of vindication began to boil over as she realized what was happening. It was the artifact, her own ancestors, telling her she was on the right path, and it was all the confirmation she needed to do something any sane person would call downright crazy.

The park ranger watched helplessly as the mysterious woman he'd only just met turned and sprinted toward the shoreline of the Sabine Pass, right in the direction of the glowing blue wave in the distance. It was a surreal sight to watch, although he couldn't help but hope she was right. After what he had just seen with the artifact, he wasn't sure about anything right now. So how could he justify stopping her? Rose finding anything out there in the water would have to be a confirmation this was something worth seeing through.

Luckily, Rose was headstrong and willing to do just about anything to accomplish exactly that without so much as a second thought. What she was about to try, swimming so far into the middle of the night for a bunch of algae, was borderline delusional. While she ran further and further from Davy, leaving him by the roadside with the artifact after what had just happened, she wondered if she should even be trusting him to watch it. It was at best a rash decision made out of excitement. With a quick look back, she saw Davy still standing there holding the torn-through bag with an outstretched arm. He was just waiting, watching her run off.

"Be careful!" Rose heard his voice faintly in the distance. The ground was sharp and rocky against her feet, drawing lines of blood with every heavy step; it didn't slow her down any. Within seconds, Rose had reached the shoreline and leaped in headfirst to begin the long swim. Salt pursed her lips as she fought to put one hand in front of the other, keeping her eyes fixated on the bright blue glow emanating in the distance.

Davy was caught between trying to dig up the map of the Eternal Flame and scanning the waves in a panic, looking for where Rose could have gone in the vast horizon. His stomach sank as he realized she'd disappeared entirely.

Unaware of the fear coursing through Davy at her disappearance, or his desperate yells to catch her attention by any means, Rose had already reached the glowing wave that had drawn her like a moth to a flame. With one last deep breath, Rose forced her body far beneath the water as hard as she could. Saltwater stung her eyes and clouded her vision. The glowing was even brighter underwater, making it easy to follow and terribly alarming all the same. Hues of light blue turned to deep red before it burned away into an intense white. She pushed further against resistance that felt increasingly unlike anything she'd ever experienced. The whiteness that engulfed her vision became a part of her very existence and before she could realize what was happening, it no longer felt as though she was swimming. She was floating in the empty whiteness with nothing but her own thoughts. The silence that she found in such an inescapable place was deafening, until it was broken with a stark cry of a woman that was nowhere to be found.

The cries sounded muffled, as though mixed into the swirling saltwater that undoubtedly had already filled her ears, distant, but full of sorrow. The cries only grew louder, and before long, they turned to painful wails. The emptiness that Rose found herself floating within turned to static. It felt like she was lost in this stagnant consciousness for hours. Her breath swelled in her chest as her lungs started to burn fiercely, unknowingly suffering from the effects of the ocean bearing down her. Seconds ticked by in agony. The burning coursed through Rose's entire body and she started to flail her arms to find any sense of balance as best she could. A salty taste began to form inside her mouth, causing her tongue to twist and writhe without reason. The static that had come to encompass her entire sense of being suddenly started to fade into blackness, second by second.

"Take hold of what is yours," a voice drifted faintly into her ears. That's when she felt it. Amid the rushing saltwater and phantom voices lost in the blackness overtaking her, Rose's fingers grasped a small object buried in the sand. It was asymmetrical, finely shaped, and cylindrical with etched markings no larger than a flick lighter—but she didn't have time to examine it any further before her body lunged upward.

Everything inside her begged to reach the surface for a fresh breath of air and it was all she could do to clench her fist around whatever she had found. If she had been able to keep her eyes open, Rose would have noticed the strange glow that had brought her to the place swell back into reality.

It felt as if she'd been struggling against the ocean's pull for several minutes before the pressure in her chest began to cause vertigo to set in. Panic was starting to find her at last. Just as the final moments felt as though they were passing her by, she felt the influx of oxygen pour into her desperate lungs. She'd reached the surface at last, but when she opened her eyes there was nothing around. The glowing wave that brought her into the waters was fifty yards out, a hundred tops, but when she emerged from beneath, she found herself stranded at sea. Panic lodged itself in her throat at the realization. She ignored the object still clutched in her and picked a direction to swim in at random.

The saltwater burned her eyes every time she came

up for a fresh breath of air. Rose's swimming had turned mad as she fought to find her way back to shore. Anger began to form in the pit of her stomach for Davy not being there like she'd asked him to be.

Where was he?

The swim dragged on and on taking her nowhere. Each time Rose allowed herself to tread water and find her bearings, she could only see an infinite horizon in every direction she looked. This went on for an hour at first, then another hour painfully passed by and she was nowhere near closer to the shore. Her muscles were giving out with every kick and every paddle through the torrent of water that stood in her way. Another hour came and went. Davy was still not there to pull her out of the ocean. Although the saltwater continued to sting her eyes, she felt an infuriating sense of relief that it also washed her tears away. The panic lodged in her throat had long faded away and she was left drowning in hopelessness.

Rose knew nothing other than to continue swimming. It became her. The need to make it out of the water went to her core, deep down to define her entire existence. Gritting her teeth and ignoring the pain she felt in every muscle in her body, she pushed forward swimming into nothing, relying only on her own will to persevere.

Without any warning or sign of what was to come, her frantic swimming was interrupted by Davy's hand tightly grasping her shoulder to pull her up from the ocean. Her body went limp immediately and the ranger did his best to swim them back to shore on his own strength. They hadn't even finished crawling into the dirt on their hands and knees when Rose started in on him.

"Where were you, asshole? I told you! I almost drowned out there," Rose was still catching her breath as she yelled at the sand, squeezing her eyes shut and clenching her fists. "I told you!"

There were a few seconds of silence as the sounds of the gulf made their way back into focus. It took a bit of time before Davy actually realized what Rose was trying to tell her.

"What do you mean? You were only out there for a few seconds, Rose. I came to get you as soon as you popped back up."

"A few seconds?" Rose was confused by the words she heard. Davy continued his worrying next to her, but his voice faded in the back as she realized her right fist was still clenched hard enough to draw blood that dripped from her hand.

"It was *her*," Rose said out loud to no one in particular. "I heard everyone who mourned her when she died, I heard them calling out to her. Then she spoke to me. She's why I'm here."

"There is no one out there." Davy gestured widely in every direction with his arms. "Look, it's just us. Who would be speaking to you?"

"I heard her just as I got my hands on something at the bottom of the ocean in the sand. I found this."

Still slightly dazed, Rose lifted her hand and turned to open her first. She stared down, watching her blood-soaked fingers unravel slowly, and started to feel heat suddenly come from the palm of her hand. By the time she was able to see what she held, it was glowing red hot and searing into her skin with furious heat, but she remained still.

"The map," Rose said clearly. "Bring it to me."

Davy was stunned when he saw what was in her hand. It looked like a molten hot pendant that stretched down into a point. It took a few seconds for him to snap himself out of the shock and reach for the artifact still nestled deep into the sand beside them. It had cooled enough now to be handled, but when he lifted it from the hole in the sand, he couldn't help but feel the glasslike surface it now rested on. Rose's hand was unwavering as she grabbed it from Davy and moved the artifact closer to the missing piece she'd just found.

What happened when the two were brought together was unlike anything either of them had ever seen before. Rose had pushed the small piece into the top of the map of the Eternal Flame like a key into a keyhole, and with a firm clockwise twist, locked it into place. A flash of light and a wave of heat rushed by them. Before Davy had the time to recoil in shock, everything had fallen silent. Rose was kneeling, holding the artifact in her hand and staring down endlessly. Her chest heaved up and down as she tried to catch her breath.

Davy wasn't sure what they should do next, but he did know that standing out in the middle of a field next to the shoreline wasn't the answer. As Rose continued to stare at the artifact in her hands, he glanced over her shoulder to see the ocean in the distance stretching far into the horizon. Behind them the end of the winding Sabine River that stretched into deep East Texas. As the cool breeze eased the sweat at his brow behind the park ranger hat resting on his head, he noticed something in the distance. The glowing wave that lured Rose to swim out to the ocean had disappeared completely. He knew the algae out there couldn't be turned off like a light switch and wondered what really was in the water that had caused their night to go so awry in such a hurry. A chill slowly made its way down Davy's spine as he came to the understanding that something stranger than a treasure hunt really was happening to him.

"Rose..." Davy started. "What just happened?"

Rose just sat there. Davy sighed in relief as she twisted the artifact and rolled it around in her hands. It had returned to its normal graying color and didn't even show any signs of damage from what had just occurred; the markings on its surface had changed, though.

"I wish my mom was here to see this," Rose said. "And my grandmother. They both wanted this so much. This is exactly what they were so obsessed with finding for ourselves. They fought so hard for it."

"They're here," Davy told her. "All of them."

Rose was finally beginning to feel the momentum at her back—after all these years of coming up short only to try it all over again—and was starting to believe even for herself that what she was after would soon be hers. A smile slowly formed across her face.

"You're right."

CHAPTER 11

To say that Rose and Davy's return to the old lighthouse a few miles back was a welcome one would be a far cry from what they really felt.

The Sabine Pass Light would prove every bit as useful as Davy had hoped when they'd arrived in the area only hours before. It was about as far from a warm and cozy hotel room as they could get, but they had plenty of camping supplies and both agreed that a night of privacy would do them some good after what they'd discovered.

Several stone structures dotted the area beside the aging lighthouse that rose above them. Their makeshift camp sat just to the side, still under the stoic watch of the old tower. The lighthouse had seen far worse than their arrival in its lifetime, but that didn't stop them from trying to be as inconspicuous as possible. This camp had no fire and no gazing up at the stars, no stories to be shared, and no smoked meats to pass around. By the time they had a chance to sit down and process what had just happened, they were both inside the tent hiding from swarms of mosquitoes and whatever else threatened to invade from just outside the nylon fabric walls.

The tent that stretched out across the back of the SUV turned out to be rather handy in situations like this. It didn't offer much in the way of protection from the elements, but it was enough. Inside had space only enough to hold two sleeping bags resting on top of body-length inflatable pads and headrests. In between them was a small lantern casting a faint yellow glow throughout the tent.

Rose twirled the now half-completed artifact in her hands against the dull light of the lantern, analyzing every detail on its surface while Davy watched on in silence. As he stared at her, he thought of what she said to him about the story he told back in Daingerfield. If there was a sense of truth to it that he had never suspected, he wondered how much of this story he really knew. After a few seconds searching his memories as best he could, hoping to remember anything from the day his dad took him to Tyler State Park that would prove useful—it hit him. He knew Rose wasn't going to enjoy it one bit, but he had no choice but to catch her off guard.

"We're going to the Big Thicket tomorrow, aren't we?"

Rose glanced at him with her eyebrows raised and head cocked to the side.

"Why do you say that?"

"It's where he got shot. The outlaw Hank He...or

Henry Hunter, I mean," Davy answered. Rose looked over at him but didn't say anything. Her facial expression told Davy he should continue telling the story and he got the hint just fine.

"He was hiding there, waiting for a time when he could pass through and return home. He was staying with a group of Jayhawkers, a bunch of locals who had different feelings on the Civil War raging on at the time and hoped to wait it out in the woods. It was a place that the outlaw had used from time to time before, but one day, he got caught up in the middle of a fight between Confederate recruiters."

Rose was listening, that much Davy could see, but her face was blank and impossible to read. He had no choice but to keep talking and hope he ended up at a place where Rose would give some indication that he was on the right track. For now, she only stared at him with an occasional nod.

"A fire broke out. Not one that burned down a camp or anything like that, though. This fire eventually burned down over three thousand acres of the Big Thicket. In the fray of everyone escaping, there were shots fired in every direction. Friendly fire and enemy fire collided as the trees around them burned to the ground in ashes."

Davy shifted in the tent as he spoke, pausing only long enough to look at Rose who was listening intently. The tent wasn't the most comfortable place to be, but he wasn't one to complain. He knew Rose was most likely already impatient to get to the point, so he tried not to waste any time.

"Henry Hunt was one of the unfortunate victims

that day," Davy said. "He caught one of the stray bullets in the stomach as he tried to ride away. It always struck me as a mundane end to a life that was anything but. His death wasn't a quick one, though. He rode from the Big Thicket all the way to their home with a bullet in his belly to find the woman he fell in love with."

Rose perked up.

"And he did it carrying that map," Davy said with his finger pointed right at the artifact in Rose's hand. "He brought the map of the Eternal Flame back to her. It was with his dying breath that he placed it in her hands."

After listening to his story for the past few minutes, Rose was holding back the flood of emotions inside her. He knew things no one else had ever known and it continued to surprise her. She tried not to betray the feelings in her eyes, but she knew her shock was written plain across her face. The man who'd stumbled into her life unpacked her family's most important history, letting her see another side of him as he did. The ranger continued detailing what her family endured and how it had put her on the path to finding what they would leave behind. The details he gave from his old west tales were uncanny to the ones she learned on the reservation as a kid.

"This place was where it all began, and if I had to guess, that place was where it came to an unfortunate end. So, we go to the Big Thicket for his piece of the map, then high tail it to the treasure," Davy said, hoping to veer the conversation away from the troublesome past and encourage her just a bit.

"It won't be that easy."

"It can't be that hard either. Right? We've only just gotten started and we're halfway done. Henry was shot not too far from where the Jayhawkers used to camp out at a place called Bad Luck Creek. We can get to it from the Big Thicket, so that's where we need to go next, right?"

Sitting across from the park ranger who was getting more and more pushy about where they were going, Rose smiled at him for a split second. The details he knew about the story of her ancestors were so intimate and he shared everything. As much as she hated to admit it, they made a good team. Though Davy couldn't see it, she was debating how much she could tell him at a time like this. There was so much she wanted to say.

"It sounds like that's exactly where we need to be, Davy," she said, agreeing to leave it be for now.

Rose didn't pay much attention to what happened next. She watched the ranger continue on rattling off random facts about the Big Thicket. He was either just showing off his nerdy knowledge of the area, or still trying to prove that he could find a way to help. Regardless, she knew this was all going in her favor and she had Davy to thank for it right now—for better or worse. So, just to humor him, she played along asking questions and listening to his lengthy answers about how many hundreds of trees were at the Big Thicket, along with an endless number of other facts about the ecosystem at the nature preserve there. It was all very informative and sometimes even fascinating, but the sun's daybreak would come early in the morning and the two had yet another long day ahead of them. She had to interrupt one of Davy's bewilderingly detailed descriptions of a popular ghost story that had lived on through the decades just to let him know they needed to get some shut eye.

The sounds of the sweltering Texas night filled their tent. They were still close enough to the gulf to smell the salt on what little of the breeze could make its way inside. Exhausted from the thrills of the day, yet undeniably eager for what else was still to come, Davy fell asleep thinking only of what more of their adventure awaited them in the morning when the sun would finally rise.

Their short night of rest would end before the sun could rise in the east to wake them, though. Davy groaned after a gentle nudge on the shoulder from Rose who turned away immediately to complete her chores before he could even open his eyes. The morning was quiet between the two as they rolled their sleeping bags and stowed the tent away into the back of the SUV. It would be only a matter of minutes before they had nestled into their seats, prepped for the drive into the Big Thicket.

"You ready?" Rose finally asked.

"As I'll ever be."

"Don't expect the next piece of the map to be found so easily," she said. "I'm worried we may have used all our luck here."

"I like your positivity in the mornings," Davy responded with a dry tone. His park ranger hat was resting in his lap and he was still wiping sleep out of his eyes as he spoke.

"Davy, I haven't thanked you yet for everything you've done so far. I want you to know, I won't forget it."

All Davy could do was smile in return.

The light from the dawn was a couple hours away from burning through the heavy clouds that hung around them. The early morning just barely let them see beyond their headlights. It was cooler than it had been before, something that just came with the territory of being so close to the oceanfront. The drop in temperature was a welcome change from the overbearing heat of the sun that was sure to come later in the day. The drive put the old Sabine Pass Light far in their rearview mirror and had started with a usual sense of mundaneness. It was too surreal to think about what his life had turned into, so Davy did his best attempt not to overthink and keep his thoughts focused on the task at hand. Just as he started questioning why he was so enthralled with such a dangerous, probably illegal, adventure with such a strange woman, he turned his head quickly to the passenger window. Something had caught his eye, or rather, someone.

A man—unusually young for such a mean glint in his eye—passed their SUV in an older model farm truck that had undoubtedly seen better days. His eyes glared to the side directly at them as a smoldering cigar hung delicately out of the corner of his mouth. When they passed right by him, the man's cold stare betrayed his youthful age. His eyes locked with Davy's just briefly, going right through him, and forcing him to consider that maybe everything he knew didn't matter in the face of someone as dangerous as him.

"Hey Rose…" he started.

"Yeah?"

Davy watched without answering her, unable to shake the feeling this person was someone they should steer clear of. Something just didn't sit right with him and it sent a chill down his spine. As quickly as the two crossed paths with the mysterious Stranger, he was gone.

"Nothing, never mind."

Rose stole a glance at the ranger sitting next to her as she felt her stomach drop—she'd have no choice but to tell him soon enough.

CHAPTER 12

The sun was hidden behind a wall of gray clouds poised to rain at any moment when the mysterious Stranger's pickup truck came bouncing through the local neighborhood that followed the Sabine Lake south, just on the other side of Port Arthur. It was a day where you could smell the coming storm on the horizon and see its dark threatening skies in the distance, but it was also just another day on the job for the Stranger who was steadily gaining ground on what he was after.

His old Chevrolet farm truck handled the rough terrain with relative ease. The road that wound its way down to the shoreline at Sabine Pass gave him but one direction. While he wasn't certain of what he would find in such a place, he knew he wouldn't be staying long. His next destination wouldn't come from any oceanside discoveries, but instead, from a single phone call yet to be made.

For now, he followed the only road he could,

keeping a close eye from under his low-sitting cowboy hat for anything out of the ordinary while puffing every so often on what was left of the cigar in his mouth. It had burned down to just an inch long with ashes dropping occasionally that would sit on his chest or flutter to the ground. His tendency to smoke the long tobacco filled cigars had given both him and his pickup a unique scent that likely linger there forever.

The Stranger was still youthful despite his roughened exterior. His short time alive so far had only hardened him more than most his age. He was mean and merciless when he needed to be, but always cold and quiet no matter who was around. His years had betrayed him more often than not, and he carried himself in a way that made no attempts at hiding this from whoever he met.

When the tracks he was following down the dirt road veered off course, he did his best to follow them until they came to a sudden stop. He put his truck in park and killed the motor before climbing out and pushing his worn leather cowboy boots deep into the muddy ground. With his calloused hands on his hips, he gazed up at the clouds rolling in before setting off toward the shoreline where the Sabine Pass gave way into the gulf. Although he was alone for now, he could easily see the area had been walked over heavily in the last day or two with tracks trailing right down to the bottom.

The Stranger made his way up to the waters that rolled in the wind of the coming rain and glanced back and forth to check for any other evidence from recent visitors. He allowed himself to pace up and down the shoreline and consider the possibilities of not just what the people he was after had found in this place, but where it would be sending them next. Everything that had happened so far was predictable and suited him just fine. With a crunch of his boot coming down on what he thought was sand and turned out to be closer to glass, all of that changed.

"The hell was all that..."

Somehow, he'd managed to trip himself in a hole just large enough to wedge his boot down into. A crackling sound escaped when he lifted his boot and it was instantly all he could focus on. The Stranger kept his eyes locked on the ground in front of him, taking only quick glances around while searching for any indication of tampering that might give insight into what those two were doing—or what they had found. It was this determined focus that led to one of the few mistakes he'd ever made out in the field. It left him completely oblivious to a black vehicle that had turned onto the same road which brought him here and was now making its way toward him at an uncomfortably rapid pace.

By the time the Stranger did finally look up, the ones who were driving the black vehicle had already spotted him and it was too late to do anything other than confront them directly. This was made painfully clear when the headlights started flashing as soon as he lifted his gaze. They were watching him, that much was clear. As the dust from the road swirled up behind the dirt-spotted black car they drove, the Stranger made sure not to move too suddenly and spook them into escalating the situation even further.

When the car pulled to a stop and two men climbed out, he quickly realized this wasn't just some security guards or parking lot police. These were familiar hired hands, and in fact, they were most likely hired by the same hand who'd sent him—they were Pinkertons. Things had a way of working out like that in this life and he had grown accustomed to it by now. The only problem was, the men standing across from him probably hadn't. They would die without even the slightest understanding as to why.

"Mornin' y'all," he called out first to set the tone, masking what was really happening.

"We know two people were up here trespassing last night," one of the men started right in with his fluffy beard pressed against his neck, bunched up against the collar of his button down khaki shirt. He had the look of someone who didn't deal with confrontation all that often, and when he had to, he didn't handle it well.

"How long you been here, sir?" the other asked, trying to show some politeness. He was skinnier than his partner and wore thick black-framed glasses with a matching shirt.

"Just got here a few minutes ago," the Stranger said. He decided the truth was the best option for now, given the circumstances.

"So you don't know nothing about a couple of people who stayed here last night, taking the liberty of walking all over the place, going for a little night swim, and doing just about whatever they damn well wanted?" The larger man was more forceful and it was coming out in spades already.

The Stranger's head dropped in response. He knew exactly what brought these two out to meet him this morning, and it was the same reason he was there— the artifact.

"Nothing worth passing on to a couple of try-hards like you," the Stranger commented, still sticking to the truth as far as he could tell. "Am I free to go?"

"You wait just a minute now," said the other man.

"I'm running late, just so you know. I can't be stuck here dicking around all damn day."

"What the hell are you doing here anyway?"

"What does anyone do out in a place like this? I'm going for a walk somewhere that isn't the same damn beach," he said, still trying to keep his calm. "That illegal now or something?"

"We're going to need to ask you just a few more questions," the pushy one told him, bristling his stature as he spoke. "We're after some real bad people and we have reason to believe they may have been here last night. Our boss isn't as understanding as we are, so you just play nice and answer our questions."

As the scattered gray storm clouds continued rolling in to cover the sun from beating down on their confrontation, the Stranger took a moment to square up the two men who seemed a little too eager to pester him while he worked. They were armed, but spotless in their attire and composed in a way that only proved their lack of responsibilities. They may have been Pinkertons, but they were also grunts. He wasn't threatened by them. He did know this could all derail quickly if he wasn't careful though.

"Why don't you try us anyway, tough guy," the bearded one let out, unable to help himself.

For a split second, the Stranger actually considered what the man had said. Just when he was ready to disregard it, maybe even turn and walk away, the second one casually rested his right hand on his hip just above a holster tucked into his waistband.

It was this moment when the Stranger knew things had no chance of going as smoothly as he'd hoped.

The view behind the two men facing him was getting darker with each passing minute. Rumblings of thunder had begun to ease into the area sporadically and the sun's light had given way to the inevitable, taking with it all the day's warmth. As a cool breeze picked up around them and the waters of the gulf turned to choppy waves, anything that was once inviting about the place had crumbled away. There were only threats that remained.

"I'm afraid I can't do that," the Stranger replied. "This is work, and even though your boss may force you to ask all these useless questions, mine demands otherwise."

"This ain't something you can just talk your way out of," said the bearded man with fiery anger pouring through every word.

"I don't know if you think I'm just playing around or what, but you really should just get while ya still can," the Stranger told him, getting colder as he spoke.

"You don't seem to understand what's happening here," one of the men replied. "If you won't tell us what the hell is going on, maybe you will talk to our boss. He has a way of sorting out people like you. Hell, this time I might even *enjoy* watching it happen."

The men were both standing with their hands on their hips now and the situation was escalating. While there weren't many options to take when this whole confrontation started, there were even fewer now. As the fleeing birds chirped away overhead signaling the rain about to pour down on them, the Stranger stood motionless and let the cocky man contemplate what he had just said for a few moments.

The Stranger let a half-smile curl up on his lips. He bit down on his cigar just a little harder and let the ashes fall to the ground in front of him carelessly. He wondered if it was worth it to tell them they worked for the same boss—that it was all for the demands of one man that the three of them were willing to gun each other down in cold blood right there. In the end, the Stranger knew that would ultimately not mean a thing. This was going to play out like it always had and there wasn't anything he could do about it, other than make sure he was the one who walked away.

"I'm only gonna tell you one more time," the Stranger muttered. "Get."

"Or what?" The first man wasted no time in letting his anger get the best of him. The smaller one leaned over to his partner and whispered out of the corner of his mouth. Though the Stranger couldn't make his words out, he knew it was done out of fear. He had started to grasp the situation and had a bit more sense than the man he rode in with, now it was starting to show. Unfortunately for them, it was already too late.

The next few seconds saw each man standing at the points of a triangle across from one another with their hands hovering over their hips. Each second ticked by excruciatingly slowly for the two clueless men who had gotten into way more than they bargained for. Each one trembled from a dangerous mixture of overzealousness and fear, something that had gotten the best of men far greater than them all throughout history. Today would be no different.

The Stranger's hand sat still, never faltering, ready to move at even the slightest sign of trouble. His cigar burned down further, leaving almost nothing left except the bit he held between his teeth. Smoke trailed out of his lips only to be lost in the winds of the coming storm.

Staring ahead at one another without so much as a blink, the men found themselves pausing for what felt like an eternity. No one wanted to make the first move, to do something that couldn't be taken back, and to risk the chance of never leaving the shores at Sabine Pass again. There were plenty of opportunities to strike the match of violence in this place where no one would see, but hesitant anxiety from those trying to face down the Stranger had hit hard.

Standing quietly and refusing to move, the three of them focused only on who would draw first. The Stranger suddenly felt a single cold raindrop land on his shoulder as a deep growl of thunder shook above them. Raindrops fell few and far between at first, bouncing off their hats and hitting their hands still hovering above their waists.

Tink. Tink. Tink. The two across from the Stranger

listened to the sounds of the rain falling onto the car they stood next to as they judged the threat. Another round of thunder rocked the skies above them, this time more violently than ever, making the men flinch by just a hair and drift their hands even closer to the firearms strapped to their hip.

The Stranger stood still.

This gave the larger cocky man a suicidal sense of confidence that finally pushed him over the edge; one that he was all too ready to drag his friend over as well. He knew he could make the first move now. He'd gained an advantage over his opponent that wasn't just simple numbers. It was just what he needed. The brief time that was left was spent waiting on the next sound of the storm to set them in their fated motions. Their wait was cut short by the sharp crackling of a lightning strike less than a hundred yards off. The bolt slammed into the field between them, starting a smoking fire surrounding the charred remains of the strike.

The bearded man drew his gun first, and his ill-prepared partner was just behind him. Their fingers cold and wet, their hearts racing in fear, but their loyalty to a cause the Stranger didn't understand was stronger than ever. Before they could get their firearms out of their leather holsters and pointed in the direction of the Stranger—two piercing shots rang out in rapid succession.

Pop. Pop.

The Stranger stood in place, facing the two armed grunts who stood opposite from him. For a couple seconds, they stayed firm with their guns pointed forward, but the determined focus in their faces soon turned to a mixture of frightened panic and confusion that can only wash across the face of a man who knows he's about to die.

The storm had started to pour down now, rain blanketed the area and all three of the men as thunder continued to roar above them. When the next lightning flashed around them followed by another cracking sound in the distance, the two grunts fell to the ground lifeless.

With an old revolver in his right hand and his left still hovering carefully just above the exposed hammer, the Stranger hesitated before slowly pushing it back down into the holster set deeply on his hip. His cracked leather cowboy boots were planted heavily in the wet mud, sinking deeper with the rain drenching the ground even more. As he turned to walk back to his truck, his heels twisted in the dirt and left marks behind for anyone who cared to see. He never looked back at the men he had just killed. The blood of their lethal wounds flowed into the mud and mixed with the rainwater making a hundred tiny streams in the ground, turning deep red as they ran.

As the Stranger strode back to the truck he came in, he pulled his phone out of his pocket, ignoring the rain while he dialed the number of Damian De León and pushed it up to his ear.

"Mr. De León, I have a plate for you," he said without elaborating. "And tell your other goons to stop trying to kill me. It won't work that easy, dammit."

"Where is the damn artifact?" Damian answered

without acknowledging his request. "We're running out of time. I don't need to explain to you what would happen if we lose it now, not when we're so close. You *need* to tell me where they are."

"Tell me where the plate is then," the Stranger told him bluntly. "I can't hang around here all day anyway. Tell me where and I'll go fetch. You better hold up your end though, you hear me?"

"If you fuck this up," Damian answered, a cruel twist in his voice.

"It's me we're talking about, remember? Send me the location."

"It'll be messaged to you from a new number. Lose this one."

"We'll be seeing each other soon."

"We better be," Damian threatened.

avy was gushing about the Big Thicket as he and Rose drove into the National Preserve, surrounded by pines and oaks, maples and dogwoods, sweetgums and just about every thorny vine Texas could hold.

"It's one of Texas's most underrated gems, the place is basically a natural showcase of just about every wildlife and forestry species you could ever imagine. In the late 1800s it attracted the meat industry because of all the hunting opportunities being capitalized on by Natives and frontiersmen. Then, in the early 1900s the logging industry tried their damndest to wipe out the woods. Swarms of people cut down just about anything they could swing an axe at for years."

"I'm not really sure how any of this is helping," Rose admitted.

"During all of this," Davy continued, ignoring Rose's offhanded input. "The oil and gas industry had their boom of production in the area that was just about as destructive as everyone else's. That's just where all the real money was."

"Are you done?"

Rose was getting impatient with the history lesson, unsure if it was actually going anywhere useful. Davy could see it on her face and he knew he better get to the point if he was going to make a case worth listening to.

"It used to be millions of acres, but the National Preserve is just over a hundred thousand acres now. That much land has had more than enough time to gather some stories over the years too. The history of the thicket is full of folklore that has been passed down through the ages, stories that most chalk up to tourist traps. Those people don't know what I know, though," explained Davy.

"Davy, you already told me this is where we need to be to find the next piece of the map but take a look around. There's so much to cover here," Rose said while letting her eyes scan the trees stretching endlessly out in just about every direction, hiding the creeks and swamps stagnating in their depths along with the animals who called such a place home. "We need more than just stories to tell each other, we need somewhere to actually start looking."

They passed a sign that read Honey Island Swamp I 1/2 Mile as Davy acknowledged her by doing pretty much the opposite of what she'd said, continuing his stories about the Big Thicket.

"Remember Bad Luck Creek? That's the place we start with, but honestly, that's not all there is to it. A man named James Kaiser set fire to the Big Thicket to chase the Jaywalkers out not too far from this place. In that fight, good ol' Mr. Hunter caught a bullet to the belly and made it his final mission in life to return home one last time."

"Davy, I need you to get on with it," she told him. "We seriously don't have time for this shit."

"Just listen, please," Davy pleaded. "Treasure hunting and killing people isn't exactly my specialty like it is yours, but I know this place, and I think I can give us somewhere to start. The stories people have who visited here are almost unnatural, but after everything we just saw down at the gulf, after what you told me happened to you out in the water—I think all of this is connected. Actually, I know it is."

Rose pulled into an abandoned parking lot to what looked like an old general store, taking in the dense woods that surrounded them. For the last hour, they never seemed to get into a clearing that allowed them enough to see further than a few feet ahead. It was the kind of brush and thick trees that would blot out the sun and suffocate you with humidity just a few minutes in, making for a rather strenuous hike even when it was just for recreation.

Davy may have thought they had time to chase old folk tales, but Rose knew better.

"There are so many outlandish stories surrounding the area, most of them all center around Old Bragg Road with this mysterious light that has been seen over and over again floating in the dark. Those who call it the Light of the Saratoga say it's the remains of a railroad worker who was decapitated in a train wreck on the Saratoga line. They say that he wanders the thicket every night looking for his lost head. Others say it is from the Spanish conquistadors who traveled into the area as part of their journeys into Texas and the wealth they brought with them. They say some were lost to a fate of always searching for what they could never have." Davy had been all too eager to explain the tales, but this time he dropped his tone. "But the story that I haven't been able to stop thinking about since back at Sabine Pass is of the undying light. It has been kept alive for people today to bear witness of the ghost of a man killed during the Kaiser Burnout."

Davy could tell that Rose was resisting the urge to groan, so he decided to ask her outright what had truly been on his mind.

"What if that undying light is actually him? What if it's Henry out there and Bad Luck Creek earned its name through an unspoken tragedy about him? Judging from the last few days of my own life, crazier shit has happened."

His question caught her off guard. Rose had to pause and force herself to think for a moment, fighting not to follow her instinct to dismiss it as complete nonsense. She knew they were lucky to have avoided the grasp of those who were after their artifact, but now she was starting to feel guilty that she'd kept information from Davy, which seemed even more important considering what he was telling her now. There was a risk that he just wasn't aware of and it was distracting her from chasing what really mattered.

Rose sighed and looked at him, preparing herself mentally to deal with his reaction.

"Before we go chasing ghosts into those woods out there, there is something I haven't told you yet about the men who tortured you," she started.

"What do you mean?" Davy questioned. "Where is this coming from?"

"His name is Damian De León. He is the head of— let's call it a corporation—that is really just a front for an enterprise of criminal organizations. My family got involved with him a very long time ago over this," she explained while holding up the map of the Eternal Flame in her hands once more.

"Okay, let me guess, and now he wants it for himself?"

"And that's not all either, actually," she answered. "I made a stupid ass promise to the man, if you can call him that. When I was at my most vulnerable, I told him that he would get his investment back more than tenfold if we could strike a deal. I gave him every-thing. Then I failed. I failed again, and again, and again. I failed in ways I didn't even understand. Now Damian De León doesn't just want his money back, he wants everything that was ever mine or ever will be. And when he's had all of that, he will try to kill me."

"My god, Rose." It was all Davy could muster up as a response.

"Damian is in the business of conquest, of empire building. We're just a single link in the chain of his control, extending it ever so slightly and by doing so, giving him the opportunity to take over more than any of us could've realized. In his eyes, even one link at risk is too many though. You don't have to understand all of it just yet. For now, you just have to beware— and be ready."

Davy sat quietly, listening to what Rose had to say before something clicked in his head. He realized Rose had a larger degree of responsibility in his capture than he'd considered, and within moments he began to feel an all too familiar frustration building up in his belly. The brand on his stomach and Rose's role in his torture played over in his mind, but there wasn't anything he could do about it now. All he could do was hope it wouldn't happen again and trust this strange woman he was with was telling him the truth. He had to force himself to remember the only reason he had escaped the research facility back in Austin was because Rose showed up and basically killed everyone to set him free. She may have been the reason he'd gotten into this mess to begin with, but she was also the only reason he was still alive.

"If I find everything promised by the map of the Eternal Flame, it will bring freedom. Something my family has too often had stolen from us, or worse, twisted and exploited beyond recognition," Rose confessed. "It's something I won't allow to happen again. But his money, his loyal supporters, who are nothing more than damn henchmen, they're nearly unlimited and we can't afford to keep up the fight against them much longer. There is too much at stake, so I pressed on as best I could by myself. Then you turned up with the artifact of my ancestors and changed everything."

"That means if I hadn't carried what turned out to

be a treasure map wanted by a bunch of bloodthirsty asshats down to Austin, I wouldn't know what it's like to be tortured. And I might still actually have my job."

"Well, there's that too. I know this isn't easy to hear," Rose conceded. "I know I'm somewhat, maybe even mostly, to blame for what happened to you, but you have to believe me when I say this man has hurt countless others far more—me included. Damian De León can't be allowed to keep his life."

Davy could see the hurt in Rose's eyes and the remorseless anger welling up in his belly began to subside. He could never understand what she'd been through, but he'd felt what this man Damian was capable of firsthand, and he knew she was telling the truth. If he was going to be onboard with actually following this map of the Eternal Flame all the way to maybe even finding a lost treasure of the old west, he would have to confront this evil as well—and he'd be damned if it was something he was going to shy away from.

"I have something to admit too, while we're at it," Davy said.

"Can't be anything worse than mine."

"You're right, it's not even close," he agreed with Rose. "But the truth is, I volunteered to take the map to Austin because I was getting ready to request a transfer to another park. I needed to get away."

"To do what?"

"Anything. I was looking for an adventure of my own. I've sat around in parks for years now telling the same stories of cowboys in the old west chasing down gold, which were basically delusions of grandeur, hoping to get lost in one of my own."

"Why are you telling me this now?"

"Because I think I finally found what I was looking for. I'm on a real-life dangerous treasure hunt for an outlaw's lost gold. We're going to find the last piece of the artifact, the freedom you've been looking for, and this Damian guy isn't going to be allowed to hurt anyone else," Davy consoled her. "I'm telling you this because I want you to know what you'll be doing to me if you screw me over in all of this."

There was a silence that fell between the two and with it, an unspoken mutual understanding.

Up until this moment, there had been a pang of guilty regret for joining Rose in this admittedly foolish journey up until this point, but now, Davy could see there was still hope.

It was the same hope that Rose had felt since the artifact had been uncovered. Somehow, she had found someone who was on her side even when she was guilty of almost never telling the entire truth. She found comfort in it.

"So, what do you say, we doing this?" asked Davy.

Rose nodded without hesitating. "Damn right we are."

"Luckily, this has become a tourist trap more than anything else, so the ghost road isn't all that hard to find," Davy explained, as he climbed out of the vehicle while staring at a map that Rose had no idea where he'd gotten.

"Ghost road? Come on, I can't believe we're actually doing this," Rose let out.

The two started off toward the Old Bragg Road. There was still plenty of daylight left and it was the perfect time to slip into the woods of the Big Thicket unnoticed. The light hadn't yet started to fade, but within the shadows beneath the brush and trees, a cool breeze still found its way in. The trailhead was marked only by a small sign on top of a stack of rocks indicating the start of just one of many paths that wound through the overwhelmingly large preserve. Surrounded by yaupon brush so thick that Davy nor Rose could walk through it without a hatchet, they stuck to the well-maintained dirt trail for at least the first mile to make sure they were in fact on their own.

"Give me a second." Rose finally broke the silence between them after listening to their boots hit the ground for almost an hour.

Rose was kneeling in front of her bag, holding her 1911 pistol and checking the magazine to make sure it was loaded one more time before slowly pushing the slide back to ensure one was still in the chamber. When she was satisfied, she pushed her jacket back and pulled her shirt up to tuck it into her waistband, hidden from sight. Without saying a word, she glanced up at Davy as if she was expecting something from him.

It took a moment before Davy realized what was happening. He reached down and grabbed the small revolver that Rose had given him out of his pants and popped the cylinder. With a nice spin to check all five rounds were still loaded, he pushed it back into place.

"All good here," he commented, trying to ease Rose's mind a bit.

"Like I said before, you need to be ready," Rose told him. "Sometimes it's a big group of assholes and sometimes it's just a few, but this has been going on for a long time now, and I can tell when it's coming back around. We've had a good, quiet run so far, but I can almost guarantee Damian's goons are on our tail. They'll either be waiting on us to get out of these damn woods, or if they are really stupid, which is typically the case, they'll be following us in."

"What kind of goons, exactly?"

"There have been just about all kinds through the years," Rose said. "Here lately, he's been favoring the Pinkertons to do his dirty work."

"Shit," Davy muttered under his breath at the name Rose just dropped. "In that case, I just wish I had something other than this little five-shot revolver to see me through."

"Well, if your gun hadn't been stolen before we ever got started that wouldn't be an issue. You'll remember that next time you carry your gun in your bag. Also, don't forget that's my little five-shot revolver, and I'll be wanting it back, so don't fuck it up," Rose said with a half-smile forming on her lips. "Besides, you don't have anything to worry about. I came prepared."

Before Davy could comment on her last remark, Rose had knelt down again in front of her bag and reached in. What she pulled out caught Davy off guard at first, but he didn't object all the same given who was after them. Rose was holding an AR with a folding stock that made it fit nicely inside her backpack, well out of sight. With a quick slap under the magazine, Rose yanked at the charging handle and popped a round in the chamber, then checked the safety.

"You never know, really," she said without looking up from the rifle. "This is only so we can get outta here alive, but it's not going to make much of a difference if we don't get the last piece of the Eternal Flame before they do. Understand?"

Despite his apprehension, Davy did feel a bit comforted knowing they would be more prepared than just his five measly rounds would allow. While he hadn't exactly been in a firefight before, the way Rose talked about the people following them, it seemed that facing this reality was just a matter of time. No matter what, he'd be ready, or at least that's what he was telling himself over and over.

There were songs of the local warblers in the air around them, and despite getting more humid by the second, it was a serene environment that was easy enough to appreciate. Davy wasn't alone in this sentiment either. Rose joined him for a brief moment to look around and consider the magnitude of where they were, the history of those who had walked the place before them, and how nature just had a certain way of humbling you no matter where you were in life. It was as if the twisting branches above and winding path at their feet did more than just understand your own misshapen circumstances but accommodated you at every turn in a way that no one else ever could. The sheer scale of it was both intimidating and magnificent, making anyone who walked through the place feel both as small as an ant crawling on the ground and as significant as a hundred-year-old oak standing tall in the woods.

With a deep breath and a much longer than usual exhale, Davy took a slow step forward to nudge himself onward down the path to uncertainty.

Rose stayed still just a moment longer, allowing a glimpse into what it was like to enjoy the feeling of having a peace of mind before forcing herself to snap back into the reality of the situation and catch up to Davy.

The two walked for an hour more, stopping only to catch their breath or take small sips from their beat-up water bottle, trying to conserve as much of their strength and resources as possible in case the worst of their imaginations came storming into reality. The sounds of their boots created a monotonous rhythm that lulled them into a false sense of safety, listening only to the birds and the occasional scatter of a critter catching their scent only to bolt away as quickly as they could. Their hike in the Big Thicket would be cut short when Davy suddenly stopped in the middle of the path and began looking from side to side.

"What are you doing? We need to keep moving," Rose said.

"This path runs alongside the Old Bragg Road. Tourists run up and down the road looking for any scares they can get out of it in the middle of the night. This ain't where we need to be though," Davy said, his tone changing to a stern seriousness that caught Rose off guard. "We gotta go deeper into the woods, trust me."

The two stepped quietly off the path and continued

on their way as Davy stared down at an old metal compass he gripped firmly in his right hand, extended out just slightly enough for him to read its directions. With the path behind them, they stayed quiet and watched their steps, ensuring they were as quiet as possible. When she felt comfortable with how far off the trail they were, she caught up closer behind the park ranger.

"Not that I don't trust you or anything, but I don't even know what we're looking for out here. Can you tell me something?"

"It'll be dark soon," he answered without looking back at her. "We don't want to be on

the path for just anyone to find when it does get dark. And besides, we're after Bad Luck Creek, remember? Just look for water. It would've been just north where the Jayhawker camp sat. That's where we need to be. I'd say this is a shortcut there, but—"

"A shortcut is never really short," Rose cut in.

The two continued on their way without stopping until daylight started to fade from view. Thick woods that cut and scraped at their skin every chance it got made the sun even harder to see. Once all of the light had gone and darkness crept up around them, the woods shifted to a much creepier environment that put them both on edge. Growing shadows filled their eyesight and the scattering of leaves and sticks were no longer endearing, but unsettling.

"We need to go just a little further," Davy pushed. "There is a small runoff just up ahead, that's where we can stop for a bit and wait it out. I don't expect to be sitting around for too long, in all honesty. I doubt it's managed to stay a rumor for this long out here because of luck."

The two found a secluded area right before the woods opened up into the dirt remains that led to Bad Luck Creek straight from the Old Bragg Road. The creek itself was surrounded on either side by towering brush and vines with clusters of trees jolting into the sky. It was in these dense woods that both Rose and Davy would be settling down for the night. Davy spent a few minutes chopping away at the branches with a dulled knife to create a small clearing, just spacious enough for the both of them to lie down for a bit. Before long he motioned to Rose to join him.

"We need to take watch," Davy told her just as she sat down. "One at a time, until we see the light we came all this way for."

"And if we don't?"

"Then we try again tomorrow. And the next day. Until we find it and follow where it leads."

"Didn't we talk about this? We don't have forever to sit here and wait on a literal ghost story to come to life," Rose groaned. "If it doesn't show up by tomorrow, we have to try something else, *anything* else."

"What else can we try? I'm all ears. Until then, I'd say get comfortable, because it's going to be a long night. And besides, I have a feeling it won't take very long at all to see what we're after. Not with that thing in your bag," Davy explained while he gestured toward the artifact in the bag slung across Rose's shoulder.

"You enjoy this, don't you, Ranger?"

"I would be lying if I said otherwise. To be back in

a place like this, surrounded by trees and everything else that calls this place home. It's just good to be back where I feel like I belong, ya know?" Davy tried to explain as best he could. The feeling he got staying under the stars perched against a tree soothed his soul. He could feel the burn on his stomach actually healing for the first time, silently confirming his own suspicions that it was a health hazard to avoid such places for too long.

Rose nestled down in the sticks and stretched across the sleeping back that was laid out to keep her from lying directly in the ground. The nighttime soundtrack in the Big Thicket began to pick up as crickets and cicadas sang their songs for all to hear just a little too loudly. That was all right with both of them though, as there likely wouldn't be much sleep between them anyway. The next hours would be long, humid, and full of flying insects that no one wanted buzzing around their faces. Rose had steadily grown more annoyed by the minute for well over an hour, sitting in the silence of night and unable to do anything apart from staring at a patch of dirt that wound its way through the woods. Davy, however, was just as enthralled as he had been when they first arrived.

"Still nothing?" Rose questioned, trying to hide the irritation in her voice.

"You asked me that question about five times already," Davy answered as calmly as he could. "You'll be the first to know as soon as I see something."

Rose grunted a small approval and sighed one

more time before deciding to suck it up for the night and see if what Davy had promised would actually come true. She was staring at what could barely be called a creek in front of them—what amounted to a dirt patch with more brush all around it—unsure of what to watch for, yet trying her damndest to stay focused all the same. Suddenly, a shift in the wind sent a chill down her spine. They both felt it, the cool air tickling the hair on the back of their neck made their eyes widen immediately. Davy glanced over at Rose and squinted his eyes without saying a word, but she shrugged it off and looked back in front of them. The temperature dropped a few degrees first, then ten, and twenty degrees, before reaching a point where both could see every exhaled breath as a fog blown out into the darkness surrounding them on all sides.

"What on earth is happening here," Rose whispered.

Both were staring dead ahead, unflinching despite getting colder by the second. Though they didn't even realize it, both Rose and Davy had slowly reached for the guns tucked in their waistbands in unison, knowing damn well it wouldn't do any good to shoot, but doing it anyway.

"Whatever it is, it ain't on earth anymore," Davy answered her at last.

Rose's stomach was turning and she didn't know what to expect next, but for some reason, she was comforted knowing that Davy was by her side. She'd been pushing forward alone for so long now, she'd almost forgotten what it felt like to have someone there to help her instead of fighting against her every move. His confidence was unusual for what he had gone through so far. Since their night by the lighthouse at the Sabine Pass though, it was like something had changed. He'd changed.

The chill in the air only continued to get worse, unnaturally so, and the woods only got darker behind the branches that tangled together above their heads. It was pitch black before Rose realized it and she couldn't even see her hand in front of her face. The sounds of the woods died out entirely. Crickets and cicadas no longer made themselves known and the stars overhead were blanketed in black clouds. It was unsettling, but Davy was stoic throughout it all. Rose could see that he was in his element in these woods and she began to find her trust in his instincts from within such a place.

"Get your things," he whispered to her.

Just as he did, the sounds of a horrendous scream from a horse pierced the air, coming from every direction. They both clutched at their ears in fear and shock, scrambling to find one another while looking around frantically to find the source. There was none.

The screams of the horse were violent and getting louder as if it were running right at them, only stopping for broken breaths to continue its screech at a higher pitch with each renewed effort. It was becoming unbearable and only getting worse, but just as soon as it had started, the screams of the horse lost in the darkness of night came to a sudden stop.

Davy looked at Rose who was showing signs of feverish unease in her eyes, and felt himself just the smallest bit lucky because she hadn't noticed his own frightened glare.

Before he could offer any consolation, a strangely shaped shadow began to rise across Rose's face, high-lighting her features in an odd, ghoulish way. It started softly, almost otherworldly in its movement and glow, but then it flashed across her like the passing headlight of a car in the night. As he stared at Rose's face, he watched her try with all her might to lift a finger gently in the air while staring into nothing ahead with only a blank expression painted onto her face. Her index finger extended out without warning and Davy knew what was happening. The look in her eyes was undeniable. This wasn't some touristy old folktale about a ghost—this was something else entirely.

The only thing left to do now was follow it.

CHAPTER 14

Damian De León had just slammed the phone back down on his desk in unfiltered frustration for what had to be the tenth time that day. His patience wasn't running out anymore, it was already long gone.

He was sitting at an oversized oak desk stretched out at either side of him, longer than one person would ever need, and much heavier than even a few people could ever lift. The lamp sitting at the corner of the desk cast a soft yellow glow throughout the office, the only light that gave any indication that someone was lurking within.

Damian had been after the map of the Eternal Flame for as long as he could remember. He'd spent more than a fortune on finding the artifact that had plagued his existence for all his life. After what had happened to his family so many years ago—the jeopardy they had been placed in despite all the power at their very fingertips—he was still chasing what had always eluded his grasp. The traitorous Rose had only used him every chance she got. Now, Damian could only think of all the years his father had spent doing the exact same thing. He refused to continue the cycle even for one day longer. Things were going to change and it would start with him taking control of the lost map once and for all.

This was the motivation that had pushed him to do whatever necessary and he wasn't about to stop now, not when he was closer than ever before. There were no other options remaining though. He had no choice but to find what was rightfully his. The De León dynasty would live or die on it. This was because Damian knew something that no other soul still walking this earth would ever know.

The De Leóns had run out of money.

It was an inescapable fact, one that had followed him with every decision and around every corner. At first it was a distant threat, one that he'd have his entire life to deal with. As the years dragged on with no end, the threat began to loom closer and closer, weighing heavier on everything he did. It had become an inevitable danger made real by a single number driving him to a dizzying madness—zero. That's all that was left after everything was said and done. He'd leveraged every bit of credit he possibly could, every bit of goodwill his family's name could afford, and spent all they'd ever known on what he and God alone knew was a righteous mission. The wanton violence he'd unleashed at anyone who dared to stand in his way was more than just a necessary evil he'd been forced to enact; it was justified in the only eyes that truly mattered.

A blaring ring of his phone turned his attention from such dreadful thoughts. His life had started to feel like one long distraction from the fate he'd been born to stare down. This particular distraction was every bit as welcome as any other, so he jerked the phone back up from the desk and pushed it to his ear.

"It's Damian," he said.

"So, you finally decided to answer a fuckin' phone call?" a shrewd voice on the other end replied.

"I've been busy, Pinkerton. I'm closer now than anyone's ever been before. You helped my father, and his father before him when they called for you. Don't you think for a second I'd forget what you did for me after we've found it."

"I'm about done listening to the fantasies of the De Leóns."

"And I'm about done listening to your threats, you sorry sack of shit."

"This isn't a threat. You've forgotten you're surrounded by *my* army, not yours. Old money will only go so far before all those hired hands you keep sending to an early grave turn and do the same to you."

"There's only one grave left, Pinkerton, and I'm going to need you to send every gun left to make sure we get it filled. You hear me?"

"One? Has no one told you about the man she's got following her around like a little puppy dog now?"

"Don't you worry about what I know. You only do

what I pay you for, remember? Not a damn thing else."

"Well, Damian, it's gonna cost you," Pinkerton's harsh voice came through.

"When has it not?"

Damian yanked at the top drawer of his desk to find a wrinkled white envelope opened one too many times. With the phone propped up to his ear against his shoulder, he thumbed through a few bills tucked inside, finding far less than the amount he was hoping for. It wasn't nearly enough to pay Pinkerton what he'd likely demand.

"I've got it all right here, down to the penny," Damian fessed up. "You send all of them, and they better be ready to work. Not like that last bunch of cadavers you called men."

"It's been a good run, Damian. Our father's fathers worked together and got rich doing it, but times have changed. Today, men like us are a thing of the past. There just isn't any room for error anymore. If you fail, or if I catch word that you're lying to me right now, I'll be sure the De León bloodline ends with you."

"You do what I tell you, you hear me, you stupid son of a bitch," Damian yelled suddenly, unaware that Pinkerton had already hung up on the call.

All Damian heard in response to his rage-filled threats was the buzz of a dial tone ringing in his ear. It was a dull sound that infuriated him more and more every second it continued. He forced down the anger of being hung up on and stared into the wall at the other end of his office, contemplating his next moves and trying not to think too much into how many people he'd already lost trying to find that forsaken map.

The wall he stared at to avoid spiraling into a pit of doubt was truly an inspiration to behold. It was a small shrine to his family's conquest adorned with trophies of what had become theirs. An original coat of arms from Castile and León sat gracefully in the center of the wall, surrounded by antiquities through every era in history across the state. Yet, that small taste of what was once signifiers of greatness from so many, had simply become wall art for the De Leóns. His family had known success that few others could dream of, but it was on the verge of collapse unless he could find the Eternal Flame—alongside what it protected—to secure their future. All that his family had created was built on riches with an unstable foundation. They knew this, and they did it anyway, like men tend to do. The only difference from Damian and those who came before him was it had become his job to finally fix things.

In order to do exactly that, Damian De León had tracked Rose damn near all over Texas, and was finally just days away from getting his hands on what he needed. That was of course until some unknown pain-in-the-ass park ranger ruined all of his plans. The rather intimidating man glanced down at his desk to stare at an aging picture frame propped up on the right-hand corner of his desk.

It was an older picture, blurry from outdated printing and jagged around the edges from its wear. The wooden frame looked even more dated than this picture itself, but it still did its job decent enough. All he really needed from it was the reminder it had instilled in him day after day.

The photo showed off a much younger Damian De León from what seemed like a lifetime ago. He had a full head of slicked-back hair almost no different than how he wore it to this day, and he was dressed in a plain black suit. Damian stood next to an old church building made of falling boards and crumbling brick. It was a place of worship, and you could see the tall wooden doors behind them extending up to the church bells at the peak of the old building. Damian rarely let out as much as a smile, but his black felted beaver fur hat was clean and it looked expensive for where he was, which gave his stern demeanor a sense of hardened dignity. With the sun in his eyes, it was difficult to make out whether he was actually happy or not in the picture, but he wasn't alone.

Just a few steps in front of Damian in the old picture, smiling at the camera with an empty, cold look in her eyes, was a young woman with long black hair that reached past her waist. While there may be some who wouldn't have recognized the girl from the picture, who would've just considered her like any other little girl, this one had an unmistakable stare. A face that was unforgettable. The young woman in the photo was Rose, and in her hands, she cradled a newborn baby swaddled in blankets almost beyond recognition.

It was a baptism ceremony for the child. Not only did Damian attend this ceremony at their local church out west, he also brought his closest friends and family to witness it in a demented display of power that no one could have asked for, least of all Rose herself.

Damian De León looked at the photograph inside the old frame with fondness in his eyes before his face turned sour and his brow furrowed. These were times that didn't turn out well for anyone in the end. The picture served as an always present reminder of just how much had gone wrong in their relentless search.

The De León empire was built on global-level expansion in oil and gas, infrastructure, and most importantly, real estate—the very industries which drive the engines of societal progress. He could be pouring his time into one of the dozens of companies he owned instead of chasing this Wild West fantasy nonsense, but he knew they would all cease to exist if he couldn't get his hands on the Eternal Flame. Everything he had in life was all on the line. If he wanted to continue to pull the levers of power that he had always known, and if he hoped to leave those levers to his own lineage, it would all depend on him getting his hands on the ancient artifact. His family had done everything they possibly could to ensure there was as much as possible at risk, going all the way back to when they first crossed the Guadalupe in the 1820s. It seemed unreal that so many had given their lives for it, but Damian was in too deep now. Too much was riding on what it would provide. Finding the Eternal Flame was a mission that was impossible to let go of.

Damian stood from his desk, holding his gaze on the picture as if he needed the feelings that burned in him while looking at it, as if he had no other choice but to stare at it in order to continue pressing on. He reached up with his hand and slammed the picture face down on his oak desk. The sound shot through the office and left Damian looking down at the floor, fighting back his emotions.

Anything short of capturing the traitorous Rose and claiming the lost treasure would be unacceptable to him—and every De León who came before him.

CHAPTER 15

T he lone SUV lingering in the back corner of the Big Thicket general store parking lot practically screamed of someone who didn't want to be messed with, which was just what the Stranger had set out to do.

A thick fog had set in across the area, bringing with it a cool air that was unexpected for the time of year. The dim headlights of an old truck pierced the darkness of night as it entered on the only street leading into the area known as Honey Island. A bright glow from his truck's headlights wound through a small road leading to the old general store that was nothing more than a steel building with a matching awning. The dark orange hues of a gently glowing cigar was the only thing visible in the cab at this hour. Its inevitable trail of smoke that followed was lost immediately into the fog outside.

The Stranger drove stoically. He was focused

completely on the SUV, already determining his next move to flush the woman and her new ranger friend out of the woods without exposing himself more than was absolutely necessary. He pulled his truck into the same lot as the SUV and parked a few spaces back, just far away enough to watch for a moment while he gathered his thoughts. The cold night air would've given anyone with any sense a shiver, but the Stranger sat still and looked at the vehicle he'd chased down without moving. His cowboy hat was pulled low over his eyes. Resting in the seat to his side was the kind of hunting rifle you could find in just about every truck in Texas. A .270 Winchester with wood furniture, one of the most popular hunting rifles in the state, which made it the kind of gun that wouldn't draw any attention in most cases.

"Probably now or never," he muttered to himself as he looked around and grabbed the rifle on the seat.

There wasn't much of an indicator for where the two he was after may have gone, but it didn't take long to figure out the best place to start was in the woods. Luckily, he wasn't there to hunt them down himself. He was there to flush them out.

With the .270 slung over his shoulder using a worn leather strap, the Stranger climbed out of the truck that had brought him to the middle of the Big Thicket and walked silently into the wood line behind the store. It took just a few minutes until he had reached the wall of oaks and pines that reached far above the beech and sweetgums made impenetrable by yaupon brush and just about every thorny vine imaginable.

When he pushed his way in, the shroud of the trees hung over him almost immediately. The world that he left behind had almost been lost to the dense overgrowth he climbed through when the flickering of lights caught his attention. He fought the brush and struggled to turn around to see where he had come from. Though it was difficult for him to see anything of use, he could make out another car pulling into the same parking lot he'd just left behind.

"The hell?"

The black car pulled in directly behind the same SUV the Stranger had been following. All he could really do was shake his head at the chances of it. This wasn't a coincidence, but there wasn't much he could do except watch how it was going to play out. The black sedan's headlights turned off, but nothing else happened. It just sat there. As the seconds ticked by, the Stranger watched without even blinking from just inside the woods. After staring at the intruder for what felt like an hour, he began to feel a knot in the bottom of his stomach begin to tighten. Something about this car made him uneasy. He had always been someone who was just a little more on edge than anyone else around, so he tried his best to be patient even in times like this. It didn't come naturally to him —only the anxiousness to act did that for him—and this simply wasn't the time for such measures.

As he stood there in the woods listening to the swell of cicadas, the Stranger began to rethink what would happen next. As far as he could see, he was stuck waiting. He couldn't risk continuing on after the artifact with whoever this was trailing right behind him; he also didn't have all night to deal with the problem though. His mind trailed off in a thousand different directions as he considered who was inside the car that pulled in. It was dark and quiet beneath the woods that surrounded the parking lot and the Stranger was doing his best to keep it that way for as long as he could manage. Just as he decided to look through the scratched scope of his old hunting rifle to get a better view of the driver, the headlights of yet another car peeked through the fog. Its headlights grew brighter as the second sedan pulled into the parking lot.

"What in the *fuck* is happening," the Stranger whispered in frustration.

The next car came in identically to the first, and within moments, was parked in the spot just beside the first. Its headlights clicked off and it sat there in silence no different than its apparent counterpart. The Stranger had seen enough to set his suspicions on high alert and lifted the stock of his rifle up to his cheek to push his eye against the scope.

He was still far enough back to keep an advantage on whoever was sitting inside those cars, but if he wanted to get the artifact out of the woods, he may have to sacrifice that. While he debated the options in his head, a flicker of light reflected across the scope he was looking through and he clenched the stock just a bit tighter.

It was *another* car.

The third mysterious car was no further behind

than the last one and it followed suit just as the others as it entered the parking lot. The headlights clicked off and together, the black sedans had started to form a row lining the back of the general store. Over the next few minutes, the Stranger watched in contempt as another car pulled in behind them, then another. He watched through the scope of his rifle from behind the trees that hid him from view as five more cars parked silently behind the SUV. Within minutes, the row of five cars had turned into ten.

Despite their sudden appearance, whoever was driving the black sedans with tinted windows weren't in any kind of a hurry. The shadows of the night had started to shift as their wait dragged on and on. The Stranger knew he was outnumbered just from the number of drivers that pulled in, not to mention whoever else was inside each of the cars, but that wasn't going to stop him by any means. If he played his cards right, they might even be just what he needed to make his next move.

Between the hunting rifle still pushed up to his shoulder and a six shooter on his hip, the Stranger knew he wouldn't ever be able to shoot his way out of a situation like this. He was willing to bet that no matter who these people were, or what they had been told, they damn sure wouldn't know his face. Anonymity would be the only thing that could keep him alive.

"Goddamn you, Damian," he muttered.

Those same thoughts were playing over and over in his head, and he was quickly becoming half tempted to turn around and drive back to the man's office. He knew better though. He knew exactly what they would get him. Instead, he turned and made his way deeper into the never-ending trees to try his shot at what was undoubtedly the definition of a half-cocked plan.

The shroud of night made it difficult to appreciate everything that the Big Thicket had to offer. As the Stranger disappeared into the woods to the sound of every creature imaginable echoing through the branches above, he felt the chill in the air creeping in around him dip unnaturally low for a brief moment. At first he considered it unsettling, but he let the thought go as soon as it came. There were larger problems than being uncomfortable that needed tending to.

The moon's light cast veiled shadows on the ground that helped to guide the Stranger's every diligent step forward. With a sharp turn to his right, he started walking north, unaware of the direction the artifact was taking those he followed. He placed each step from heel to toe without making a sound where others would do well to avoid the crackling of leaves beneath their boots. His pace quickened when he got the feel for where was at and all that was left to hope for was to make it far enough into the depths of the woods with enough time.

There was a clearing just ahead that seemed perfect for what he needed. The Stranger stopped and allowed himself a moment to look around, making sure he was in fact still alone one last time, because all of that was about to change in a hurry. The men waiting in the cars were likely all too willing to wait out the night until those two stumbled into something more than they bargained for when coming back. It would be near impossible to follow the two into the Big Thicket in such darkness, but the Stranger had a feeling these were the kind of men who would do just that if they were tipped off in the right way.

The Stranger unslung the hunting rifle from his shoulder, lifted the stock up once more and aimed into the night sky full of stars, away from the parking lot. He took a deep breath, exhaled slowly, and squeezed the trigger.

The thundering *boom* that followed rang out with a bright flash from the barrel before silence fell once again.

The Stranger paused for a few seconds. When it felt like just long enough, he yanked the bolt back on the rifle to send a shell casing flying into the air, then pushed it back in and locked it down to chamber a new round. He lifted the rifle again and fired once more with another loud *boom* that rocked through the woods.

All he had to do next was wait right where he stood to give the newcomers the best chance at finding him tucked away in the trees. It would likely be only a matter of minutes, so he went ahead and found the couple of empty shell casings that had fallen to the ground and stuffed them into his pocket. After taking a few deep breaths and chambering a third round as a precaution, he listened closely to catch the sounds of car doors slamming shut. It didn't matter if they were professional mercenaries, amateur bounty hunters, or just some guys who needed the cash for their next fix, they were still people, and that meant they were predictable.

The pounding of boots trampling through the branches quickly followed. What must have been a dozen armed men came sprinting toward the sounds of the gunfire, alarmed and ready to find their target to make it a quick night filled with easy money. Instead, they found someone younger than all of them, holding a hunting rifle and looking like he had just seen a ghost. The Stranger could see confusion hit each of them like they'd just collided face first into a brick wall.

The closest one to him spoke first, he was short and to the point. "Tell me where they went, goddammit!" The end of the sentence was punctuated by the barrel of a pistol pointed right at the Stranger.

"My god, they said you would be after them," the Stranger responded with a dumbfounded ring in his voice that disarmed the men. "I didn't believe them!"

Just as the words rolled off his tongue, he realized he knew exactly who was standing in front of him. Damian De León had played his hand. He'd made the call to the Pinkertons to go all in and the ones who answered were only after one thing—to collect.

"Tell us where they fucking went, boy," one of the other Pinkertons with a puffy beard said.

"The man and the woman?" The Stranger led them on a bit more. "They both took off together; headed west I think, that way…"

He went to raise his hand to point the direction but before he could show them the way, the group of men were already running off deeper into the woods. They signaled with their hands and whispered directions as they moved in unison, holding their firearms up at the ready for anyone or anything they came across. They had plenty of firepower and the numbers were on their side, but the Stranger had something else in mind.

"Dumbasses," he muttered under his breath as the men ran off.

The Stranger slowly made his way back to where he'd come from, walking in the opposite direction the Pinkertons hurried off into looking like fools chasing death dressed in black only to mock the one who would be taking them. He was taking a chance in doing this, but he felt rather confident about knowing the type of people he was dealing with. They'd accomplish their mission of getting those two out of the woods one way or another. There was enough money floating around those kinds of people to make sure it happened. His only job now was to make sure everything else went his way.

The night air had only gotten colder in the meantime and it was getting harder not to notice. With most of the moon's light blocked in the thick woods, there wasn't much else to look at other than every exhaled breath sweeping out into the air in front of him. It had even gotten cold enough to quieten all the chirps and screeches that usually carried through these woods at night. The Stranger suddenly stepped out into the clearing of the parking lot to put the dense woods at his back. He gazed around the general store and silently confirmed his assumptions when he saw a single car that stayed behind in the parking lot with its headlights still shining directly on the SUV.

At first, the Stranger wasn't too sure if he should approach the vehicle. He'd surely set off a firefight that would ruin his plan to send the Pinkertons into the woods, something he'd hoped would make for an easy night on his end. The black sedan idled quietly one row behind the vehicle he was following. When the Stranger peered through the scope of the rifle to get a look inside the car, he couldn't help but let out a scoff just loud enough for only himself to hear.

"Could it be this easy?"

The Stranger shouldered the rifle and clutched the cracked leather sling as he did. His stroll through the woods and into the patch of dirt behind the general store was as casual as a tourist who just came off the trailhead. When he made his way up to the sedan still idling in the parking lot, putting to rest the problem at hand was as simple as knocking a couple of times on the driver's-side window.

When the creaky glass slowly rolled down, the Stranger almost couldn't believe his eyes. There was just one man sitting in the sedan with his cell phone glowing from his lap signaling his own fatal distraction. He had just enough time for shocked bewilderment to wash across his face and before the passenger side door of the sedan swung open and the Stranger climbed inside.

Pop.

A flash of light inside the car and a red splatter against the windshield put an end to any worries the Stranger had about the Pinkertons foiling his plans.

When the young gunslinger climbed out of the sedan, he adjusted his worn cowboy hat to sit lower on his face, allowed a deep breath of cold night air to fill his lungs, and gazed up through the limbs of the Big Thicket into the stars above.

All that was left now was to figure out which direction Rose and the ranger would come running from before the sun came up.

CHAPTER 16

"We have to follow it."

"I know we do," answered Rose. "I just don't want to."

Neither Rose nor Davy could truly believe what was right in front of their eyes, but they both knew there was no time to waste on their own disbelief. The freezing air hung heavy around them and their breath plumed outwards with every exhale. The temperature seemed to still be dropping, but it didn't bother either of them as they stared ahead, focusing on the light hovering no more than ten feet ahead that had only just made itself known. Davy took a step forward and the leaves crunched beneath his leather boot. Rose's arm instinctively reached out to stop him, but she paused and watched as the light floated half a step away and hovered once more. Davy moved forward with another step and Rose stared in shock as it once again drifted further away, beckoning them with every movement.

"Let's go," Davy said. "Now."

Step by step, Davy and Rose followed slowly through the night across a path that didn't exist through the Big Thicket. Rose still couldn't believe what she was seeing. She did her best to not get lost in her head about how any of this was possible. Davy's stoic demeanor seemed to help her at a time like this. He may not have always been the confident type, but tonight he was, and it was showing from how he carried himself to how he spoke. She stole a glance and saw him focused intently ahead with the soft glow illuminating his face in a strange way.

They continued walking together as Rose tried to consider every possibility of what could be happening, but the only thing she could focus on was the sound of steps that weren't their own.

"What is that?" Rose asked with a tilted head as she felt a jolt of fear shoot down her spine. "Don't you hear it?"

"Don't stop, we have to keep going if we want to find that last piece," Davy whispered.

"Shhh…" Rose hushed the ranger. "Listen."

It was the rhythmic sound of hoofbeats pounding into the dirt floating in the wind. Each step echoed into nothingness, yet somehow approached closer and closer to the two all the same. The hooves soon passed them by, leaving Davy and Rose to exchange a worried glance.

Davy paused for just a moment as the light ahead of them danced across his face to the tune of their own near-frantic breathing. He turned his head in curiosity. They were following someone, or something, deeper into the woods, even if they couldn't see them. He had to believe it was the one who inspired the name of Bad Luck Creek, the very one they were after tonight. But he was also hoping for all its worth they wouldn't discover the reason why it got that name for themselves.

"It's guiding us," he finally spoke up.

The sounds of a horse walking through the woods came and went in waves as the two continued walking after the light that drifted lazily around overhanging branches, floated through thick trunks, and passed into the distance. They each patiently listened to the clacking of hooves echoing out into the darkness and kept a steady enough pace to not fall behind. The cold night seemed to lose all sense of time as they walked— oblivious to the minutes ticking by into hours—yet the light lingered on as if it had no other choice but to continue.

"*No,*" a desperate scream of a man suddenly came from the depths far within the woods. "*No!*" The estranged man's voice bellowed louder. "*No, no, no!*"

Davy and Rose froze right in their tracks. Rose started to whisper to him but was cut off by Davy's fist jolting up, motioning her to stay quiet.

"*No!*" The scream came again, this time closer to them. "*No! No!*" The man's voice wailed horribly into the night air, coming from nowhere and everywhere all at once.

Davy stared wide-eyed at Rose as she returned the same look at him, both lost in ragged breaths laced with uncertainty, knowing they had to push on, but too startled to move. The light had continued on its unearthly journey without them, moving in the same direction as the man's cries, all too willing now to leave them behind if they would only allow it to happen.

The man's scream repeated over and over again in deadly disbelief as they forced themselves to continue onward. The voice was tragic, and after the wave of fear it struck in each of them, it was difficult to fight their feelings from turning into disheartened pity. It was the ghost of a man who wasn't ready for what happened to him. It was a man who was doomed to repeat losing everything he'd ever had every night— alone. Rose and Davy knew they were in the right place, though neither was prepared for what they'd found. Their uncertain hike dragged on for hours through the Big Thicket. It was three in the morning before the light finally came to a stop, forcing both of them to speak up again.

"There's nothing out here," Rose told the ranger as she looked around the woods, unable to see further than ten feet into the branches that circled them both. "There's nothing out here," she repeated as though trying to convince herself.

The light had taken them on a winding maze through the woods seemingly at random. They followed it intently, hoping it would lead them to a place where they could find the next piece of the map of the Eternal Flame. Instead, however, they only found more questions deep within the trees. There were no sounds, not even the crickets that had followed them for hours were chirping anymore. The cool air had lifted to reveal a muggy heat that caused beads of sweat to run down their faces. There wasn't anything out of the ordinary in their sight, and it was starting to alarm both Rose and Davy.

Bam.

A loud clash rang out through the woods and the light they had followed began to slowly rise into the air. First gradually, almost unnoticeable, then faster and faster until it was almost out of sight. There was no time to react. Davy did the only thing he could think of.

"I'm going after it!"

Before Rose could say anything else, Davy was bolting toward the closest tree where the light was rising to join the stars hanging over Texas. It was a tall pine that reached what looked like a hundred feet into the air and Davy had only a small length of rope pulled miraculously from his bag to help him climb. Much to her surprise, he made quick progress ascending the tree. When he reached the first limb, his unhinged climb continued even faster, but his eyes stayed focused on the light emanating from just above his head.

"Be careful!" Rose hollered, trying to be of some use. Just as she did, she started to feel a familiar heat coming from the bag slung over her shoulder.

"Oh shit," she let out for only herself to hear.

Davy couldn't hear anything over the grunts that escaped him while climbing as fast as his aching body would allow. It was a skill he learned on his own, playing in the woods at their family home, and it had come in handy only on sparing occasions in his career as a park ranger. He trusted his abilities and his technique that propelled him up the tree. The key, as they always say, was to not look down. A fear of heights wasn't exactly the best compliment to the skill set of climbing a tree, though he'd done his best to manage. As sweat made its way into his eyes, the ranger climbed only on instincts. He passed through the tops of other trees nearby and noticed the burning stars that extended out in almost every direction above him. The light some claim to have seen, but none had experienced quite like this, climbed higher nearly parallel with the tree. Davy followed without slowing, sliding the rope up furiously and hurling himself up.

With one hard push, he saw the night sky above reveal itself like a gorging beast, swallowing every-thing around them. Though he couldn't go any higher, he watched as the light continued rising, lighting the tops of the nearby trees and casting its soft glow down on his awe-struck face. He could hear Rose calling out from down below but couldn't make out what she was saying. It was a beautiful night and though he was exhausted, covered in sweat, and nervous about what he was following, it was impossible for Davy not to appreciate the view that reaching the top of the pine gave him.

The light they'd followed from Bad Luck Creek rose for just a moment longer before it rocketed up into the sky at impossible speeds, leaving him shrouded in darkness staring wildly into the sky trying to find where it went.

It was a strange moment of surreal silence that followed, giving Davy just enough time to bewilder himself at the situation, before an explosion of light burst out in the night hanging over the Big Thicket like a firework blowing up in space. It was silent, yet blinding, causing the ranger to shield his eyes in a split-second reaction. When he lifted his hands, his grip on the tree slipped unexpectedly and he was forced to scramble to hold on. He struggled against the tree while looking desperately at anything he might miss in the brightness of the flash above him.

That's when he saw them.

"Oh my god," he let out.

The remnants of light burned off into what looked like a thousand new distant suns

flickering in the darkness. Against a backdrop of stars shining bright over the Big Thicket, the burning light created a constellation portrait in the night sky. At first almost indistinguishable, the vision born of a force of nature he couldn't possibly understand quickly became unmistakable. There were streaks illuminated to portray a recognizable silhouette of two people stretching out across the horizon holding a striking gaze, each one with suns for pupils—and they were looking right at him,

Davy was fighting for a grip on the tree, leaning into it with all of his weight and trying to look up to find whatever message he knew had to be hidden among the stars and in the faces staring down on him from above. He committed the constellation from the explosion of light to memory as best he could. The eyes looking back at him flickered weakly before disappearing entirely. Just as the last light gave way to swaths of darkness, Davy heard the same man's voice that led them deep into the Big Thicket call out into nothingness.

"Reach out your hand," the voice beckoned.

Davy instinctively obeyed the voice, slowly stretching out his hand with his palm facing the sky, risking what little grip he had while clinging to the tree. Before he could blink, he felt something smack him in the forehead with surprising force and a jarring sound that he only hoped wasn't a hairline fracture from the impact.

Just like that, his grip finally gave way and he fell.

The slide down the tree was painful and jarring. He smacked branches and scrapped his legs and forearms against the thick bark that acted like razors against his skin.

"*Davy!*" Rose's fearful cry rang out as she watched helplessly from far below.

Sound of cracking branches and groans from Davy pierced the air around them and a few excruciating seconds later, a loud thump echoed out when his body crashed to the ground. Immediately afterward, a small object fell right next to him with a much softer sound as it smacked the dirt. It was the other missing piece of the map of the Eternal Flame, the same unique, key-shaped size as the one they found at Sabine Pass. Davy's arms and legs were bloodied, and he was dazed from the fall, but he rose quickly and started shouting at Rose while staring at the ground.

"Bring me something to write on!"

Rose was shocked he was even conscious, but she dropped her bag to the ground that was getting hotter by the second and started digging around inside.

"Hurry, Rose!" Davy yelled with his eyes closed, still facing toward the ground.

By the time Rose had grabbed her notebook and a pen from her bag, Davy had sat up with his eyes squeezed shut, fighting the urge to crumble from the pain of the fall he had just endured. She looked past all the damage and threw the pen and paper at him, then watched as Davy began to sketch wildly.

"It was a portrait of something," he said as he finally opened his eyes to squint at the paper. "Of someone."

"What do you mean? Who did you see up there?"

A few quiet seconds fell between them as Davy focused on the paper in his hand. It was haphazardly sketched, and difficult to distinguish at best, but Davy had done his best to recreate what he'd seen burned into the night. He didn't say anything to Rose at first, but his eyes lifted to meet hers and he slowly turned around the paper to show what he'd seen in the stars.

Rose looked down at his hands and saw the sketch of something that looked strangely familiar, like someone she had seen so many times before in passing but couldn't remember their name. Like the flip of a switch, her stature sank, and she was left speechless. What Davy drew so desperately on the paper with such uncanny detail were the faces of her own ancestors.

"We need to go," she demanded. "Now."

Her tone told Davy everything he needed to know, and it didn't take much to realize that they had made yet another step in getting closer to finding the treasure they were after. His heart raced at the prospect. It wasn't so much the riches that enticed him, but the thrill of the chase and the thought of the possibilities still yet to be explored. It was the adventure he was after and every second of it was living up to his wildest imagination.

"Do you know who these people are?" he asked immediately, trying to stay focused. "Does this tell us where we need to go next?"

"No, it doesn't," she told him as she reached down beside where he sat to grab the object out of the dirt. "But this is what knocked you down the tree, and it will take us right where we need to be."

Still slightly stunned, Davy's face turned from battered confusion to excitement in an instant when he saw the bag slung over Rose's shoulder glowing from the burning heat of the artifact it held. Light barely escaped from within and the glowing was more intense than even before. With the last missing piece of the map of the Eternal Flame that had fallen from the sky grasped in her fingers, Rose watched as the artifact melted its way through the last of their spare bags and sunk into the earth once more.

Rose knew better than to waste any time now. The map of the Eternal Flame had turned into what looked like molten steel as it burned its way deeper into the dirt like a meteorite cast down from the stars themselves. Rose jammed the missing piece of the artifact shaped just like the first inside with a slight twist and once more a bright flash of light shot out around them, causing the map to change again.

"There are some things I still haven't told you," Rose admitted without acknowledging what had just happened, instead staring at the park ranger, who was still trying to get back to his feet.

"What do you mean? Was it something you should've told me before I fell out of that damn tree," Davy told her as he pointed up at the pine they stood under.

"It's about the people coming after us," she said while looking around the trees that encircled them with a nervous twitch in her eye.

"We talked about this. I already know we gotta get the artifact out of here, Rose. These people tortured me. What else could I really need to know right now?"

"Well…" Rose tried to say before trailing off.

"Wait," Davy cut her off. "Let's just wait until we get out of here, then you can tell me everything once and for all. For real this time"

"You're right, let's just get back to the car in one piece first."

The hike that had taken hours following the light back at Bad Luck Creek took half that time to trace back to the old general store at a more urgent speed. The pitch black of night they had gotten used to was finally starting to give way to a grayish haze that cautioned the coming sunrise. It had been a long night, but they were finally making their way out of the Big Thicket and leaving their personal ghost story behind them.

"I wish we would've had time to dig down where the light stopped back there," Davy chimed in casually, paying no attention to the awkward talk yet to be had that hovered between them. "There could have been something from the old outlaw back in that area, you know?"

"Now that we've found the last missing piece to complete the map of the Eternal Flame, if we can get to the treasure it protects, we'll definitely have enough money to buy a couple of shovels. You help me finish this, and I promise you, I'll come back out with you to dig up whatever you want," Rose bargained.

"You're gonna regret telling me that," Davy said, holding back a smile. "You got yourself a deal."

The two kept up with one another as they walked at a pace closer to jogging than anything else to make their way through the woods. It wasn't long before Davy suspected they were no more than an hour away from where they had left their SUV. He looked over at Rose and watched as she walked carefully through the woods, her focus staying on the ground just ahead of her next step. She wasn't running, but she was walking so quickly that Davy had started to breathe just a bit heavier than before while trying to keep up with her. After a few minutes, he saw Rose steal a sideways glance over at him.

"We're going to do this," he said, trying to encourage her a bit more. "Think about it, we're closer to that treasure right now in these woods than you've ever been before."

"You're right," Rose agreed halfheartedly.

"Yeah, I mean the hard part is basically over now if you think about it," Davy said as he tried to keep the mood light and their spirits up.

Rose started to allow herself a laugh at Davy's naivety. A smirk was just beginning to form at the edges of her lips when she looked over at him and saw a shadow move in the distance. She froze and Davy reacted without missing a beat, stopping in place and staring at her in silence.

Another shadow sped behind a tree just behind the ranger's wide-brimmed hat.

"*Get down!*" Rose screamed at the top of her lungs.

Davy fell to the dirt just as the blasts of gunfire rang out through the woods and shattered the silence that had followed them most of the night. Deafening shots came from all around and fiery muzzle blasts flashed like bursts of hell in the distance. Davy fumbled with his hands, grabbing at the revolver tucked away that Rose had given him. Just as he got his fingers wrapped around the grip, he looked up to find Rose ready to fight.

She was kneeling down on one knee and calmly shouldering the rifle she had stashed in her backpack when they first entered the Big Thicket. Shots continued to pop off in the woods and the occasional bullet whizzed by, putting Davy even more on edge, but he watched as Rose never flinched.

With a rapid turn to aim the barrel just over the ranger's head and the unmistakable clicking sound to flip the safety off—she opened fire.

CHAPTER 17

The screams of an unknown enemy unexpectedly struck by a bullet and left bleeding into the dirt echoed through the woods for only seconds before it was drowned out in a cacophony of raging gunfire.

Davy was lost in a haze, unable to see straight amid the chaos that had suddenly erupted.

Rose, however, was hard at work. Her reactions were rapid and her aim was dead on. She fired again and again, almost always in bursts of two before changing targets, but she could only stay kneeled down out in the open for long.

"We gotta fuckin' move!" she yelled at Davy in between firing off rounds into the trees around them.

He was looking at Rose and watching her mouth move, but he couldn't hear anything other than the ringing that pounded in his head. He couldn't make out anything she said and just sat there in the dirt trying to find his bearings.

"Now!" Rose screamed at him again, still firing cover rounds.

It took a bullet slamming into the ground in front of Davy to snap him out of his daze. A cloud of dirt flew up into his eyes and he fell backward, scrambling to find cover that didn't exist in the middle of a firefight that he wasn't ready for. The next thing he felt was the harsh grasp of Rose's hand on his arm as she yanked him up to his feet. He looked her in the eyes and finally heard what she was telling him.

"Are you with me?" she asked him with a slight tremble in her voice that had never been there before. "We have to run for it."

"Rose..." Davy struggled to let out.

"Davy, if we don't go now, we're going to die. It's that easy."

"Let's get the hell out of here," Davy finally told her.

Both of them took off at the same time, stomping their boots as they ran. Rose was behind Davy, slowing only to shoulder the rifle occasionally and fire a few rounds to cover their sprint. He caught on to what she was doing and gripped his five shooter in his right hand a little harder. The blasts of gunfire rang out all around them in the woods as bullets splintered branches and pounded the earth at their feet. After getting just a few more paces ahead of Rose, he stopped and extended his arm in the direction of whoever was shooting at them. He squeezed the trigger once and the recoil sent his arm upward, but he steadied his aim and fired again.

"Keep it moving!" Rose yelled while staring down

the sights of her rifle, still shooting in double round bursts to keep whoever was after them pushed back as long as possible.

The morning light hadn't yet started to filter in through the trees, the gray shadows that lingered only made it more difficult to spot anyone who was more than thirty yards away. The stench of gunpowder filled the air and random flashes of light from muzzle blasts dotted the area sporadically. It was the kind of firefight that anyone who knew what they were doing would want to avoid at all costs. Exposed out in the open, facing dwindling ammunition, and sorely lacking in firepower were just the beginning of their problems.

"Shit, shit, shit," Davy kept saying as they bolted through the woods.

Rose was running as fast as she could while going through the motions of reloading her AR-15 for the first of what seemed like several times to come. She slapped another magazine into place and chambered the next round before turning to unload four shots back at their attackers. One bullet went dangerously close to her shoulder causing her to turn in its direction and nearly fall to the ground, but she spotted the man who was gaining on them. In less than a second, she had her rifle trained on him and put two shots into his stomach. When he clutched his gut and fell, she turned to keep running.

Davy never stopped running. He couldn't seem to find the opportunity to look back for Rose and was worried he'd gone too long. He was scared and experiencing the symptoms of fight or flight with intensity that he'd never felt before. Just when he got a chance to glance back and see Rose running after him fifteen yards back, he watched as her face twisted in terror. She was lifting her rifle right in his direction.

A man dressed in black with a thick beard had stepped out from behind a tree holding a handgun tucked into his chest. He was about to fire. Davy's chest tightened and his fingers clenched around the pistol that held just three more shots. Without hesitating, Davy kept moving toward the man as two bright flashes burst in front of him.

The man dropped his pistol and grabbed at his neck, then stumbled and fell to the ground bleeding out into his shaking hands. Davy looked down and saw his revolver still pointed forward with smoke trailing from the barrel and realized he'd been the one who had fired. He'd probably killed someone for the first time. It was something he fully expected to rattle him to his core when the reality of what just happened had time to set in, but he didn't have time for that. He knew he couldn't stop now.

Rose shoved him as she caught up and sprinted past without waiting. He watched confused, as she continued running, leaving him further behind. Before he could force himself to run after her, a searing pain flared in his left shoulder and he howled in pain.

Rose knew immediately what happened. She turned to look where Davy had been hit and wasted no time in calling out to him.

"It's just a scratch," she said over the gunshots. "We gotta keep running."

Davy wasn't listening to her though. The park

ranger held his hand out in front of him and saw it covered in his own blood, stained red within seconds. He felt woozy but did what he could to disregard it. Instead, he made himself put one foot in front of the other. The sounds of men running through the woods and an occasional gunshot pushed him to move as quickly as his body would let him.

The sprint was furious between the two. They were outnumbered and outgunned, exhausted from the long night, and too far from their SUV to have a chance at escaping. Davy ignored the warm blood falling from his bullet wound and caught a desperate glance from Rose. She seemed to know that following behind them was most likely not just their capture, but their own death. The look in her eyes would be burned into his memory forever. It told Davy she didn't have the heart to tell him it was hopeless, like she knew everything he was going through was her fault, and that she couldn't do anything about it.

They made their way as quick as they could move through the woods as the gunfire began to circle around them. While neither could distinguish the faces of the men who were trying to gun them down, Davy figured it would only be minutes before they would know his and Rose's face all too well. One foot in front of the other, they both ran with heavy breath and fought back panic from taking control of every move. Their luck was about to turn, however, as their hurry to find even the faintest glimmer of hope for safety would lead them to a creek just ahead—Bad Luck Creek.

"There!" Davy shouted and half-ass pointed in a

hurry to the creek that had helped lead them here. Now he could at least hope that would also be their route back.

Rose didn't say anything, but instead darted toward it suddenly and never looked back. Within just a few paces they both had jumped into the creek that dipped steeply a few feet down. The water that ran through the creek was only inches deep and their boots splashed hard when they landed. Davy crouched low and listened closely to the noise of the men clamoring through the woods, still trying his best to ignore the gunshot wound in his shoulder. They may have been trained to kill, but they clearly didn't care about doing it quietly. There wasn't much to say to each other at this point, though Davy wasn't exactly looking to talk anymore.

"Give me your gun," he gently told Rose.

A wave of confusion washed over Rose, and she hesitated to respond.

"It's okay," he reassured her. "Here, I'll trade you."

He held out the revolver he was carrying and gestured for her to take it while reaching for her rifle. After a quick swap, he checked the magazine to make sure it was loaded. With a slight tap on the bottom to lock it back into place, Davy pushed the bolt release to chamber a new round with a sudden slap of metal.

"Stay here," he told her with a determined sense of focus about him. "Only one shot left in that thing, by the way."

The park ranger stood up with ease and positioned the rifle slightly over the edge of the steep drop into the creek. It was just his height and gave him plenty of cover without costing any visibility in front of him. He leaned his head over a bit and rested his cheek on the stock of the rifle to find the iron sights.

Just as his skin pressed against the cold polymer rifle stock, the memories of his first hunt with his dad back at their homestead came rushing back to him. He thought of the doe that bolted from the woods and his dad urging him not to shoot when it was running. He remembered feeling where he needed to put the shot, and the feeling of squeezing the trigger. All he had to do was line his target up. It was like he could smell the foggy morning of his first hunt, taste the humidity in the air, and feel exactly what was supposed to happen next. He was right where he needed to be.

Rose sat beneath Davy holding the revolver she had taken back, looking up at him, still unsure what the next move was going to be. The quiet that hung around them was short-lived, however, as another man took a shot in their direction just moments later. The bullet slammed into a tree ten feet away while Davy sat still, gently breathing, seemingly unbothered by the round. She watched as he moved the end of his barrel to the left slightly, exhaled, then squeezed the trigger sending a single shot blasting out into the woods.

Almost immediately following Davy's first shot were the sounds of a grown man bellowing in pain. His screams rang through the woods. Rose flinched at first, but before she could do anything about it, Davy sent out another single shot from the rifle and the man's screams fell silent.

Davy's perspective overlooking the thick green

foliage in front of him afforded a view of everything he needed. The time to dwell on what he was doing would surely come back to bite him later, but for now he would have to ignore those thoughts if he wanted to get out of the Big Thicket with Rose alive. Firing his first two rounds set in motion a flurry of gunfire that forced his mind to focus on the task at hand. As bullets rained down around them and silhouettes of the shooters began to pop up left and right in Davy's field of vision, he put his long-standing philosophy of shooting—honed by years of hunting in the backyard woods of his family's home —to work.

Each shot from his rifle echoed through the woods and caused both Davy and Rose's ears to ring violently. Through the iron sights, precisely trained on one man after another, Davy watched as they each fell one by one to the ground with every squeeze of the trigger. They ran from one tree to the next scrambling for cover, but not a single one of them saw the bullet with their name on it coming for them.

"There's about a dozen more of 'em," Davy told Rose between shots. "They'll close in around us before I have time to say hello to all of them."

Rose knew exactly what that meant. She clutched her fingers around the revolver tighter and clenched her jaw, nodding silently.

Davy's shots continued to sound off through the woods as he gently leaned the rifle to either side of him aiming at the men making their way closer to them. He had downed three men with relative ease so far, four if you count the one he shot with a revolver. It seemed like every time he dropped one, another would take his place though.

"This isn't going to work," Davy told her. "We can't take down all of them like this. We won't last."

"You have any better ideas? I'm all ears," Rose shot back, her jaw still clenched as bullets continued pelting around them from the distance.

"We thin them out here as best we can, then we split up to keep moving."

"We can't split up right now Davy, we don't have the damn ammo for something like that. And I'm damn sure not going to leave you dead in some random ditch. We'll figure something else out."

Davy waited to answer. He fired two more rounds off and the two listened to the screams of another man who sounded much closer than the one before. Only this time, Davy didn't end his pain so quickly. The man continued yelling for help as the other gunmen started to surround them just as Davy had described. There were only a few with the heart to help their wounded, and they were the next ones to fall by Davy's hand.

"Just a few more seconds and we'll have to make a break for it." Davy turned from his shooting to tell Rose, his voice rising as bullets continued to hit too close for comfort around them.

"You just say when," she answered.

The next two minutes were a chaotic shit show that pushed Davy and Rose beyond a point of true fear for their lives. The men they were fighting weren't like the assholes Rose took out so easily at the bar, or even when she found Davy being tortured. This was a different group. They moved like they had been trained for years, were relentless even when taking casualties, and despite their losses, kept cover fire from what seemed like every direction. It was a wonder how either had lived as long as they had against them.

Davy had reached a point of rapid fire not too long into their firefight and he was shooting from left to right at hard angles. He wouldn't be able to keep the fight up much longer and Rose knew it.

"Now! Now! Now!" Davy shouted with renewed urgency.

Rose wasted no time in sprinting as fast as she could. Davy watched her from only a few feet behind while lugging the now scalding hot rifle still pouring smoke from the end of the barrel. He tried his best to keep up with her, ignoring the bullets flying past them and the searing pain in his shoulder where one had burned a hole right through him. Branches scratched at their faces and the trees crowded their run, offering both cover from the gunfire and obstacles to avoid in their desperate run for safety all at once. The sounds of the men chasing them haunted their every step as they listened to them yelling out directions they couldn't understand.

Davy tried to pay attention to them so he could stay a step ahead. He knew that the parking lot was getting closer. It had to be. Rose stopped ahead of him all of a sudden and fired off a round for cover from the revolver. Someone was getting closer to them and her bullet shattered the tree just to his left, sending him diving for cover.

"Coming to you!" a man yelled into a device on his neck from deeper into the woods. "Repeat! Coming in hot!"

They were running into a trap.

"Rose!" Davy shouted, trying to get her attention.

"I know I heard too!"

"We gotta do something," Davy hollered while trying to keep from losing his breath from running. He was long past the point of getting tired, but he couldn't stop, not yet. The burning in his calves and back would just have to wait.

"It's my turn, Davy," Rose answered while turning to hold out her revolver again. "And don't think we're not talking about what you just did back there either," she said as she grabbed at the still burning hot rifle.

With a fluid motion, Rose dropped the empty magazine from the rifle with the push of a button and grabbed the last one she had stuffed into her back pocket—a last resort. She slammed it into place and slapped the release. Bullets had stopped flying and the only sounds that made their way through the thick woods were the shuffles of the Pinkertons running as fast as they could to keep up.

"What's the plan here, Rose?" Davy asked loudly. "Please tell me you have something."

"Just keep pushing!"

Davy looked down and checked his revolver to see the one bullet remaining in the cylinder and knew he'd have to make it count.

In a matter of seconds, the tree line came to a sudden end and the two ran out into the opening to see the parking lot no more than a hundred yards in the distance just behind the old general store. Both Rose and Davy noticed the SUV was surrounded by black vehicles at the same time and gave each other a disheartened glance.

They kept running anyway, panting heavily with every step that slammed into the ground and straining to see through the sweat pouring down their face, stinging their eyes. The SUV was getting closer. When they were halfway to the parking lot—their only remaining lifeline—the men chasing them through the woods of the Big Thicket emerged from the trees and opened fire again. To Rose, this might have been just another run-in with Damian De León's goons, but these men's disregard for anything other than killing them terrified Davy to his core. The bullets raining down from behind kept his mind focused on one thing —escaping. Shells rocked and shattered the pavement they were sprinting across.

"We get in the SUV and we fuckin' go, okay?" Rose double-checked with Davy.

"You don't have to tell me twice!"

The next few steps were the most treacherous of all, but they were damn sure worth it. In just a few seconds, they had both made their way around the cars in the parking lot—including one that looked like it had been shot up from the inside—and ducked their heads into the SUV to avoid incoming gunfire. Rose jammed the key in the ignition and cranked it in a panic.

"Go, go, go!" Davy hollered as soon as he heard the engine fire up.

Rose didn't waste any time. She pulled it into gear

and jammed the gas pedal down into the floor. The engine screamed in response. They were finally pulling out of the Big Thicket and they had managed to do it alive against all odds. Davy couldn't believe they made it. He was fighting the surge of adrenaline that made his hands and knees shake. He tried his best to ignore the gunshot wound in his shoulder in between ragged breaths, watching the mirror out of the passenger window with a feverish intensity. The car was hauntingly silent after what they had just gone through and the radio carried on like a drug-induced dream in the background.

"Fuck those assholes!" Rose shouted at the front windshield while hammering her fists into the steering wheel.

Her screaming shocked Davy back into a state of awareness that he wasn't ready for. As their car sped out of the Big Thicket and trees raced by his view, he found himself hoping they'd never come up with a reason to return.

"I think we actually did it," Davy said with exhaustion heavy in his voice. "We lost the bastards."

Just as the words escaped his mouth the dreaded lights of two more vehicles came into view, reaching closer and closer in their mirrors. They weren't out of the fight just yet. Davy immediately jumped to reloading both of the firearms they had. Their ammo was limited in the vehicle, but it would have to be enough to get them just a little further away.

The light from the cars speeding up to them filled the cabin of the SUV cast shadows across everything around them. Davy couldn't help but feel the creepy sensation that they were being watched. It was the feeling that lingers in you after waking up from a nightmare of being chased to no end. The feeling you can't shake no matter how many times you turn around in fear. Despite knowing it was all in his head —assuming it was likely a side effect from the blood loss in his shoulder or his body coping with the pain— he allowed himself a quick glance behind him expecting to see only the cars chasing them down.

What he saw made him freeze in fear.

Drowned in the white light of the car's headlights behind them was the silhouette of a man in a cowboy hat sitting in the back seat of the SUV—staring right back at him.

CHAPTER 18

U nable to say anything, due to either complete disbelief or the panic that had painfully lumped in his throat, Davy let the SUV fall silent only for a few seconds as he stared blankly at the man's silhouette in their car. The unwelcomed silence was broken by an unknown voice.

"Y'all just keep on like you were," the Stranger threatened with a devilish whisper along with the distinctly familiar sound of a revolver's hammer locking back.

"What the…" Rose yelped.

Davy and Rose both fought to turn around and see who it was, only to find the end of a gun barrel pointed at them. The gun was held in the hand of the Stranger that had been following them. His face was covered by the cowboy hat tucked down over his eyes and his trigger finger was just begging them to move an inch so he could put an end to their adventure right then and there.

While Davy was understandably shocked to find someone hiding in the back of their car, Rose had an entirely different look of fear wash across her face. There was no time to react any further though. Two cars filled with the same Pinkertons who'd attacked them back in the woods were catching up quickly.

"Rose," Davy started before he was quickly cut off.

"No, no, dipshit," the Stranger said with a mocking tone and a wag of his revolver. "You turn right around and face that way."

Rose was staring wide-eyed ahead of them. She refused to even glance at Davy and instead, focused on driving as best she could with her foot heavy on the gas. The RPMs in the SUV's engine became louder in the cab as they sped through the forest leaving the Big Thicket.

It was a terrifying sound, but at this point, Davy wasn't sure what should be more afraid of—those who were chasing after them, or the one who'd already caught up to them.

In the blink of an eye, the Stranger leaned in to push his cowboy hat-covered face just a few inches behind Rose and Davy, his pistol still trained on them with deadly intent.

One of the cars had pulled into the next lane facing oncoming traffic to catch up beside them. Rose knew they wanted to take a swipe at them to knock them off the road. She wasn't about to let that happen. The SUV they drove was easier to handle than the sedans these guys were driving. It just wasn't as fast. Out of the corner of her eye, Rose could see the black car inching its way up. When she looked quickly out the driver's side window to her left, she saw the hood of the car as it pulled nearer to them.

Bam. Bam. Bam. Shots fired from the Stranger in the back seat echoed through the vehicle.

The car that had been pulling up next to them slowly drifted off to the left and within just a few seconds had slammed into a ditch. The front of the car lifted high into the air when it lost control and went off road, coming down hard and causing smoke to pour from the hood almost immediately. A dark laugh came creeping up behind them from the Stranger who was a little too pleased with his shots.

"Just one more," the Stranger whispered, looking over his shoulder to find where his target was moving next.

The SUV took a hard turn and all three passengers slid violently in their seats until each one managed to catch themselves before it was too late. Rose floored it again to get back onto the road leading to the highway headed north. The second car was gaining quickly behind them. Out of nowhere, the Stranger had rolled down the back window and his head was hanging out, trying to aim one of his revolvers back at the car and screaming obscenities the ranger didn't care to repeat.

"Rose, they're coming up quick over here!" Davy called out.

"I know, I know, Davy," she answered, looking worriedly into the mirror to her right. "Shoot what you've got left at them, buy me some time."

"I only have three rounds," Davy admitted.

"Better make 'em count."

"I'll do my best."

The roads they were driving were blocked from any sunlight and curved in dangerous and unpredictable ways. There was only one car left behind them and it had the full attention of Rose, Davy, and the Stranger. Bright headlights swerved back and forth behind them as the car frantically searched for a way to bring them off the road. The winding country roads that waited on them were more dangerous in a high-speed chase, but they didn't have a choice.

Bam. Click. Click. "Shit!" Davy yelled out right after the shot, his upper half leaned out of the window. He slid back into the passenger seat and looked over at Rose.

"Count was wrong."

"Yeah, I got that much."

"Y'all watch this shit," the Stranger interrupted.

With everyone's attention on him, the young man tucked one revolver back into his leather holster on his side but held another in his right hand. With a gentle click back of the hammer, he aimed the barrel backward over his shoulder right behind his head, and closely watched the mirror that Rose had used to stare him down. After a small adjustment of the gun pointing behind him, he winked in the mirror and fired. The rear glass of the SUV shattered in the fraction of second while Rose and Davy both recoiled in shock. It took a few seconds for each of them to regain their senses, and when they looked back, they saw the car that had been racing after them slow down drastically as if the driver had stomped on the brakes. There was a small hole in the windshield from the Stranger's bullet—stained in red. Just as they were about to leave the car behind them, it rolled off slowly into the ditch and crashed with the driver dead behind the steering wheel.

Davy was lost in the sounds of the shattered windshield. The wind rushing in made it difficult to process what he had just gone through, but there was no time to stop. There was a dangerously violent man who seemed barely of age sitting right behind him, ready to kill him and put an end to anything he hoped to accomplish in this life.

"This wasn't supposed to happen! You can't be here," Rose yelled at the windshield.

"Just shut up and drive, Rose," the Stranger said coldly from the back seat. His eyes pierced right through both of them.

"No," Rose shot back. "We're so not doing this right now."

The SUV began to slow down and Davy started to snap out of his daze. By the time they had pulled over to the side of the road, he was more than alert enough to realize this wasn't a smart move. "We can't stay here, Rose! There might be more of them coming."

"We aren't taking orders from this one," she told him firmly. "Trust me, you'll thank me later."

"Look at y'all acting like you actually have a choice here," the Stranger mocked them from the back seat. "Now, drive."

"Don't do this, not yet," Davy tried to reason with her. "Not when we're right there. We're so close, closer than ever, remember?"

"You don't understand," Rose told him before

looking into the mirror with her trademark piercing stare. "None of you do."

The gentle motion of the SUV pulling off the side of the road was the first indicator that Davy could finally release the white-knuckle grip on his revolver even after it had been emptied of all shots. He refused to part with it just yet considering who sat behind him. The park ranger knew even if it was fully loaded —he'd have his hands full if it came to a fight.

"Do you have a name?"

"No," was his cold reply.

"What do we call you then?"

"You don't."

"No sense in trying, Davy," Rose said, cutting off his questions.

"Maybe he can help us."

"Just give it up. The only thing he is going to do is lead us to our death. He works for Damian."

Rose turned her head to glance back at the Stranger who was watching them from beneath his cowboy hat, his revolver resting in his lap with his hand crossed over it, just listening.

"Isn't that right, little guy?" She mocked him with her tone, knowingly pushing his buttons to see if she could get a reaction.

"Rose," Davy pleaded with her, slightly nodding his head to the gun pointed at her back.

"I don't think we should be making this situation worse than it already is."

The inside of the vehicle fell silent. The sun had started to show itself just beyond the tree line and its warm light was more than welcome. It was a night that Rose was anxious to put behind her. As she drove endlessly on the highway taking them from one small town to the next, her mind raced with what they needed to do next. How could she get away from this? Even worse, how could she get away from this without making Davy never want to speak to her again? She still needed him. Impatience began to set in. The miles were ticking by and Rose had given up any sense of direction. The drive was now a game of keeping the compass headed north without giving away any indicators of where they needed to be. She looked over at Davy to see how he was handling it. He didn't look good.

Davy couldn't stop thinking about the revolver. Not the one in his hand that had claimed a life at the Big Thicket though. He was thinking about the one he couldn't see, the one aimed at his back and ready to fire at any moment. He knew Rose was the one they wanted and that meant he was disposable. There was no chance of talking his way out of this one. It seemed his only hope at getting out of the situation unharmed was for Rose to pull off something miraculous. Luckily, that wasn't too far off from what he knew she could do.

"You're bleeding you know." The words swirled in his ears without holding any real meaning.

He knew what they were meant to trigger in his mind and he realized Rose had spoken to

him, but he didn't react. He had gone numb in all the panic and forgotten that a bullet had gone right through his shoulder. It was a flesh wound that likely needed stitches, but fortunately, not one that would kill him. Somehow, Rose's words flipped a switch in his brain. Just as she reminded him of the gunshot wound on his shoulder, the pain flooded his body causing him to grunt.

"Oh shit," he let out.

"Wrap it tight. It's not serious, but you need to stop the bleeding. You're lucky it didn't hit you a few inches to the left."

"You keep using that word, but I'm not feeling so lucky."

The blood on Davy's arm had seeped through his ranger uniform's long sleeve button

down. The cut it caused on the shoulder of the shirt revealed his broken skin and it was clear the wound needed to be cleaned. It was the closest he'd come to dying in his entire life. Aside from when he was tortured not too long ago of course. The surreal feeling of being stuck in something so far over his head didn't mix well at all with the fact that he had killed multiple people today. It was all too much to process at a time where his mind wanted nothing more than to focus entirely on something simple—on anything other than his own mortality. He and Rose almost didn't make it out of the Big Thicket alive, and they'd be lucky if they didn't die before the next sundown. It was all he could concern himself with.

Rose continued driving as Davy did his best to wrap his shoulder and stop the bleeding that had made its way down his arm to spill on the leather seats and mix into the carpet. The Stranger sat silently in the back with his head tilted down, his revolver in hand pointed at them, daring them to make a move he didn't approve of.

Highway marker signs came and went while Rose ignored them all. She just had to wait for the right moment. Davy wouldn't be the one to make the first move, she knew it had to be her, but it couldn't be now. With the Eternal Flame finally completed in the bag at her side, the stakes were higher than ever. They had driven for over two hours now, giving Rose enough time to contemplate, and Davy enough time to become a makeshift nurse to stop the bleeding in his arm. The Stranger never said another word. He just waited.

Rose held onto the same hope that the constellation in the sky had sparked within her. They were the only ones who could use the map of the Eternal Flame, not only to find the lost treasure, but to unlock its fullest potential. No one could take that from her. The thought of where Davy heard the story of the treasure it protected back at Tyler State Park by the lingering ghost of her own grandmother entered her mind. Her ancestors had ensured the park ranger was by her side when she least expected it for a reason—like it was meant to be. After a few minutes, Rose was ready to speak up at last, but the Stranger's phone rang and threw a wrench in that.

"Yes." His cold voice rang through the SUV once again.

There was a brief pause as Rose and Davy listened, wide-eyed and worried for entirely different reasons even if it wasn't clear by looking at them.

"All of us. And the key."

"You made my life so damned difficult when it didn't even have to be. Don't think I won't remember that kind of shit," the Stranger admitted. "We have what we need now, finally."

Rose and Davy risked another look at each other.

"Are you ready?"

The Stranger nodded in approval and allowed a slight smirk to cross his lips.

"We'll meet up with you before going to the old vault. We'll be there in a few hours. Congratulations, by the way," the Stranger told the person on the other end of the line. "It's finally ours."

Rose's heart sank to her stomach.

CHAPTER 19

D amian De León hung up the phone in his office with a smile so big it went clear across his face from ear to ear. Finally, after so many wasted years, so much wasted money, and so many empty promises—the artifact was finally his and the treasure it protected would soon follow. His eyes had widened with excitement, and he thought maybe even his pupils had blown out. The anticipation was almost too much to bear.

For a fleeting moment, he considered what it must have been like for the Stranger to catch both of them just as they found the missing pieces of the map. It was surely a confusing and difficult time for him knowing as little as he did. There was even a distant, faint feeling of pity that Damian found at the bottom of his belly, but there was no sense in any of that. He chuckled at his desk and shook his head in disbelief. With a gentle lean backward in his chair, he propped his exotic leather boots up on the edge of his wooden

desk and rubbed at his goatee. He was finely mani-
cured in every aspect of how he presented himself.
The gray hairs that just recently became the majority
of his hair were all slicked back. His suit was one of
money despite the fact that he didn't have any, and
that was the point, as hard as it was to swallow for
him. He may not have been immune to failure, but he
was a man who wouldn't accept anything other than
results. Even if it took generations to find them.

"I told you I'd get it all back one day," he affirmed
to his father, and his father's father, from just beneath
his breath.

He couldn't help himself but to bask in the accom-
plishment that had been laid so diligently right before
his feet. It may have taken longer than he'd anticipated, but the dull grind and ruthlessness of leaving
no stone unturned and no punches held back had
finally paid off after all these years.

Rose was young when Damian took her away. She
was frail, exhausted, and hungry when he first laid
eyes on her so many years ago. Her mother had
desperately continued a doomed-to-fail search for a
mythical lost treasure of the Wild West that her family
filled her head full of as a child. In doing so, she
destroyed any chance of normalcy for the family that
instilled it in her. Unfortunately for them, that was the
least of their worries. He knew Rose's mother was just
as crazy as her grandmother who single-handedly
started this whole fight, but even he underestimated
just how far they would all go to steal what they felt
was theirs.

The De Leóns of Texas were a family dynasty who

knew only of success all throughout their history, and Damian wielded their generations of economic conquest without remorse. He hedged his bets whenever he could—sometimes even when it didn't make any sense—and Rose had been only a piece of the results those behaviors yielded. The treasure of the Eternal Flame felt like it was pulled from a dime novel right off the frontier, but Rose and her entire family were radicalized by it. The lengths they would all go to in order to find it were extraordinary, but they paled in comparison to what he was about to do. He'd already discovered much wilder things in life and he, more than anyone, knew he had to find that damned artifact if there was any hope in preserving the De León dynasty for the next generation.

It wasn't often that Damian De León had to put himself in the field to get his hands dirty. This was a situation that warranted it, though. Decades of an impending feeling of the family empire crumbling beneath him had become impossible to ignore any further. He allowed himself a couple of minutes to enjoy a few meaningless puffs of a cigar, exhaling each one with a gravitas that he felt was at long last truly earned. Once he felt like he had smoked the cigar down to an acceptable point, De León smashed it out on a glass ashtray resting on his desk. The smoke trailed up as ash floated into the air around him. It smelled of a deep, rich earthiness that portrayed a sense of masculinity he was desperate to exude. The scent was soaked into everything around him. After half of a suppressed cough he reached for the black corded phone once again on his desk and pushed it to his ear.

"Start it up, I'm leaving now," Damian said bluntly before pausing just long enough to scrunch his face in sudden frustration. "I know it's the last tank, goddammit. Do it anyway."

He refused to wait for a response before slamming the phone down with an odd sense of satisfaction he knew few would ever feel for themselves. He wasted no time in standing up as if a hundred pounds of weight had been lifted off his shoulders. Before leaving, Damian tried his best not to stare at the picture frame that still rested face down at the corner of his desk, the one of him standing a young girl named Rose and the child she held in her arms. He thought of how they got to such a place, the bloodshed, lies, and betrayal that had everyone at each other's throats. The look on Rose's face in the picture was one of young naivety, but the look on his own face was the same that he wore today. It was the look of purpose, and of determined willpower. It was also the look of a man who knew something the girl in front of him didn't. He knew their entire family's obsessive search for a treasure no one even believed existed would be their downfall. Destruction ran in that family's very DNA. Rose's grandmother had only cemented it further for generations to come by what she did. She'd been the one to run off with the Eternal Flame artifact long ago when it had just fallen into the De León family's grasp, setting off a vicious cycle with no end in sight where everyone was fighting for a way to find the map and claim its horde of wealth for their own. Damian was prepared to do damn near anything to finally bring that cycle to a close.

At one time in his life, Damian De León hadn't been aware of this old west tall tale of a lost treasure that had been circulating behind his back. There were rumors about an old vault which was protected by a familial bond that transcended time to make it one of Texas's—possibly even the United States'—few remaining preserved historical secrets. The vault's door sealed off unthinkable riches which a family claimed to keep alive with what they called an Eternal Flame, something beyond anyone's imagination when it was assembled by an unknown outlaw in the late 1800s. As he became of age and rose in the ranks of his family's company, that story followed him everywhere he went. It was something that was interwoven into their dynasty that would never leave. It was around every single corner and lurking behind every decision. Everything hung in the balance of what could only be described as myth for so many.

As he organized the same stack of past-due bills and disheartening tax documents that had sat on his desk the last six months and started to collect his cell phone and jacket, Damian De León thought back to his own venture in that muggy swamp Rose's family loved so much. He thought about all that filthy place had given him—and what it had kept from him.

If Rose's grandmother hadn't set everything in motion, he may never have had to deal with the situation to begin with, but he'd also have never actually found the place for himself. Although he couldn't have ever known it at the time, visiting the family's

207 LATE AND A BULLET SHORT

burial vault turned out to be a pivotal moment, and a
blessing in disguise. It was one of the earliest signs of
his God-given inheritance and the righteous mission
he'd been next-in-line to see through.

He took a moment to look around with a single
deep breath. It was the De León headquarters found at
the heart of Victoria, Texas, a building further south
than anywhere Rose or her family would live. It was a
sign of their earliest subjugation of the land at their
feet. His office was filled with priceless antiques and
historical artifacts that were born of his own ancestors'
feats of conquest throughout the state. They inspired
him to do whatever was necessary, and now he was on
the cusp of cementing his own mark to the family's
legacy. The story that had been whispered behind
closed doors, the asterisk on their name, was about to
be put to rest at long last and solve the financial pains
that had become a scourge on anything they did.

Damian straightened the collar on his jacket and
glanced from side to side in order to make sure he was
still the only one in the building. The trip to the burial
vault where the treasure would be found was
normally a six-hour drive, but he couldn't risk such a
long time to travel today. The boy he sent after them
may have been good, but holding both Rose and this
mysterious park ranger at gunpoint for so long
wouldn't be an easy feat, even for the best of
gunslingers. He was never one to hang his hat on just
one plan, though. That's why he had one more stop to
make before leaving for the vault.

He made his way to an empty hallway where he
would find a nondescript door. It was a door that few

who worked in the building—even those who worked directly for him—would ever use. What happened on the other side involved the work of the most depraved and twisted men Damian would ever come to know. It was a place made of only nightmares that few would ever have the misfortune of experiencing. He used this place only in times of necessity, or at least he always had in the past, but these days it seemed there was always a reason to be found.

He followed a trail of blood through the hallway to the other side of the door until he found smeared handprints and heard the sounds of running water. It was a familiar situation for what these men were paid to do. There wasn't much to be found inside, a countertop with a sink against the wall where two burly men were hunched over washing their hands, a small table full of red-soaked tools that looked as though they belonged in a dentist's office, and one small stainless-steel chair propped up in the center of the room that held what remained of the men's work.

"Did you know it looks like a damned bloodbath in here?" Damian asked abruptly. "You used to be more professional than that. Now look at you. I sure hope to hell you know something about this asshole after what you put him through. You spilled enough blood to know every damn detail of that man's life."

"We know enough."

"What does that even mean? You have a name? Address? His fuckin' favorite movie? You better tell me something after all this you sons of bitches."

One of the men dropped his eyes and held out his hand to show a driver's license grasped in his orange fingers. It was from Texas and about to expire, but more importantly, it had a name.

"Tom Wayne," he said aloud as he tried to see if it rang a bell.

"The last call the ranger took was to this man before they made off with the map. Turns out, this is the chief ranger back at Daingerfield and he suspected something was going on," the other one finally spoke up. "He tried to warn him."

"Couldn't take his own advice," Damian answered. "Clean the mess up and get me something I can use right goddamn now."

In just a few short seconds, Damian was climbing multiple sets of stairs that led him to the roof of the building with a stride like nothing had ever happened. When he stepped out into the sunlight and windy weather, the sounds of the swirling blades of a helicopter filled his ears. A nameless pilot, loyal to a fault, stood next to the door ready to accompany him to the cockpit, unaware of where they would be heading, but ready to go all the same. Damian De León checked the stainless revolver tucked into his side to ensure it was still loaded, pulled a pair of dark sunglasses down over his eyes, and jumped into the cockpit of the helicopter.

Within seconds, they were rising into the air and taking off northeast, high into the clouds that dotted the sweeping blue sky. The town of Victoria faded in the horizon behind them as Damian flew toward deep East Texas—toward the always destined burial vault near Caddo Lake—where he would finally close a chapter that was long overdue.

CHAPTER 20

Being held at gunpoint was a fate that no one ever wanted to be on the receiving end of. Waiting on the gentle squeeze of a trigger to determine whether you see tomorrow was a level of anxiety that few were able to withstand for more than a few minutes without succumbing to shock. The constant thought of what may happen if you made the wrong sudden movement, or if the car hit an unexpected bump, was enough to drive anyone up the walls. It wasn't just concern that began to send an unsettling chill down the spine, it was dread, and it was panic. Unfiltered, burning, unquestionable panic. Because bullets were unforgiving and mistakes aren't always so easily rescinded, and when combined, they can only become inseparable for eternity. If more people understood these simple facts of life, there would be more than a few less regrets in the world.

But Davy did understand these facts of life, and that meant he was panicking—severely.

The dreadful car ride Rose and Davy were forced to endure at the end of arguably the most unfriendly of gun barrels ended sooner than anticipated. There wasn't any discussion or fighting, no more phone calls for the Stranger, and no more guessing about where they were headed next. At this point, the only thing left for any of them to do was to wait and find out what was in store.

Rose knew what no one else in the car knew though. She understood the dangers faced by herself and Davy, even the times when he was able to remain blissfully unaware. Sure, he knew there was a pistol aimed at his back from who could be a total madman for all he knew, but if he understood how much worse it could get, he probably wouldn't have been able to keep his cool quite so well. It was something she had grown to admire about the man who sat next to him. She couldn't explain exactly what it was. Rose was starting to find herself caring about keeping Davy alive more than she ever expected to. It was far from the place or time for such thoughts, but they were there regardless, even now.

Davy had already come to terms with why he had become so willing to help Rose on a deadly chase for a treasure that he would most likely wouldn't get much of. It was something he understood quickly, especially compared to Rose's own understanding of what was happening. But Davy also knew that this wasn't the time for such thoughts. He knew they would only see the next day if they worked together. While this isn't what they had originally planned, his mind was hard at work to deliver a solution that would keep them both on the same side and throw their captor off long enough to either kick his ass or find a good escape route.

Following three hours of silence into their drive, one of the three finally spoke up on their own volition. The other two stiffened with anxiety at his own announcement.

"Take the next exit," the Stranger demanded from the back seat, flicking the pistol to the right in a motion toward the upcoming sign directing them off to the right-hand shoulder.

There was so much Rose wanted to say. She wanted to tell Davy she was sorry, for everything, including dragging him all into this to begin with. She wanted to say that she was sorry to the Stranger, for everything he had to do to get to this point, chasing something he didn't even understand. She knew holding the two of them up at gunpoint wasn't what he dreamed of doing when he grew up, and she also knew it was likely to only get worse from here for him if all of this continued. Now wasn't the time for liberation though—now was time for survival.

"You aren't trying to go to Shreveport, are you?" Rose said, glancing back at the mirror to see the Stranger still staring forward.

"Shut up and take the next exit," his cold voice came again from behind them.

Rose drove in silence for the next two miles then followed his directions, taking the next

exit that put them onto a country road with a speed limit that matched the highway's. The trees racing by their windows never got any shorter, always seeming to reach high into the sky no matter what the weather was like. It was easy to see why someone like Davy would fall in love with a place like this. Rose only wished it didn't take the threat of death to make her appreciate it more. Up until this point, she'd only seen a different side of the place he called home. The historic and admittedly wondrous piney woods of East Texas cast a long shadow indeed, a shadow that you may not see at first, but would soon come to understand how it manages to cover the underbelly of the worst that people are capable of. It was a place where time moved slowly just like people always say, where families could spend generations without any interference—and where some things that shouldn't see the light of day can find unnatural ways to thrive. Even so, it was as magnificent as anything anyone had ever laid eyes upon. If the adventure to follow the map of the Eternal Flame was to go up in fire for whatever reason, she could at least take comfort in the fact that she was in a place such as this.

Meanwhile, Davy had spent just about every minute going through each scenario in his mind and how he could play his cards right to make sure both he and Rose walked away alive. The Stranger had put them in a bad situation, and as the hours ticked by, Davy was only feeling more and more desperate to get on the other side of the gun that was pointed at them. He wondered what Rose was thinking about, if she was formulating the best way to get out of this whole ordeal in a way only she could pull off. The time he'd spent with her following this Eternal Flame legend had shown him things he'd never dreamed of seeing, and made him do things pulled only from his nightmares. None of it seemed to matter though. Everything they had gone through would come to a meaningless end with a bullet lodged into his spine. If Davy was going to do something about any of it, his window of opportunity was closing rapidly.

His plan was a simple one. It would require Rose to catch on quickly to stomp on the brakes and give him the upper hand when everything started, but as long as he could manage to get in the back seat, he was sure he could make the difference to change their situation. It wasn't much, and he was willing to risk his life to even the odds with the cold, trigger-happy gunman behind them, but there wasn't anything else he could do. The only thing he needed now was a distraction.

The most recent sign they passed had told Davy they were headed to a small town called Uncertain up near Caddo Lake. It was a drive Davy hadn't made in years. He racked the depths of his memories to scrounge up anything useful from the last time he was in the area to watch the paddlefish get restocked at the lake. They had gone far from the highway where there wasn't anyone in sight by now and worry was starting to set in. This wasn't the typical route to Caddo Lake, that much he did know. With his timeframe to act getting shorter by the minute, he braced himself to create a distraction of his own, forgoing any chance at notifying Rose ahead of time. Just as he took a deep breath to make his move, the distraction he would have never asked for happened.

"Pull over," the Stranger said gently, shattering any plans that the park ranger had been debating. "There."

Davy's chest sank with dread, and Rose's followed soon after with fear. If both of them could have spoken freely at the time, they would have known that a single word ran through both of their minds at the same time—*shit*.

The Stranger gestured lazily with his hand, directing them to pull the SUV over into the ditch. There was no shoulder on this country road and that meant they had to put the vehicle entirely in the grass, just a few feet from the thick woods that lined the asphalt as far as anyone could see. They may have been out in the middle of nowhere, but it was still deep East Texas, and that meant dense trees with brush so thick it wouldn't let you walk through them without a few cuts and scrapes of the greenbriar and yaupon as a memento.

Rose glanced sideways at Davy to make sure he hadn't totally lost it and started freaking out. He was still calm, somehow, or at least that's what she saw when they locked eyes for no more than a second.

The road, empty as it was, stretched out in front of them to no end and was lost behind them all the same. The flickering light and annoying tick of the blinker on the SUV changed the atmosphere, and for some reason, made their situation more real than the ranger had come to understand. Davy may not live to see the next few hours, much less the next day. He knew he was an accessory. He knew he was disposable in what was unfolding around them.

"Look, I know where you're going with this," Rose

said while looking into the rearview mirror. "The park ranger was a wild card even for me, I'll admit that. That doesn't mean all bets are off. You hear me?"

"What are you talking about?" Davy wasn't keeping up.

"This is about Damian De León. Always has been. Don't forget that."

The Stranger offered only silence in return. His eyes were locked forward and his face didn't even as much as twitch with emotion at Rose's words.

"Rose? You're scaring me more than you usually do. Why are you saying all of this?"

"Davy, do you trust me?"

"I really do want to."

"That's gonna have to do for now."

The SUV gently swerved to the right and drifted off the road. Everyone inside the car bounced in their seats in silence as the vehicle came to a stop. For a strange few seconds, everyone sat there without saying anything.

"Go on," the Stranger spoke up at last. "Out."

Rose yanked the door handle first, climbed out without a word, and walked in front of the SUV without locking eyes with him. Davy watched her in shock. Instead of attacking the Stranger when it was just the two of them alone in the vehicle, he watched Rose simply walk around the front without any indication of what she was planning. Before he realized, Davy found himself focused instead on the swarm of gnats and mosquitoes that surrounded her in the muggy air. Anything, so he could avoid the thoughts of what was about to happen.

"Now you," the Stranger's words came without pause.

It took everything he had to reach up and open the passenger door and climb out into the tall grass on the side of the road. He stared at Rose. His face contorted into a dumbfounded expression as he made his way over to her. He knew she hadn't given up—not like this. She just looked forward with a blank face and gave him nothing to go on. It was frustrating beyond belief, and the fear for his own life in the middle of everything made it entirely worse. As Davy walked forward to stand beside Rose in the weeds that brushed his shins, he felt a tinge of regret. Doubt crept through his spine and he thought, for even a single second too long, that he had risked his life for a childish dream that wasn't even his.

All of this surprisingly made Davy only yearn for the tall pines of the Daingerfield park, the cool waters of the lake at its center, and the inconspicuous outdoor amphitheater where he used to tell stories. The feeling of a strong breeze wicking the sweat from his brow and the smells of the campground barbecues—even the occasional invite by a welcoming family to try some for himself—all made him think this entire ordeal was just one big mistake on his part. More than anything, he just wanted to be back there, in the wildlife where he could do no wrong. Staring into the brush ahead of them with an empty road at their back and a ruthless killer with a pistol in his hand, he wondered if this really would be the end, if he would never again look up to see the pines tower over him in the sunlight. He wondered if he'd ever go back to wishing for an adventure to fall in his lap ever again, or if those days were now long gone.

He shook his head in defiance. None of that mattered. For all he knew, he was about to take a bullet to the head and all of this would be over in less than the blink of an eye.

Rose, on the other hand, was getting impatient. Her lips were curled and she struggled to keep from rolling her eyes at everything this Stranger was doing. He was visibly younger than his penchant for shooting would suggest, but that didn't stop him from forcing his hand by any means necessary. Assuming the park ranger was most likely shitting bricks and contemplating his best chances at sprinting into the woods ahead of them, Rose considered it best to avoid any eye contact which might inspire a rebellion that would send this whole thing to hell even worse than it already was. As long as he didn't act up too badly, they should be safe for what was coming next. She knew it'd be best to get it over with as soon as possible —for both their sakes.

"Oh come on, for fucks..." Rose started complaining. But she couldn't finish the sentence before the Stranger raised his arm into the air, gripping his revolver tightly, stared down at Rose with black eyes. With a sharp lunge, the Stranger interrupted her complaining with a downward strike right onto her skull. Rose collapsed immediately to the ground with an abrupt thump.

Davy could only watch on in horror.

A black bag suddenly fell on Rose's back, tossed by the Stranger's own hand, and Davy shuttered at what it meant for him. He took a second to glare down the road, begging in his mind for a car to drive by at the right time and see what was happening to them. After everything they had been through in a matter of only days, from his own realization the map was real down in Port Arthur, to just barely escaping the Big Thicket with their lives, he hoped with everything he had they could pull off one more surprise. But, as he looked down at Rose's unconscious body lying in the dirt and the Stranger standing over her, he couldn't help but feel doubt sneak its way back in.

"Put it on her," the Stranger told him.

He reached for the bag to forcefully pull the fabric over Rose's head and down to her shoulders. Her hair fell down further than the hood, and a pang of unbridled guilt shot through him when he rolled her over into her back to pull the front down over her closed eyes. The sight of her knocked unconscious shook him to his bones and something inside him said that he'd never go through such a thing again. When he was done with the task given to him, he glanced up and held his hands out in bewilderment to sell his white flag offering.

"The back seat," the Stranger said in return, flicking his revolver toward the SUV still flashing its emergency lights on the side of the road.

Davy let out a sigh. It was a long one, comprised of exhaustion, fear, anxiety, and burning anger. Hoisting Rose into the back seat of the SUV took only a few seconds, and while he struggled to get her arms and legs situated to buckle her into the back seat, the Stranger hovered behind him watching closely. Just as the seat belt clicked around her waist, the ranger made his move. In the blink of an eye he swung his body around in a circular motion with his hands outstretched, ready to grab at the Stranger's gun to catch him off guard. He put all his strength into his attack, every muscle in his body screamed with fury as he tried his best to get close and take the gunman down, fighting as hard as he could to disarm him. The frantic struggle on the ground lasted only seconds. Suddenly, Davy felt a blunt force to his nose and then the warm trickle of blood down his face and neck. His vision was blurred and his entire body dazed.

Davy watched as the Stranger stood over him, looking down with an unnerving glare that revealed no emotions behind his cold eyes. For just a split second, Davy felt as though the Stranger's eyes somehow pierced through him in a familiar way. Before there was any chance at recovery, however, another blow came down onto Davy's face, and blood spurted out once again, soaking his clothes deep red. Breathing through the mess on his face was difficult, and the bleeding wouldn't stop no matter how hard the ranger clenched at his face.

Thoughts of Rose filled Davy's drifting mind— stunned from the blows to the head by the Stranger's revolver—yet he could only find himself worrying for her safety. His eyes couldn't even focus, but he desperately searched for any clues of her wellbeing all the same. Davy was falling in and out of consciousness, soon to join Rose in an unwilling nap brought on by a violent hand all too willing to leave them in a puddle of their own blood. He couldn't see her. He couldn't hear her. His face pulsated from the beating, but he had lost most of the sharp feelings to the numbness that was starting to overtake his entire body.

"Rose..." He moaned through gurgled breaths before allowing himself to drift away on waves of darkness that carried him into nothing.

CHAPTER 21

I t would be hours before Rose found her way back to consciousness again. A swaying bounce that turned into a violent shake forced her to grunt unexpectedly, and with it, a rush of memories, pain, and shock poured back into her without remorse. Her body curled in on itself in reaction.

The steady sounds of leaves and twigs crunching beneath hooves played in an endless loop in her ears, a familiar gait that someone could only really come to know so instinctively through experience. A sound that was unmistakable to anyone who'd heard it over and over again formed the rhythm of each step. It didn't take long to piece together the fact that they were on horseback, and they were riding in what was undoubtedly the least comfortable—or logical—way imaginable.

Sweat ran down her face and into her eyes, stinging them enough to make her wince even while still half dazed. In an effort to take her mind off the pain, she allowed herself to finally look around to see where they were, and who they were with.

It was barely dusk, a gray fog hung around near to the ground, floating in the silver light that washed out the trees surrounding them. Everywhere Rose darted her eyes, she could only see more men traveling with them. Some were on horses, others walked diligently without complaining, and all of them were heavily armed. Most cradled an AR-15 in their hands with handguns strapped to their hip and one even carried a rifle that had a scope on it as round as a baseball. They were the favorites from Damian's preferred goons of today, the Pinkertons, and that didn't mean anything good for her.

Before she realized it, her thoughts turned to Davy. It was as if she'd been dealt the cruel hand of a loved one knocking on death's door. There was only one question that blared in her thoughts. Was he alive? Her head swirled in panic. The man that dropped his life and joined her to find a lost treasure he may or may not have believed even existed—someone she had personally forced to get involved in her treacherous mission—had been taken alongside her. She was sure of it. What she didn't know, however, was if Damian De León allowed him to live after everything that had happened.

"Davy..." Rose whispered in fear of what may have happened while she was knocked out.

When she was finally able to turn her head to the right angle, she caught a glimpse of Davy's limp body strung over the back of a saddle. Her head was hanging upside down so it was difficult for her to make out any specifics, but she at least knew for now that he was still with her. That would have to be enough.

He was the most unpredictable part about this entire circumstance for her. He had been ever since they crossed paths at Daingerfield. An air of naive trustworthiness in everything he did was inexplicably disarming to her. For a few fleeting moments, she allowed herself the luxury of a daydream where everything would turn out as it should. A time where she wasn't running for her life and she could finally be with her family. It was a simple wish for her, but one that felt as though it would never happen regardless. Being ripped apart from so much you've ever loved has a way of putting everything you want to love behind a wall that only gets harder to climb. But this time, in a daydream she'd only granted herself sparingly over the last few days, she saw Davy alongside her. He was droning on about the plants or birds or whatever was alive around him, but he was there, nonetheless.

A burning, searing feeling of worn rope rubbing back and forth across her wrists and ankles killed Rose's daydream and forced her attention back onto herself. She'd been taken hostage, or so they thought. While there had been some wildcards, including Davy of course, she did actually know what she was doing. Rose needed to get close to Damian, but only when the map had been completed, and only when she allowed it to happen. Anything less would play into his games that twisted her mind for so long.

She felt relieved that Davy was knocked out right

now. It gave her the chance to get her bearings and figure out what to do next. The only problem was she had no idea what was happening to them at the moment. Bringing the map of the Eternal Flame to the De Leóns had to happen at some point, but they weren't supposed to know where the treasure was already. Rose closed her eyes first, then squeezed them shut so hard a tear forced its way out.

If these people knew where the treasure was, it only meant they needed her to bring them the map because they couldn't get in. They were chasing her to get what they couldn't find, to learn what they wouldn't understand. It only made the knowledge— and who held it—more crucial in actually getting the treasure. Thinking of what she'd been through because of this fact under the hands of Damian De León made her blood boil.

"Rose!" came a hoarse whisper across from her. "Are you alive?"

Rose struggled to force herself to the side and look at Davy who had woken up in dramatic fashion only to immediately try and get her attention. This also drew the gaze of the man riding the horse he had been slung over, who glanced back, visibly annoyed, and lifted the butt of his rifle. The only thing Rose could do was widen her eyes in shock before the rifle came down on his head. The ranger was knocked out cold once again just like that.

Rose did her best to not make Davy's painful mistake while bouncing up and down on the ass-end of the horse, just barely staying on, tucked behind the saddle of a gun-for-hire who probably had never ridden a day in his life. Although every ounce in her body wanted to rage at everyone around them until no one was left standing. The constant crushing of hooves dragged on for the next hour where she could only see the ground at their side and a handful of other armed brutes. They had to be the same ones who chased them through the Big Thicket. Although she couldn't tell one from the other, they were just the type of guns that Damian De León preferred—obedient, trigger happy, and not too bright. He had a type. It seemed they were accompanied by half a dozen or more of them.

"You already knew where the treasure was? I'm sitting here trying to imagine one reason why you wouldn't just dig the damned thing up yourself years ago." The voice came from a couple riders ahead of Rose that she recognized immediately. "Can't think of a single fuckin' one."

Of course Rose knew who it was, it was an unmistakable voice even after all this time. The Stranger may be just another gun that Damian De León unleashed on her in a fit of blind fury, but even he had a lot to learn about why she was doing what she was doing. She had to break the cycle. She'd die to do it.

The stale smell of swamp water filled her nostrils as they rode. Musty, stagnant air that felt humid against the skin hung around them. It was the air that surrounded a lake. If the men holding them hostage were hoping to keep the location of where they were going a secret, the very air betrayed them all with embarrassing accuracy. They could never know the land like she did, or even like the park ranger did.

"If you say it was worth all those people dying and all that money, it must've been," the Stranger spoke again, perking Rose's attention. "I would've just dug that shit up myself though, by hand if I had to."

Rose fought to ignore the screaming burns on her wrists and ankles while listening to the one-sided conversation unfolding in front of them. For some reason, the thought of Davy's rendition of the story behind the map of the Eternal Flame entered her mind instead, the silly one he told back in Daingerfield. Embellished didn't even begin to cover it. She forced a slight smile across her lips as she remembered listening to his sincerity when they were back at the amphitheater. It was the kind of story that inspired belief, even the kind of story that would bring a bunch of murderous assholes together in search of a fabled treasure of the old west.

"If we don't get what we're after here..." the Stranger said before his voice quieted, and Rose couldn't make out what the end of the threat was.

Damian De León had to be the one he was talking to. They'd made it to Caddo Lake, a place that man absolutely shouldn't be at the same time as the artifact that brought them here. Even she couldn't deny that they were closer than ever to finding the treasure her family had been after for generations, but what would have to happen next wasn't going to be easy. She would need Davy's help when it came time, and she hoped that all of the lies she told to him wouldn't prevent that from happening. If there was a right time to tell him, it'd probably already passed them by.

Their forced ride on horseback with the lake on

their side carried on in similar fashion for another hour. The blood that had all gone to Rose's head from being slumped over the horse made her dizzy and her vision blurred. Every few minutes she would crane her neck around to try and get a glimpse of Davy for reasons that were becoming painfully clearer. He was still unconscious, rocking back and forth with the sway of the horse, but still breathing. He looked strange without his ranger hat—something he'd worn since they first met—but it was strange in a good way, and she was finally ready to admit it.

The ride had mostly been quiet other than the occasional complaint from a random gun-for-hire. There hadn't been many clues that Damian was actually with the group. His presence was usually felt by all— whether they wanted it or not. He had the type of showmanship that made him a favorite among corporate donors and hated by almost all who worked for him. If she had to take a guess as to why they were even on horseback right now, it would be Damian's own ego and penchant for boastfulness. He probably viewed this as a victory lap hundreds of years in the making, a triumphant moment which deserved to be memorialized. To some he was just a good businessman, to others he was a pioneer, but everyone knew him to be ruthless. It was how he had gotten where he was now, with her hogtied on a horse and him leading the way by exploiting everything she had ever done or become in life.

"Isn't this just magnificent!" A boisterous holler from a man at the front of the group came out as if on cue. She had summoned the devil himself. "You can feel the touch of God's own hand right here. And it's by his hand that I will finally have what was always mine," he continued.

Rose's stomach sank with dread. Even though she knew he had to be there if any of this was going to work, she never wanted to be face-to-face with Damian De León again. Before she had time to react, she noticed Davy out of the corner of her eye. Damian's loud yells had the unintended consequence of jarring the ranger back into consciousness. He woke with a violent shake, and Rose watched, as his eyes darted all around while he tried to get his bearings back. All she could do was feel guilty.

"You know boys, the route we take today has been walked on horseback for two hundred years!" Damian wasn't even trying to hide his excitement at this point. He was giddy. "We walk directly in the footsteps of history and on the shoulders of giants! Even as we are led by the very lowest among us. If that doesn't teach you a lesson in God's mysterious ways, I'm not too sure what will."

None of the hired guns reacted.

"We have few to thank other than the dull-witted mother of the woman so nice enough to join us today," Damian continued, now mocking Rose without even knowing if she was listening. "She has laid the very path down we walk to show us the way to this glorious redemption!"

Davy was listening to the man yelling from the head of their group, still dazed and unable to move. Rose could see the pain of waking still coursing through him and knew there was still so much to tell him. She finally locked eyes with him. She wanted Davy to see that everything was okay, that he wasn't about to die, and that she had considered everything in her plan to find the treasure. But she could see in his eyes he felt none of that. He felt only desperation, and given the circumstance he found himself in, that was certainly understandable.

"Gold, silver, jewels, and cash by the truckload await where we go, and that is just the start!" Damian was up to something here and Rose knew it was exactly as she'd feared. The men may have not been responding, but there was no doubt they were listening and that meant Damian knew the park ranger would. "I should know. The woman that bestowed the path to riches on us—the mother of that unruly, ungrateful, heathen we brought with us today —was my old lady!"

Davy's face twisted, upside down as it was, into a look that would haunt Rose until she had turned gray and found a way to her own grave.

"And just wait until you hear about this one here next to me. The man who delivered the key to our future," Damian yelled for everyone to hear, including Davy who had already started to spiral. "They may be a broken family, but the De Leóns are the furthest thing from the likes of those people. Tonight, we're gonna show all of you why."

The men around him laughed as if directed by a cue card at a studio production in some warehouse in Hollywood, unaware of the irony Damian's words held. Their bellows were a horrific background to Davy's chain reaction realization of what he had gotten involved in. Rose's mom was only the beginning. As Davy's mind went from one thing to the next, he came to the understanding Rose was closer to all of this than she ever let on. It wasn't just some angry people chasing after her for a bunch of money—it was personal. In the middle of all of that, she lied to him over and over to get what she needed. He obviously knew something she didn't when it came to the legends of her own family, and he had no idea why he'd been chosen to know anything about it. The only thing he did know was that his life was on the line here and he likely couldn't trust the one person who got him into this mess.

What the fu... He mouthed silently in response, knowing Rose was watching him.

While Davy could see Rose cringing into the bounds of her restraints, he looked beyond her into the lake that stretched out behind them. The drooping cypress trees scattered through the area barred any sunlight and covered everything in sight with a sense of ancient majesty. The lake was one filled with history —from the first people of Texas to the world's first real offshore oil well. This place changed history itself more times than one. For just a few more fleeting moments, the ranger allowed himself to be lost in that history and how they might find their own place in it. Then, for a few regretful seconds he would love to have back, he even pondered the fate of his trusty park ranger hat.

"We walk into the ghosts of our own past tonight," Damian De León cried out again, breaking Davy's distraction. "I should warn you all, if you are afraid of things that go bump in the night and need to run back to your bed to hide under the blankets like little girls—do it now."

The men laughed again in the exact same manner as before. It was on cue once again for each and every one of them. Whether they listened to Damian's warnings or not, they seemed to be of little concern to them.

"But stay, face the demons themselves, tame the death throes of the Wild West with bullets at their feet to make them dance, and I will lay claim to more money than you would ever think possible."

Rose and Davy finally locked eyes again.

Only this time, neither one could tell what the other was thinking—and it was probably for the best.

CHAPTER 22

They traveled the length of Caddo Lake almost to the Louisiana border into Buzzard Bay before turning south. For the next few hours, Rose and Davy rode on the back of their horses in silence until the light of day faded away, first into a dull gray before the darkness of night fell on them. Neither Rose nor Davy could see the stars above or feel the cool night breeze on their faces. Spending so long hunched over the back of the horses had made both of their body's ache with soreness. They were growing impatient and each minute ticked by in agony.

When it got dark enough outside to no longer see a difference between the tops of the dense trees and the night sky filled with enough clouds to blot the stars from shining through, the group began to slow their pace to a crawl.

"Rose," Davy whispered out of nowhere.

"Quiet, Davy," she whispered back, unwilling to

give him the hint that she wouldn't dare try to explain herself under these circumstances. "They'll stop for the night soon. That's when."

The next few hours took them deeper and deeper into the woods away from Caddo Lake. The bald cypress trees that hung low with sweeping Spanish moss shading acres and acres around the lake gave way into the pine trees that dominated the East Texas area. They were accompanied by oaks and elm trees, yaupon brush with greenbriar, and the occasional hickory which twisted its limbs in contorted ways unimaginable to the eye. The horses didn't seem to mind the thick woods they pushed through even in the cover of night.

Their ride came to an abrupt halt. Though Rose and Davy couldn't see it, bound as they were, the place Damian De León and the Stranger had taken the group was a mystery tucked away from time. Shrouded in darkness was a two-story log cabin that was built to stand through the ages, and it had done exactly that. The porch extended out far into the front, resting on top of gray stone overgrown with vines and bushes. It had a wide chimney attached to the far side that was made of the same stone. It was charred from use, but that was only the smallest of concerns with the state of the old home. More than anything, it was a sad sight. Shattered windows and broken-down doors adorned the front, which had been left untouched for who knows how long, and rampant weeds had overrun the yard. Abandonment had taken its toll on the place. Even the home itself seemed to weep at the approaching crowd of armed men on horses, arriving like thieves in the night, coming to sort through the picked apart remains of a corpse looted long ago.

Helmed by the current De León heir hailing from a line of conquerors he'd give everything to be, alongside his second in command, the Stranger, the group rode up to the house with guns lifted in the air. The only thing they were missing to become a full-fledged posse were the torches.

Neither Rose nor Davy could make out where they were at this point. Amid the hollering of men settling in for the night, they were each blindfolded and knocked forcefully to the ground off the ass-end of the horse that had carried them. Their bodies hit with a hard *thud* nearly in unison and both struggled to catch their breath with faces pressed into the dirt. Then, as if choreographed, they were dragged away by their armpits in the opposite direction by burly men with beards and no discretion for their wellbeing, or apparently, their own hygiene.

The rest of the men gathered in front of the old log cabin looming eerily above them in the background. Their presence made the place one of disheartening proportions, almost apocalyptic with all the self-righteous vindications to suit, but attended only by those willing enough to be manipulated to be there. Nonetheless, they all cheered each other on under sprouting lights of lanterns, flashlights and even a growing campfire. It was an alcohol-fueled celebration of nothing. This carried on until close to midnight when the men were just drunk enough to be cheerfully compliant and Damian needed another jolt of attention to accompany his hubris.

Summoned by the chants of the last drunken force of men he could afford, Damian De

León stepped in front of the crowd all too eager to give them exactly what they wanted. It wasn't a rousing speech he delivered to inspire his followers. Instead, he gave them a twisted promise he had no right to ever make to a single soul, least of all the thieves and mercenaries who stood around him.

"The victory lap we took today was earned by too many years of failure," Damian spoke up at last.

The crowd cheered wildly—and blindly—in response to the would-be conqueror's words. They were all too eager to drink themselves happy while on the job.

"Some of you know firsthand what I'm talking about, and I'm sure the others who just got here are probably wondering what the hell they've gotten themselves into. It's true, I've replaced the dead among you by the dozens, and I doubt you trust me to lead you through the night alive. But you don't have to trust me, I've earned something else from you all, something you want for yourself. So, please allow me the opportunity to show you a small taste of what you showed up for today, of what you have fought and died for, and of what can finally be yours…"

The drunken men had fallen silent by now.

No doubt they were trying their hardest to under-stand what was happening right in front of them. They knew they had been paid to go into the woods with a crazed megalomaniac. That was just the job, but this was something else entirely. Damian's bravado really only served to confuse his paid army, despite his best intentions. No one had promised them anything more than a chance to make it to the next pay period. This was made abundantly clear in the awkward silence that followed his most bizarre offer yet.

Damian paid no attention to the dull quietness that served as the only feedback to his words. It was safe to assume there wasn't much in the way of expectations on his part, so he continued on without hesitation.

"I will offer you a taste of not just the money or the jewelry this fabled treasure promises, but power. Power bestowed by God himself, the kind of power that can only be commanded by a single source in this world we've all been cast out into—respect."

That's when it clicked, and the men shook their heads vigorously in agreement, mostly not to stand out among their peers as the only one who didn't know what was going on. The cheers were growing louder and louder as Damian De León walked back and forth in front of them with a curled smirk and a stern look in his eyes. The fire behind them swelled as if it was fueled by the mercenaries' support for the cause they knew so little about and would profit from even less. Its smoke bellowed into the dark sky above them, swallowing the area in a gray haze that filled the lungs of anyone nearby. The red glow of its flame was cast out deep among the crowd to mix with the shadows of the night for a view that was second only to hell itself. It was in this place of chaos and hunger where every generation of the De Leóns thrived.

In response to the cheers, Damian held up his right hand into the air. It first looked like a fist, but with a turn of his wrist, the crowd of hollering men could see he was holding the artifact he violently stole from Rose and Davy.

"Tonight, we will burn a path through these woods like has never been seen before, and with the Eternal Flame in my hand, we will take everything we find," the man continued as he traced his way back in front of the men. "You want my respect? Then you will earn what is yours only by doing what is necessary, by taking it."

Each one of the burly, armed men started to look around at one another. The fire burned brighter, and the crackling sounds hissed into the air around them. It fell quiet once more. This continued on for some time until the billowing smoke made one of the larger grunts with a tied-up beard choke on his breath. The distant sounds of his coughing echoed amid an uncertain crowd.

Damian looked out at those who followed him into the woods. His slicked back hair had fallen forward slightly in the excitement. His typical black suit had been replaced by black denim jeans with a pair of black snakeskin boots tucked neatly inside, and a button down of the same color that was offset only by a large belt buckle of gold and silver. At his hip hung a brilliant pearl handled single-action .44 magnum Colt revolver resting neatly in a charred leather holster. It looked as though it had never been fired before, but the men who stood before him in all of their blundering faults, at least knew that he wasn't afraid to use violence as a means to an end.

"Of course you don't know what you are supposed to do," Damian De León yelled with a smile on his face. "If you did, you wouldn't have any need for me here now, would you?"

A couple of the more loyal, sycophant-type followers gave an audible chuckle to show they were among the few who could follow along with what their boss was saying. This was met with even more side-eye glances from others in the group who didn't take too kindly to ass kissing.

"Allow me the chance to show you all the way."

Damian lifted his hands gently with his palms facing the sky and looked down at his audience. The fire that had been started behind them roared back to life, larger than most thought naturally possible, and with an unsettling force spurred on by nothing that could be seen. Inside the flickering red-hot lights of the fire, surrounded by thick black smoke blanketing the area, Damian took a step forward toward the first line of those listening and focused his darkened gaze at a cowering young man in the front. Judging by the fear in his eye, the man was new.

Yells and clapping started sparingly at first then grew into a sustained effort. Once it had reached a point of passionate contention that could be felt by anyone nearby, Damian De León acted quickly, and he acted without mercy.

In the blink of an eye, Damian drew the pearl handled Colt from his hip and flicked his wrist to send it spinning around his right hand. Before it could make two full rotations through his fingers, the revolver stopped abruptly, falling into the older man's firm grip as if it had done so a thousand times before. Before anyone could react to the fancy trick

Damian pulled off, the gun in his hand fired with a loud *bang*.

Smoke trailed up slowly from the barrel of the Colt revolver as the slight smirk on his face channeled pure evil. The red glow of the fire basked the stunned crowd in a sinister presence as they watched in horror while the once-cowardly man fell to the ground dead, blood mixed with brain matter pouring profusely from the hole in his forehead.

The gunshot echoed far into the woods and rang through the house that witnessed the man's ruthless murder. The shocking sounds of the gun rang through the shambled walls, falling ceilings, and decaying floors—from the tiny attic to the crumbling basement —awaking the home in a way it hadn't known for a long time. It was empty inside other than the dried oak leaves that had blown in through the shattered windows. No pictures or appliances filled its walls, and no furniture crowded its floors. It was as if the home had been built only to be abandoned immediately thereafter. There were two floors in the surprisingly large log cabin home. A grand fireplace and living area sat at one end opposite of a set of stairs made from the same trees of the home itself, which all showed no signs of wear. Upstairs were several bedrooms, an intended bathroom with nothing in it, and last, tucked out of the way where it was easily missed—a single broom closet no more than a few feet wide. The closet was accessible only through a heavy wooden door at the front. It was the smallest of rooms in the log cabin, if you could call it a room, and just like all the others, it was completely bare.

It was in this closet, however, where Rose and Davy sat back-to-back, bound at their wrists and ankles with heavy-duty zip ties and stained canvas bags tied haphazardly over their heads. It was impossible to see one another, but that wasn't going to delay the conversation that was about to happen.

"That guy is such a dumbass," Rose said, her voice muffled beneath the bag covering her face. "I mean seriously, did you hear that shit?"

"Someone just died," Davy let out. "Do you not care about any of that anymore? Or did you ever?"

"We're not going to die, Davy."

"You'd tell me that with a gun pointed right at my face, Rose. And you know it."

He wasn't lying. They both knew it. Her instinct was to make him feel better, and for some reason, it always had been ever since they met. From when she was taking care of the brand on his stomach after he had been tortured by Damian's goons to now, tied up together by the same man in charge, the one who only wanted to exploit what they had accomplished together. It was always that man's MO, and Rose would be a fool to think this hunt would end any other way. She knew she'd have a tough time convincing Davy of the truth.

"At this point, I think you'd tell me just about anything except what's really going on," Davy said. "Like, what the hell was Damian saying about the one who kidnapped us? Who is that and how could I even trust anything you tell me?

"You're right," she admitted. "But I had to get captured by that bastard Damian in order to get closer to this place, this house—with the right people. I had no choice, and I couldn't risk anything going wrong."

"But you could risk my life over and over again?"

"I didn't want to, Davy," Rose tried to continue. "The Eternal Flame is a family heirloom, remember? Well, when it's returned home, my ancestors take notice. All of them. I had to be here."

"You could've just told me. You could've trusted me like I did so blindly for you. You never said anything about those people. You never said you needed those assholes following us everywhere we went. You only told me they were after the artifact, that we needed to complete the map. That's all."

"I know, I've lied to you and—"

"And I got tortured, if you can remember. And then I got shot. People would call me a damned lunatic for following you like I've done. They would say I've lost it completely. And maybe I have. When I said I'd join you, I didn't think it would actually turn into anything like this. I just kept waiting for the rug to get pulled out from under me. Opportunities for adventure and riches don't exactly come by people like me often, or ever, really. Hell, even now I have a worry in the back of my head that I was meant to be killed or worse for the treasure back in Austin, because how would I know any better? But now, I honestly don't know what I was thinking following you around on some treasure hunt. Look at what's happened. You honestly think that fuckin' maniac out there will keep me alive after everything?"

"Please," Rose pushed on. "None of this was supposed to happen, because *you* weren't supposed to happen. If you can find it in yourself to trust me just a little while longer, to help me just a little bit more, we'll find that treasure, and we'll make Damian pay for what he's done."

Silence crept back in between the two for a few seconds. Tied up, facing away from one another, and left alone in a dark room to die had a unique way of bringing out a sense of honesty that wasn't normally so prevalent.

Rose stayed silent as long as she could before she had to try and take a deep breath, giving away her broken heaves and tears beneath the bag that swallowed their heads. The ranger had given something to her that she never expected, and his words were crushing.

Davy mirrored the silence, finally allowing his thoughts to run unchecked and fighting back the rage that was swirling in his belly. The mysterious woman who'd been more like a rampaging whirlwind in his life was unlike anyone he'd ever met before. At this point, all he could think about was how he couldn't let her hurt him yet again.

Suddenly, their troublesome back and forth was interrupted by a deafening crash coming from the confined attic above their heads. It was as if a stick of dynamite had gone off just a few feet from them, shaking the dust loose from the rafters and rattling the old bones of the home they were locked inside.

The jarring sounds caused both Rose and Davy to jolt in opposite directions and fall to their sides on the floor. It was an original hardwood floor caked in years and years of grime that made it not only gross and uncomfortable to lay on, but also putrid when lying inches away from it. Turned over onto the ground, each of the two struggled against their restraints, hoping to find even the slightest sign of weakness that had occurred in the commotion. Davy fought with his wrists as best he could for what felt like a few minutes before the shrill shrieks of the horses just outside the home began to echo around them. First it was just a few, then more joined the raucous, and before long, it was the entire line of horses tied up just outside the log home screaming frantically, as if they faced death itself out there in the dark.

"Shhh..." Rose let out behind Davy with a slight sniffle.

The horses continued to cry into the night and they were soon joined by the panicked hollering of men scattering throughout the area. They yelled at each other without any sense, unsure of what was happening. It was as if a killer had been let loose among them, and there was nowhere to hide. The sounds of terror carried on over a haunting few seconds as Rose and Davy listened, helpless beneath canvas bags and bound by rope.

Suddenly, between the fearful screams of horses and men alike, were the cheerful sounds of children laughing. Feet stomping through the halls and giggling sounds cut through the chaos outside the log home. Conversations began to swell throughout each room in the house. It was dark and abandoned, yet alive and thriving all the same. Gunshots fired into the night without warning from the mercenaries still trying to fight whatever terrorized them as laughter roared from downstairs in the living room. Some of the men, scared for their lives, banged on the doors trying to get inside in a hurry. Instead of an empty log cabin, however, they would find a home filled with the presence of generations past. The families who have loved there, the children who grew up there, a few unfortunate enough to not have such an opportunity, and the husbands and wives who made the house a home throughout the decades—they had all made themselves known.

"We're not alone..." Rose said with a newfound surprisingly upbeat sense about her.

CHAPTER 23

"*Get your shit together!*"

Damian De León sprinted through the encampment of what was once full of his paid goons, screaming at the top of his lungs, fighting to restore order in the distraught men firing at will and fleeing for their lives. He ran through the falling ash of their roaring campfire gone astray, and watched as the men who followed him to this place now abandoned him in a drunken fright like spoiled children.

"Get to the house!" He yelled at the men blindly running away in every direction. With his pistol in hand, he joined the sporadic shots and fired into the air hoping to get their attention.

Bam. Bam. Bam.

"Get to the house, you sons a bitches!"

It was no use.

As he made his way through the chaos toward the log house that sat eerily in the shadows, he watched his worst nightmare unfold. A man was lying on the ground with a bullet hole in his chest. He struggled to breathe and clutched at the gaping wound hoping to preserve his own life in panic-stricken dismay. Damian slowed his pace to a crawl. The next man he saw was holding onto his limp shoulder as he ran with eyes wilder than the crazed horses who screamed in the background. Blood rushed down his arm while he ignored Damian's repeated demands for obedience. When Damian turned a corner around the campfire toward the front of the house, he saw only a couple of his men running toward it and at long last, he came to see the few among them with any ounce of true loyalty. That's when he saw what those same men were running from.

Though he'd been forewarned of their presence and prepared for how to handle their arrival—seeing it all for himself was no different than winning the lottery in his eyes. There was a flicker of light trying to take the shape of an apparition from just right angle creeping down the front walkway to the log cabin with an unnerving, rehearsed presence which felt unnatural to bear witness to.

Damian watched in silence despite the frenzy around him, shivering at the dropping temperatures that appeared out of thin air. It was unlike anything he'd ever laid eyes on before, and it begged him to linger much longer than he should. His breath poured out in front of him within a matter of seconds. The chill in the air seemed to correlate with the encroaching ghostly presence, but Damian simply didn't have the time to spare to watch any longer. There was work to be done. He was anxious to find the family riches that had eluded him for decades and was determined not to let anything prevent him from doing so.

"Go!" he screamed again to the few men who remained in front of the house. "Bring the woman and that damned park ranger to me right now and put them on their knees at my feet."

The apparition making its way toward the house was then joined by another at the opposite end, one which waited at the front steps, hunched over in anticipation. They hesitantly drew closer to one another, hoping with all the life they had left to embrace each other one last time.

"Get this fuckin' door open!" Damian De León had lost all of his patience by now. "And who locked the damned thing anyway?"

The two men who'd shoved against the door with all their might shrugged in pain, acknowledging Damian's incessant pushing. Then, they returned to their task.

"They won't hurt us," the Stranger said from behind them, appearing like an apparition himself. "I know they won't."

"No shit. They couldn't if they wanted to. About time you made it," Damian answered. "They may be dead, but they're still going to do exactly what we want. You're going to make sure of it. You understand me, boy?"

The heavy oak door to the log cabin burst open and the two men, commanded by Damian De León, rushed in, slamming it shut behind them as quickly as they could. They faced the door in exasperation, both otherwise fearless, capable men, were now scared for their lives and thankful to have put everything happening outside behind a wooden door—even if they would rather die than tell anyone such a thing. The bearded men who looked like frightened replicas of one another, sprinted to the closet upstairs without saying a word. When they made it to the closet door, there were no sounds coming from inside. They squeezed their guns tighter in unfounded desperation and yanked the door open.

"Get more than you bargained for?" Rose questioned at once, still lying on the ground, bound and covered, yet somehow still smug toward the would-be tormentors in her own unforgettable way.

No one said anything as the two obedient followers grabbed Rose and Davy both by their ankles and dragged them from the confines of the tiny closet. The sounds of their bodies scraping against the floor while being dragged down the hallway carried through the house until the *thump, thump, thump* sounds of their heads banging down the steps broke it up. Both of their eyes were still covered, so while neither Rose nor Davy could see the imprints of generations past surrounding them throughout the house, the two who had them hostage knew all too well what was around them.

The house was crammed full.

Passing shimmers of silhouettes that vanished as soon as they appeared came and went all around them throughout the inside of the log home. The faces of smiling children swept by, and men with long rifles slung over their shoulder passed through them on their way out of the front door. Women shuffled through the home, climbing the staircase only to return the next second right where they were. It was packed with fragments of what looked like people one second, then wisps of air the next. But the entire home had fallen into utter silence, a reflection of the reality that still laid bare before them. While the burly bearded men who clung to the ankles of Rose and Davy watched in awe, they pushed through crowded home, passing through the faded memories of people long gone with a shrug of their shoulders.

With one more hard felt drop, Rose and Davy were dragged out onto the porch area of the log house through the front door. The apparitions had fully embraced one another right in front of what was once so clearly their own home. Damian De León wasted no time in storming right up to the both of them. With their faces still covered, Rose and Davy could only hear the violent banging sounds of his boots hitting the ground every step of the way. Within moments, they were both propped up on their knees with wrists tied behind their back. Davy focused on his breathing to keep himself calm. The fear that sat in his belly had made him nauseous and unsure. Rose, however, was eager to fight.

"None of this is yours to take, you piece of shit. You don't see it," Rose called out from behind the canvas bag muffling her yells. "It was never yours, you cursed asshole! What's here can only belong to my family, the Hunters, the family you are not a part of!"

The family of Hunters? Davy questioned in his head, still shrouded in the bag covering his face. Was her name Rose Hunter? Come to think of it, he'd never heard Rose's full name before.

"We're doing this now," Damian's voice came down from above Rose and Davy. "No more games. No more running away. It's time for you to see what God has coming for you with your own eyes."

Their wrists were then freed and each one immediately yanked the bags from their heads in order to see what was happening all around them at last.

"It can't be," Rose said as her eyes adjusted.

Davy was speechless. He knew the two figures embracing one another could only be the old Wild West outlaw and his native wife, Angelina, who he had hung up his pistols for. They each stood before him in a way he never would have believed to be real. The silhouettes flickered in the moonlight and suspended themselves unnaturally without noticing anyone other than the one they held in their arms.

"My family is here," Rose said to them before she looked right at the young man standing beside Damian. "*Your* family is here."

The ranger's head twisted in surprise, but there was no time to speak. Sensing what Rose was up to by what she said, Damian De León grabbed the Stranger by the neck in response and leaned closer toward him. His usual slicked back hair was now frayed and loose, partly hanging over his left eye. As the apparitions continued to swell and fade around them, Damian whispered quietly.

"Dare not lose sight of what matters boy, not now."

The Stranger stiffened in response, and Damian turned his attention to Rose with a fiery look. All of the money and time he had sunk into this forsaken family and their treasure was on the line, and though he would never admit it aloud—his own family's entire empire was as well. It wasn't just desperation in his eyes when he spoke to the young man. It was madness. The type of spiraling intensity that is more often lost to the depths of despair than channeled into any usefulness. Damian stood tall above them as his shoulders swelled in righteous anger. Just when Rose and Davy thought he was going to lose his senses and start raining his fists down onto their faces, the veins in his neck receded and his eyes blinked rapidly several times. His demeanor shifted completely.

"Do not lose sight like Rose did, and her snake-of-a-mother before her," the latest De León heir began to shout into the night air, speaking to no one in particular like the true madman he'd become. "They care only for their own greed, my dear God. They want everything for themselves, never to share your most humbling of blessings for the greater good in this world—our own past. People like her, and her kind, care only to hoard obsessively so that they may take it to their grave. We ask your guidance in striking them down tonight. Before the night is through, by my hand, I will enact your righteous justice."

The Stranger looked at Rose with these words. He didn't look at her as he had before though—as someone who only stood in his way—this time was different. This time he looked at Rose and Davy as if they were exactly the same. A fleeting wave of emotion swelled just behind his eyes before it passed as quickly as it had appeared.

"I told you, boy, tonight we tame the Wild West. There is nothing that awaits these two but a couple of empty headstones," the crazed De León heir told the Stranger with a gesture to the two knelt before them. "You know what they cling to. What they refuse to let the world know about. And you know it isn't right. Rose's mother, my own wife, kept the greatest secrets one could ever hide, until I pried them out of her bloody mouth. When she finally revealed the truth, I told her without a second thought I would take every generation of her family away from her until what they had hidden from the world, and from the De León empire, was mine to hold."

"You fucking *monster*!" Rose screamed at him.

"So, I took her daughter first," Damian turned his attention to Davy. "Did you know that? Did you know that I helped raise Rose to be the feisty little woman you've been running the roads so cavalierly with like rebellious teenagers?"

Davy stayed silent. He knew Rose was begging inside for him not to respond. He could at least give her that, despite what she'd done to him.

"Then, she went and failed me, just like her mother did. Disappointment disguised as opportunity runs in their family. As much as I hate to admit it, I fell head over heels for it. Because of what they had cost me, I stayed true to my word, and when it came time, I took her son and we started the damned cycle all over again," Damian said with a shit-eating grin while throwing his arm around the Stranger. "But in my defense, so you know I'm not this fucking monster Rose seems to think I am. I told her the same thing I told her mom. If you find the treasure, if you can get me back what was already mine, you can get your family back with it. It's a simple choice. Hell, it should've been an easy choice!"

Damian then turned to look at Rose, focusing all of his furious impatience into a stare that went right through Rose this time.

"But nothing with you is ever easy, is it?"

Never one to back down from any kind of fight, Rose stared right back at him and

ignored his taunts. She matched Damian's brimstone stare with one that could kill a rattlesnake. She didn't say anything; she didn't need to. The look on her face told him everything that she was thinking and she wasn't holding anything back.

Davy, however, felt more confused and alone than ever before. He was still processing what Damian had just said about the Stranger who kidnapped them, and he didn't understand how Rose could just keep lying like that to him. He'd been caught up in a family fight that was generations in the making and woefully unprepared to contribute in any meaningful way. His worries of being an afterthought, of being disposable, all seemed to be coming to light before his eyes. Now, he could only feel an urge to do something, anything, to survive what was happening.

From down on their knees, Rose and Davy watched helplessly. They were both looking for any opportunity to break free from Damian's grasp for entirely different reasons when suddenly, as if it was planned all along, their prayers were answered. The same guiding presence that had followed them both from the Sabine to the Big Thicket found its way into the home of Rose's family, right where they stood. The map of the Eternal Flame that Damian had lost track of in the middle of throwing a fit, reacted just as it did on the shores of the gulf and in the deep woods of the thicket. It was the distraction Rose and Davy so desperately needed to turn the tide in their favor. Damian De León was caught off guard. He reacted with a jerking motion and accidentally dropped the artifact to the ground in a moment of weakness that would forever haunt him far worse than the ghosts of the past who appeared around him. The clinking, scratching sound of the round map rolling down the front of the porch froze everyone in place.

It was Damian who mindlessly lunged forward with everything he had. His outstretched arm was only fractions of an inch from his reach as the artifact rolled ahead, glowing hues of orange and red, brighter and hotter with each passing second. He brushed against the escaping map just barely, for less than a second, yet long enough to burn the tips of his fingers off with searing pain that made him yelp. The smoke from his burn trailed up into the air and forced his eyes upward.

Spinning in unison off into the distance with a still sense of serenity, the apparitions of two lovers as real as the guns pointed at Rose and Davy's faces embraced each other in a dance together that could only be done in death. They glided across the pathway leading away from the home, heading north into the woods that hid in the overcast fog settling in before the sunrise in the coming hours.

"They're ready," Damian De León bellowed while lying on his stomach. "Their dance will take us right to their grave. We have to follow them!"

Before he could finish barking his demands, Rose and Davy had already made their move. Still lying on his stomach in the dirt, Damian watched as the artifact rolled away from him even further, clanking down the steps before continuing its journey down the pathway. Its red-hot glow lit the way and seared the ground with blackened burns wherever it rolled. The completed map of the Eternal Flame may not have been far from him, but Rose and Davy were closer. Before he could react, she snatched the artifact with the same bag that had been used to cover her face and they both bolted to the wood line. He watched them run as fast as they could until they were hidden by the very fog they chased the dead into.

"They ain't going far," the Stranger said calmly despite the shitstorm unfolding around them. "We'll catch up to 'em."

Damian scrambled up to his feet in a hurry, brushing the dirt off his knees and shoulders as he stood again. The aging man looked as though he could spew literal fire from his mouth, but instead, he just stared forward, deep into the depths of the trees that he was bound to follow.

"No," Damian finally spoke. "We're going to bury them."

CHAPTER 24

The trees that bordered the Hunter family homestead were the typical makings of East Texas woods. They were grouped in large patches separated by an occasional field that hadn't been touched by a tractor in years. The sounds of boots pounding to the ground, crunching leaves and sticks and pinecones, were drowned out completely by the deafening screech of cicadas that rang from every direction. It was a dizzying maze of dense trees with barely enough room to navigate and no time to find a direction. The only saving grace was the gray overcast light that peered through the tree limbs, providing just enough visibility to put one foot in front of the other without tripping.

Rose and Davy had made their escape, but it wouldn't last for long. If they had any hope of getting out of this with the upper hand—it'd have to come through force.

"Just keep running, Davy. We're not far."

Her voice was like a distant dream interrupting his own panicked confusion. Davy stared down at his boots slamming into the ground as he ran at full speed for longer than he ever should have.

"We need to be at the grave with the Eternal Flame in hand. It's the only way any of this is ever going to work," Rose said just as Davy snapped out of his daze. "Do you understand?"

They both stopped running with their next stride and faced each other in the middle of the woods. They were unwilling to make the first move, to do what had to be done, because of what it could mean for them both. It was unspoken between the two, but the odds just weren't in their favor. The cool air that had settled in before was now only a faint breeze through the woods amid the muggy heat of the coming dawn. Sweat beaded at each of their foreheads as Davy made the decision to take the first move for himself.

"Rose," Davy said, taking the initiative to speak between steady gasps for air. "I don't feel good saying this, but this is the end of the trail for me."

"Wait. What?"

"What do you want me to say? It was actually your fucking kid back there who kidnapped us, Rose. When were you going to tell me? This was never about some ancient artifact or a treasure map. You put me in the middle of something that was always gonna end with me dead. I have no idea what else you're lying to me about anymore and this time, it's a risk I can't take. I can't keep going like this."

"We're so close now though," Rose said with shock

in her voice, despite the fact that she knew exactly
what he was talking about.

"No, I think I'm done."

"Don't do this. I didn't know how much I needed
you until we were already in too deep. The treasure is
real, and my son isn't who you think he is. I told you I
just need you to hold on for a little while longer. I'll
tell you everything."

"I'm sorry," the ranger said one last time before
dropping his eyes.

"Me too."

"North is that way, just in case you weren't sure,"
Davy said with his finger pointed behind her. "I hope
you find what you've been looking for. I really do."

This time, Rose was speechless.

It was as if nothing had ever happened between
the two, as if they hadn't just traversed damn near all
of East Texas together. Without another word to each
other, they turned away and ran. Rose continued
north, just as Davy had helped guide her one last time,
while he circled back into the woods to find his own
way back to a life far from the lies and death that had
become all he knew.

It was harder than Rose had ever expected to turn
and leave Davy behind. It hurt more than she could
admit to herself that this would be the last time she'd
ever see him. With a faster pace than before, Rose
continued through the woods into the first clearing,
trying her best to run from everything in her head. She
ended up in a small pasture that led into the next
wood line just a few dozen yards away. Before taking
one more step—she screamed. She screamed to try and

cope with the loss she was feeling, to get the hurt out of her in any way, but she also screamed to protect the ranger one last time as best as she could.

Her voice echoed through the woods and pierced the area so loudly that it was unmistakable for anyone listening, including the park ranger who hadn't gotten far yet. When her cry reached Davy's ears, it forced him to think about what he was leaving behind and who he was leaving alone in the woods. After a deep sigh that only he could hear, he pushed on trying to escape it all. The ranger had no choice but to continue walking in what was his best guess at getting out of the place unscathed. With such little light and no directions to go on, he knew his chances would be slim at best, but there was no other choice if he wanted to live. He walked through the woods, pushing his way past the yaupon brush when he had to. Without any notion as to how, he tried to put the entire wasted adventure behind him. All he'd have to do now was come up with some kind of story to get his job back. He did still have the brand on his stomach as proof that whatever he came up with was truly against his will. He had been forced into all of this. That's all he had to say. It wasn't even all that far from the truth either, considering the lies he was told to mislead him into going along with everything.

He hated himself for even allowing such a thing to happen to him. All he really wanted was to believe more than anything that there really was more to life than an empty home and a nine-to-five. There had to be. That's when a few familiar words came into

Davy's head and made him stand up just a little bit straighter.

"You don't ever run," he heard his dad say. *"You might as well get used to putting your head down and gettin' through it."* His words came back to him just when he needed them most. They stopped him right in his tracks and made him consider just what he had been fighting so hard for when he first joined Rose. As fate would have it, just as he stopped, he heard the warnings of the murderous men from deep off into the woods.

"We're right behind you!"

There was an awkward pause before the meanest among them shouted into the night once more.

"You just wait right there, you little bitch," Damian hollered. "You're never gonna leave that goddamned graveyard again!"

His deranged voice reached out as if it was riding on the breeze itself, a breeze that carried itself through the woods until it brushed gently across the face and neck of Rose. All she could do now was pray for a sign to keep her going. Briefly, she saw a flash of the dead lovers embrace, dancing together through the woods in her peripherals as if begging for her attention. The ghoulish illumination making up their form appeared to her as if their entire reason was to light the way ahead, and show her to where she belonged if only she would allow it. She heard the calls of Damian creeping in from just behind her and took one step toward the direction of her ancestors spinning into the distance, then she took another step.

Rose's trek through the woods would go on for an

agonizing hour as she followed her long-dead relatives on a crazed hunt deeper into the woods all by herself. The calls from the man chasing her came every few minutes, and for some strange reason, they only came from Damian himself. His yelling was cruel, and intentionally harsh. His frenzied voice carried through the limbs and leaves in the dense woods as if it could follow her no matter where she went.

The area had slowly started to become dotted with the large, cumbersome cypress trees that signaled Caddo Lake was nearby. These were a sign to Rose they were getting nearer to the grave of her family, which was something she desperately needed by now. It took just a few more steps for the sign to prove true.

There were no ghostly lovers or splendid treasures to be found within the graveyard. Instead, there were only a handful of gravestones sprouting up out of the ground without any order. Overgrown grass hid their illegible markings, and an empty hole in the ground rested beneath a crumbling monument that looked as though it once stood as a solemn reminder for a family that once was. She was still recoiling from Davy's decision to leave her to face whatever was about to happen alone. Rose braced herself for Damian and her son to find her at any moment, unsure of what was about to happen next. The quiet hanging around her at the graveyard was deathly; the kind of quiet that set her on edge. Every second in such a place felt an eternity. Rose squinted her eyes shut, forcing everything out, and waited for what was to come. Either in response to her prayers or for all she knew, a complete rejection of them, another sign happened.

Bam.

A gunshot rang out through the woods. Its echo repeated in the distance and splintered the silence of the coming morning for miles in every direction. Stretching back to the source of the shot was one man was still holding a rifle and the other lying dead on the ground.

The man was Davy, who stood above a lifeless body and listened as the shot that took a life reverberated through the trees until it rang only in his head. It was one of the men who had stayed with Damian De León back at the log home—the one who dragged Davy from the closet—who had the misfortune of falling behind the others as they trailed Rose. He was just the person Davy was after to turn the tables. The park ranger only hoped his moment of weakness hadn't cost him the opportunity to even the odds for Rose.

With a stroke of luck finally in his favor after all this time, Davy had found himself holding a bolt action rifle equipped with a beat–to-shit scope that he hoped dearly had been sighted in within the last year. There was no time to think about what he had just done. He had to get back to Rose. Her life could be in danger, even worse, he could be holding the only thing that could save her and he didn't even know where she was.

"Rose!" he called out into the gray haze that hung above him.

The next thing he knew, he looked down at his feet and realized he was sprinting. He ran as fast as he could, headed north, where he had directed Rose not too long ago. Catching up to Rose meant he was only that much closer to the maniac Damian who was after them. This pushed him even harder. The oaks and pines started to give way to more and more bald cypress trees hanging low as he ran. With just a few more steps and a handful of scratches from the branches now drawing red lines across his face, he reached what looked like a small clearing. On the other side, walking in a single file into the wood line ahead of them was Damian, the Stranger, who he now knew to be Rose's son, and one last hired hand, seeing it through to the bitter end.

"You go ahead and lead the way to what is ours, Rose!" Damian bellowed as they walked, his deep voice haunting the woods each time he spoke. "It's all you've ever been good for in your entire miserable life!"

Davy was close enough to hear his taunts clearly. He started to think twice about rushing in blindly while they were still outnumbered, especially after seeing the lengths Damian would go to in order to continue building his family empire's wealth. The weight of the rifle suddenly felt heavier in Davy's hands.

"I'm coming for you," he whispered as he turned and started the long run around the next patch of woods to get ahead of the coming conflict.

The only thing that mattered was keeping Damian's path on his left and pushing ahead far enough to make a difference. He thought about Rose, the way he felt about her through all of this mess, and he thought about what he'd say when he saw her again. He may have felt he was owed an apology, but deep down, he knew he'd have to offer one up himself too. Tortured, shot, and sprinting through the woods holding a gun, he still had to admit it was nice to care about someone. Despite all of that, he could only manage to feel like he'd been a complete asshole. So, he ran until Damian's taunts were coming from behind him, echoing through the woods like deadly bait waiting to ensnare anyone desperate enough to stumble into him. Once he reached the top of a slight hill overgrown with thorny greenbriar that offered a decent enough vantage point, he kneeled down and checked the rifle still in his hands.

It was unfamiliar and uncomfortable. The wood grain was dented and chipped around the handguard and there was a slipcover over the stock with three rounds tucked neatly inside. With a smooth motion, he shouldered the rifle and leaned his head to the side gently. The lenses were all blurry at first. He adjusted his cheek to find the relief in the scope and stared without blinking to scan the area slowly from left to right. He saw only more limbs and tree trunks, now magnified by the scope, and tilted his head back to get his perspective again. This continued for a few seconds while he struggled to spot what he was looking to take down. Fear began to creep into the back of his throat. Anxiously, he pushed his eye back to the scope and ignored his rapid breaths until he finally saw something worth seeing.

There she was.

Standing in a small opening over two hundred yards away, surrounded by what looked at first like large rocks scattered aimlessly around the area, was the woman he'd so foolishly left on her own. It wasn't just rocks all around her though, they were grave-stones surrounding a broken, misshapen monument that he could only make out while looking through the scope. He was able to see Rose in full view and scanned to the left just a bit more to find Damian De León standing across from her. They had already come face-to-face and started speaking to one another.

Davy could only watch them motion back and forth through the scope on the rifle. He couldn't hear anything they were saying, much less make out what they were talking about from so far away. It was impossible to know what was happening between them, but he knew it had to be life or death.

Damian De León was an imposing figure. He stood taller than everyone around him and was wider than them too. He was waving his arms around as he shouted, and though he likely meant to make himself look hostile and not to be fucked with—Davy saw only desperation. He'd never be able to understand why a man as rich as Damian was out in the woods chasing down Rose for some old treasure tale, but he did know what a man like that was capable of when backed into a corner.

Davy steadied his breathing and used his thumb to click the metal safety switch on the rifle off. He rested the pad of his index finger on the trigger and let his thoughts drift to Rose one more time.

He blinked a few times, trying to keep in mind the lessons he'd learned hunting with his dad so many years ago, and knew his moment would come. It was just a matter of time. All he had to do was be ready for it. He just needed a moving target. He focused again on Damian De León who was now standing only a few feet in front of Rose. It didn't matter how far they were, or how quickly they'd move, he knew just where to put the bullet that had Damian's name all over it. Listening to his own breathing for a few seconds, Davy cleared his head while keeping the lightest pressure he could on the trigger before it would break. The thin black crosshairs of the scope moved slowly to the left until they fell right on Damian De León, swelling in response to his own steady breathing.

Over two hundred yards wasn't an impossible distance for the ranger to make, and his confidence would have been a Godsend for Rose at that very moment. He knew she was feeling more alone now than ever after what he'd done, but he couldn't give an advantage like this up.

The only thing left to do now was wait until it was time to squeeze the trigger.

CHAPTER 25

"Why have you abandoned us like this, Rose? Your own mom, God rest her soul, wanted this to stay with the family —with *our* family. You remember the things she used to tell us? I know you do."

"You aren't family," Rose told Damian De León. "Do you even hear yourself, you damned lunatic?"

"The De León legacy is on the line here in ways you wouldn't believe, Rose. Before you judge me for keeping the ground beneath our feet to ourselves, ask yourself this, where have you been? Because it sure wasn't here, taking care of what's left of your family. Hell, by the way you've treated them, I might be more a part of this family than you've ever been."

"Because you *took* my family, you piece of shit. You expected me to just be okay with that? How far gone are you, exactly?"

"I only did exactly what your own mom asked me to do. She pleaded with me to take care of you before she passed away. She begged me to keep you safe."

"Before you killed her. Also, great job keeping me safe, you sick fuck. Why are we even doing all this? You've ruined this family, taken everything from us, even my own son. Can't you just leave us alone already?"

"Don't you see? I won't leave this place without what God has already deemed to be mine. And besides, you know more than anyone that I took your son from you because you couldn't do it alone. You needed me. It was the only way. I would have never kept you from him if you hadn't done what you did," Damian explained. "I did what was best for you, and for him."

They were both standing opposite each other, face-to-face at last. Surrounded in a graveyard long forgotten, and in their own way, each of them were summoned by the ghosts of their own ancestors. It was a confrontation they seemed fated to be a part of, no matter how much they ran from it or ignored its inevitability. It was written long before either were ever born.

Despite the tragic collision of consequences unfolding through history that brought Rose to such a moment, her heart was hurting. She thought of the park ranger, David "Davy' Patton, and their short time together. She thought of what could have been, and how it was the hand of her own grandmother long passed that guided his way to her. It was this thought that fueled her to lash out.

"You fed my mom lies to turn her against my

grandmother, and then you did the same thing to my son. You're never going to stop destroying our lives until you've had it all, are you?" Rose was furious. "Take a look asshole, this is what's left of my family. All because of men like you who only want to steal, to kill, and to lay claim to what's not theirs and never will be. We've been dealing with the likes of you since long before the days of the white man's six-shooter-fueled version of justice, and this is where it's gotten us."

"That is where you are mistaken, little girl," Damian told her with a hint of a smile. "There are no men like me, and there never will be." He lifted his arms up, standing in place, and glared at her from the tops of his eyes. "You don't get it. I am the only reason we're here. I am the only reason you have everything you have, that your son has everything he has. God himself demands that what is down in the earth beneath our feet right now belongs to me," he told her before thinking twice and cutting in again. "It belongs to all of us, forever. It is His will."

"We finally have the key to unlock it all," he continued his exhausting tirade. "Now, join your son by my side and let's finally dig up all of the family secrets protecting the riches that have eluded us for so long. Or, if you must have your way and face the end of a barrel one final time, you can join your ancestors down there."

"You know, Damian, I'd heard the rumors, but even I couldn't bring myself to believe you'd fallen so far. Seeing you out here though, they must all be true."

Damian was a breath away from instinctively

taking a step toward her before he rethought his rash decision. Unfortunately for him, Rose had already seen enough to push her luck just a bit further and send him over the edge with her next words, uttered through sheer arrogance.

"It's over, asshole. You're broke. Just admit it."

What she accused him of never did really click inside Damian De León's crazed head. The time for thinking was long gone and he'd been forced to act. He was done talking, done pleading for what was already his, and tired of listening to her annoying cries. He had the numbers and the guns that she didn't, and he knew her son was loyal to him after what they'd been through together. Damian had waited for years now to put an end to the stories whispered behind his back that threatened everything he had in life, the very rumors that corrupted their way into Rose's own ears. All he had to do to finally put it all to an end was to reach out, take the cause of all of his problems into his own hands, and squeeze as hard as he could.

So, that's exactly what he did.

Rose could see it coming from a mile away, but she knew there wasn't anything she could do about it yet. If there was ever going to be any hope for her son to come through, she'd have to stay planted until she could see the whites of Damian's soulless eyes. As she watched the man across from her try his best to close the distance with his eyes locked on her throat, she couldn't help but think of Davy again, of how she wished everything had turned out differently for her, and how she always was forced to give up everything she ever cared about. All of that was about to change now—it had to.

Damian lunged with all of his weight, his hands outstretched in front of him, ready to cling onto Rose's neck and choke the life out of her. His eyes were burning with the hatred of the conquerors who came before him, wronged in both life and death, eager for blood to quench their thirst for vengeance. He wasn't the man he used to be, though. He was slow, slower than even he remembered when it came down to finally doing the dirty work for himself. As he hurled himself forward, the final betrayal of Damian De León was cut short, struck down in its most violent state.

Bam.

He jerked backward in unison with the loud boom that rocked through the woods around them and doubled over in shock as he absorbed a rifle's bullet into his stomach. Blood gushed out. In a split second, there was only red everywhere he looked.

The Stranger, never one to miss a beat and always faster than a bullet, had already drawn his revolver and with a flick of his wrist—fired a second shot at the last Pinkerton standing.

Pop.

The only remaining hired gunman, the only man left loyal to the madman Damian, fell to the ground dead.

Damian, however, was still clinging to life and stumbling through the old graveyard in a refusal to face the only thing that was left for him in the world. A trail of thick red blood followed him wherever he went. His hands clutched inches below his sternum, but the blood pouring out was too much and it soaked through his clenched fingers, pushing against the bullet hole. His breathing came only in short gasps and the burning sensation that now raged in his belly soon spread throughout his body. He was sucking in the last bit of air this world would ever offer him. Helpless to the whims of his fleeting life, he looked up to the sky for mercy that would never come.

"Looks like your friend is still somewhere out there," the Stranger said.

"Yeah, looks like it," Rose agreed with a smile finding its way to her lips before twisting sourly as her thoughts turned to her son. "I'm sorry it took so long, Cannon. I'm *so* sorry."

"Not done yet," Cannon answered as they watched the man who had caused them so much pain stagger onward.

Damian took his last step then tumbled from his knees into the hole of an open grave, making a hard grunt as he landed. It was a black hole with but a single purpose—to contain the remains of the last De León heir until even the bones of his corpse became indistinguishable from the dirt they were buried beneath.

The sounds of boots stomping into mud came closer to where he laid face up on his back, struggling in pain with each breath. Two stubbornly familiar faces leaned slowly over the edge and peered down. Once Rose and her son, Cannon, saw the way he had landed, the way his body had twisted so unnaturally, they stepped closer to the edge without much hesitation. Dirt that had turned to mud after mixing with all of the blood seeping out below began to smear across him as he writhed in agonizing pain inside his own early grave. The fight was over.

Rose looked into the trees with tears in her eyes because she knew the park ranger was watching over them from somewhere and that he actually cared about her. She slowly nudged Cannon with her elbow and gestured at the grave finally fulfilling its purpose, and spoke up.

"Well, look at that. Remember a couple weeks ago when I told you we dug the grave in the right spot?"

"I still would've put it about ten feet in that direction," Cannon said with a smirk while pointing over Rose's shoulder. "Plus, he looks a lot worse than you said he would."

"He's still lucky," Rose quipped. "Just not for much longer."

The end of the line had caught up to Damian. He gargled on the blood in his lungs, trying and failing miserably to catch his breath with heavy wheezes that went nowhere. He was lying in a grave made especially for him and he realized this fact far too late to do anything about it. All he could do now was bleed out into it. But, at the very least, he didn't have to go out in such a way so quietly.

"You...you think this ends with me?" he whimpered to them before coughing himself into a crooked bloody smile. "There will be more. They will find what you have..." He was interrupted by another violent coughing fit that spurted more blackened blood onto his lips and down his chin. "And they will take it."

"I guess I'll know right where to put 'em then," Rose answered, talking down to the dying man.

"You're just like the rest of them," Damian De León accused her as his voice at long last began to fade out of the same world it had cursed with its very presence. "You really are all the same."

The sounds of his hands failing desperately to keep his blood from filling the grave were lost in his painful groans that followed. His eyes turned from the pain and anger that had fueled him into a hateful stare that could only be described by the very best in this world as downright evil.

"Just a bunch of fuckin' *savages*..."

Pop.

A bullet pierced through the final heir to the De León dynasty's forehead before the final word could leave his lips. A thin trail of smoke lifted from what was left of the would-be conqueror's blood-splattered face, and another rose into the air from the burning barrel of Cannon's revolver. The De León's reign against their family had finally come to a violent end as Damian was left to stare endlessly into the stars above forevermore. With his last breath, the Eternal Flame artifact rolled from his hand through the bloody mud at the bottom of the grave.

Their ancient heirloom—a map that had returned the Hunter family home so many times before—was theirs for the taking.

CHAPTER 26

The burial vault's monument resting at the center of the family's graveyard wasn't anything to look at. The stone it was built of had long started to succumb to the effects of time. One corner crumbled into the ground and any markings that once existed were washed away by the elements years before. There were discolorations spreading across the surface, making it look as though it had sat there longer than the tallest trees that surrounded it. Right up on the front of the burial vault, just inches above the dirt, was a small rectangular panel loosely fastened to the stone structure.

The vault had yet to draw the attention of the only ones left alive in the graveyard, though. As Rose looked down at the grave of Damian De León while his lifeless body continued to bleed into the mud and soil, the park ranger made himself known once again after coming down from his vantage point in the woods.

"I'm sorry, Rose," Davy called out. "I should've never left."

Rose allowed herself to look away from the dead man in the grave and make eye contact with Davy. She had no idea what to say and could think of even less knowing her son was still standing there, but she could at least manage a smile. Words escaped her at a time like this. They always did. Instead, she nodded and smiled with tears welling up in her eyes.

"That was a good shot," she told the ranger through her emotions.

"It really was, wasn't it?"

Cannon watched the two stand in front of each other awkwardly for a few seconds, smiles drawn onto their faces and eyes that did all the talking for both of them. Finally, he decided to speak up.

"The Eternal Flame, Rose," said Cannon. "It's time."

"Time for what?" Davy couldn't help himself.

"The Eternal Flame holds the remains of our family's first ancestors," Rose answered. "The ashes inside fuel a flame that has burned as long as our history has existed. It's how the key works."

"Why this place, though?"

"Our family belongs here, Davy. They belong at home. My grandmother was the only one who figured out what was happening to us all. She tried to stop it, she tried to do the only thing she could and steal the Eternal Flame to hide it where few would know to look. It was too late, though. The roots of De León's hostile betrayal of our family had grown far too deep, and the world grew too big."

Rose turned away to let her words hang in the air and walked slowly toward the burial vault surrounded by old gravestones and overgrown grass sprouting up all around. She knelt down and removed the loosely latched panel on the front of the burial vault. Inside was a compartment, not large enough to actually look into, but just the right size to stick your hand in, which was just what Rose did with her face scrunched in determination.

"Tonight, all of that changed," she said as she fumbled around inside the compartment.

She pulled out a familiar dirty brown glass bottle with a cork wedged into the top. With a smile of disbelief, Rose dropped the bottle onto the ground next to her and reached her hand back inside. She fidgeted for just a second before she exhaled and jerked her arm backward, yanking a switch hidden from view with an exasperated grunt. A jarring click seemed to resonate deep inside the aged structure. Then, a second clanking of a hidden mechanism sounded off before the top of the vault popped upward with a grinding force like the hood of a thousand-year-old pickup.

"We've lost so much by not having access to this right here," Rose spoke without taking her eyes away from the opening that had appeared. She heaved against the cracked lid made of stone and it screamed in response, locked in place from time and unwilling to budge. It was Davy who quickly stepped forward to lend his weight to Rose's efforts before Cannon followed along. When it had been opened enough to peer down into, all three leaned their head over and stared into the black abyss below, eyes squinted with curiosity.

"Don't tell me you're afraid of a leap of faith now."

"It's not the faith part, really," Davy answered her. "How far down are we going here, exactly?"

"Not as far as you'd think."

"This thing is incredible, it's a design by W.S. Parker," Davy said, who had already gotten distracted by a few of the indiscernible markings on the vault. "It's early 1900s probably, made to be indestructible and hermetically sealed. It was usually made for banks and paranoid rich people. They were never this big though. What the heck is down there?"

"You know enough history to know that any treasures from the old west would never last long. Even when they're hidden away in an old contraption like this," explained Rose. "We just need to find a way down now."

Luckily, the corpse of Damian De León would prove more useful than when he was alive. He may have had the foresight to bring a decent enough rope to be repurposed for their needs, but he never stood a chance to see the bullet that had his name all over it from the day Rose met Davy back in Daingerfield. There was probably some irony there somewhere, but the group didn't wait around long enough to think of it. Within a few minutes, Rose had dropped an end of the rope torn from his cold, dead body, down into the top of the burial vault with an ear cocked to the side. She waited until the sound of the rope smacking a hard surface came from the dark hole.

"I'll go first." Cannon stepped forward.

"Then you, Davy," Rose said. "I'll drop down last."

The park ranger nodded slowly with widened eyes, still straining to see anything in the darkness they were headed toward. It only took moments for Cannon to step up onto the burial vault, wrap one leg around the dangling rope and start working his way down. This caught Davy's attention and he mimicked the movements, hoping he could replicate the technique with half as much grace when it came his turn. Cannon descended into darkness for a minute or two in silence until it was broken by his shouting from below for Davy to join him.

His attempt wasn't a complete embarrassment, but the darkness was more than he had ever expected. It swallowed him completely in seconds and made it impossible to see just inches ahead. The familiar burn of fear deep in his belly started to swell going down the rope, until suddenly, his toes pushed up against the ground in what felt like divine intervention at just the right time. The sounds of Rose sliding down the rope came next. Davy lifted his hands to avoid running into anyone as he fumbled through the pitch black darkness, trying to feel for anything that would be useful to them.

"Cannon, got a light?"

Rose's question brought Davy hope for even the slightest bit of relief from the suffocating darkness that engulfed them. A couple of haphazard flicks later and they were basked in the flickering heat of a broad, heavy wooden torch Rose was holding with two hands in front of her.

They were standing in a long, narrow hallway that stretched on into nothing, where the light of their torch had only pushed the darkness down to the other end. It hovered away from them in the distance as if scared of the fire's courageous presence. Lining each side of the lengthy hallway were the tombs of family members, sectioned off on their own, but still sharing the room. The floor was littered with the picked-through remains of a room once filled with valuables. Scattered coins shimmering in the faint light of the flame, half-burned books torn apart with pages scattering the area were all around, and what looked like several sandstone busts of unknown faces laid to rest there were tossed carelessly to the ground.

"This is the treasure?" Davy let out his premature disappointment.

"You think we would've done so much just for this?" Rose asked with a chuckle. "This is a crypt. We still need to go that way, to the actual vault."

She pointed toward the direction of the dark end of the hallway still hiding from their light and Davy's heart sank just a little. He tried to change the subject to push down the fear creeping up in his throat.

"Are these all your family?"

"They are," Rose said.

"What about the markers up above us?"

"Let's just say it's an old tradition. They aren't family up there, but they damn sure got to know our family up close and personal before they wound up buried there."

The trio walked cautiously down the hallway, placing one foot slowly in front of the other through the tomb kept alive by wood, stone, and some unnatural force holding it all together. Their torch lit just a few feet around them as they moved, revealing caskets resting in the dirt with the occasional remembrance that hadn't been strewn around through the years. Davy watched intently as they passed each burial and began to notice a pattern as they went. Although the resting places featured a carved bust to remember the face of each person buried in the family crypt, the caskets that filled it seemed to grow older and older the further down the hallway they went. When the darkness cowering at the end could no longer hide from the light of Rose's torch, they reached the last of their trials for a long-lost treasure.

"I've only heard stories about this place, to be honest," Rose said. "It's so much more different than I'd ever imagined."

"And darker," Cannon quipped.

"It's incredible," Davy said, unable to help being lost in the history of the vault.

"My mom always used to say this place was a real sight to see, or maybe it had been," Rose told him as she waved the torch around slowly to see. "It was meant to last for generations and be a place for each one to come, to find themselves, or to lose the world, even if just for a moment."

Towering in front of them at the end of the narrow hallway was an intimidatingly large steel frame that boxed in an entryway into the earth itself, hidden away in the tomb of Rose's ancestors. The bolted columns on either side were taller than any of the three standing in front of them and the door housed inside was every bit as daunting. Intricately detailed blackened steel formed the shape of a door, but there was no handle to be found. Instead, the door that blocked their way featured a locking mechanism with a five-pronged wheel sprouting from its center spindle. It looked as though it was last spun by the old outlaw Henry and his wife Angelina—except there was no visible way to unlock it.

Rose pushed the torch forward and the light revealed a cavity in the center of the wheel that was a familiar spherical shape. The five golden handles darted outwards and swelled at the end with elaborate styling for its time. The hole at its core seemed to yearn for fulfillment that would unlock the wheel and with it, rebalance the scales of power with what was inside. All it would take was a simple turn.

"Davy, I am going to need your help with this part," Rose said as she leaned forward to examine it further. "It's just a matter of listening carefully for the right click."

"Me?"

"Come over here, next to me."

She handed the torch to Cannon and pulled out the Eternal Flame artifact. It was subdued, and though it wasn't glowing like molten lava when she held it, the perfectly round heirloom turned white-hot when she pushed it into the cavity of the spinning mechanism on the door. With a loud clunk and several rapid clicks following in succession, the artifact was fastened into place. Like the flip of a switch, it smoldered and cooled in place as if it was made to be right where it sat.

"My grandmother always used to tell me stories of our family and they weren't only meant to be taken at face value. All this time, she knew it was left for me to see everything I needed in the waters of the Sabine, and in the stars above the Big Thicket."

Rose kept her eyes locked on Davy. "And she sent you to help."

She leaned in carefully to place her ear right next to the artifact lodged into the door. With a flick of her wrist, her fingers brushed the top half of the Eternal Flame and it slowly rotated against her touch. As it spun, she listened intently to the faint ticks that echoed from within. After almost a half rotation, the object found just beyond the Sabine snapped out of the artifact and a loud *thunk* echoed within the door.

"Remember what you showed me back in the woods at the Big Thicket? They're watching," Rose reassured Davy as she gestured to Davy to give it a shot. "You'll just feel it."

A second later, Davy was listening to the spin of the bottom half for at least three-quarters of a rotation. Whispers of the ticking sounds carried through the crypt second by second before Davy felt what Rose had promised. Something in his bones told him to stop what he was doing. The piece from the Big Thicket did the same thing as the half before it, slamming into the door with a thunderous echo that resonated from within. The old steel handles that seemed to point in every direction rumbled unexpectedly and then clanked forward about two inches into place with a loud boom.

Rose rested her hands on the prongs of the wheel

that stood in front of them. It was as if a bank vault was buried beneath a graveyard, an old west mausoleum beneath the ground which held the very riches of westward expansion born from the tragedy of its time. The potential at what such a vault held inside was beyond anything Davy had ever experienced. He and Cannon watched closely as Rose gripped the locking mechanism and spun it with all her might, sending dust billowing out all around as she did. The door shifted and popped open with surprising ease. It revealed only blackness inside. There was a complete void of any light or fresh air that met them in this new place.

"If I'm being totally honest, that was a lot easier than I thought it would be," Davy said while staring into the doorway ahead of them.

Rose turned to look at him while still gripping on to the wheel. Cannon did the same.

"I mean the door," Davy corrected himself before trying to take the attention off himself. "Who's first?"

The steel entryway opened into a chamber that seemed unnatural for where it was buried.

What had to be a twenty-foot ceiling—framed with the same blackened heavy steel of the entryway and packed with rotting lumber and dirt—stretched backward as far as the light of the torch would reach. Two more large, spiked torches clung to the wall at either side of the entryway, standing guard in the confines of the vault, ready to light the way. Cannon shoved the blazing flame that led them here into the torch on his right until it started to catch, then again to his left. It took a couple of minutes that nobody had the patience for to create enough light inside the room. The only thing Davy could focus on however was Rose, who'd walked deeper into the vault with a dazed look frozen on her face. Never before had the ranger seen such a forlorn look in her eyes.

In the center of the vault was an old pine box coffin, left open for the decay of whomever was inside to be seen by all who entered. What Rose, Cannon, and Davy could make out in the fleeting shadows inside the coffin were skeletal remains—too many to be a single person. The bones were delicately placed to resemble two lovers embraced through death. Rose approached the pine box on her toes as if not to disturb them with her trembling breath. Something else had caught Cannon's eye, however, and he was lured deeper inside to see more of what they'd uncovered.

The light flickering beyond him as he made his way into the vault revealed a series of flagpoles on either end of the room stretching out into the darkness. The oldest flags of Texas, of all those who tried to call the place home after Rose's ancestors, were stored away like memorabilia from a collector who lived through the ages. The Rojigualda from Spain with the arms of Castile and León gracing the corner of the flag, and a banner of the Kingdom of France never to have seen the light of day, sat on either side of them covered in layers of dust that could only build up from the passing of time. Both rows of flags carried onwards only to reveal the next like the rise and fall of each empire, and it was all just a taste of what the Hunter family had endured.

Rose was focused only on what was ahead of her with a look of disbelief washing across her face that left her eyes unrecognizable to Davy. To his dismay, she reached out with a wide-eyed stare at the coffin beneath her and touched one of the remains exposed inside.

"Y'all need to see this," Cannon called from behind the coffin.

"Is it all the gold?" Davy asked without looking. "Please, please tell me it's all the gold. Or something better. I've actually been wondering all this time if the cash that's here is greenbacks or silver certificates. Does anyone actually know when the first federal notes were issued?"

The eeriness of silence that Davy had been trying so desperately to stave off came back. Instead of suffering it any longer, Davy silently joined Rose, and they made their way over to find what Cannon had called them for. When they tried to look out into the treasures promised, they stopped in their tracks. The vault was filled with battered wooden crates and boxes piled on top of one another, unable to escape the effects of time from the musty decay to the thick layers of dirt. Once, they must have held the gold, jewelry, cash, trinkets, and priceless artifacts that filled a feared outlaw's bags over and over again. The vault had been built to preserve a moment in time for those who came next to see. It had become something else though, somewhere along the way, that much was all too clear now, because everything was gone.

Most of the crates with metal hinges were missing their lids, some of them that had been ripped off were laying on the dirt floor around them, others were missing entirely. Crumbling statues of unrecognizable figures stood around deteriorating art of little value. Littering the ground were torn pages of books well beyond any recognition needed to read them. The stories that Davy once told in jest to park visitors about a treasure of the Wild West lost in East Texas, the same legends that kindled his love of being a steward of the land, were all real. The only problem was someone had beat them to it, and they left the entire vault ransacked.

"It can't be," Cannon whispered.

"Wait a second," Davy interrupted. "Before we freak out, we haven't even looked around here. There could be *anything* in this place."

Silence fell between all three standing in the vault once again and Davy got the hint. Darkness hovered around them, always present in the musty air of the old vault, which only managed to magnify the feelings of failure and pent-up desperation settling in. They had given so much and sacrificed everything that remained to find what their family had left behind for them.

Rose could only take comfort in the fact that they could at least return to their home, so she gently made her way back over to the coffin once again to hover over the bones inside and allow herself to think.

"In the stories my mom used to tell me as a kid," Rose started talking as her eyes scanned the coffin in front of her. She could see the shadows of Cannon's frantic searching and hear Davy digging through crates, but she didn't pay them any attention. "She would tell me about the books collected by the family over the years. First editions, different translations, famous authors, they had it all. She dreamed about them every day when she was a kid."

Her voice wasn't rushed or agitated, she spoke and moved easily as she searched the coffin full of remains with an unnerving poise that graced every gentle movement.

"The most important was always what every generation referred to as the ancestor's album. It wasn't a work of fiction or a scrapbook full of pictures, it was the stories of our family that most believed were more tall tales than history. It was the only written account of our family that traced back more than hundreds of years before," she explained. "My grand-mother knew it existed, but never actually laid eyes on it herself."

The items that remained near the open pine box coffin seemed to be only sentimentally valuable, like the pair of old Colt six-shooters half buried in the ground. Only someone with an eye for detail could notice the five-number serial number on the cylinder dating it to the 1880s, and the small *"H"* ornately etched into the walnut handles, but anyone could see the pistols looked like they hadn't been fired since the first Roosevelt presidency.

"I'm just hoping no one else knew about it too," Rose admitted with a whisper that neither Davy nor Cannon could likely hear. Her voice carried like a wisp through the emptied vault. Any ghostly presence or dangers of this world had fallen away and the silence that came in its place turned the vault into an echo chamber for each of their worst fears quickly being realized.

Davy suddenly stopped searching through the emptied crates when saw torn pages from books scattered across the ground. Some were buried in dirt, but others looked to be from entirely different decades. History itself was strewn across the ground, and it needed only to be followed.

"Do you know what it looked like?" he asked as he scanned the ground. "It looks like there used to be a whole library here."

No answer came from Rose, but Davy couldn't stop thinking about what the pages were. His boots kicked up dirt as he anxiously made his way to the aged papers littered throughout the vault. When Davy knelt to pick one up, it took only a glance to see it wasn't just some torn page from a book. The official seal stamped across the top of the page stole his attention immediately. It was faded and difficult to make out. He blew on it gently and a cloud of dust swept off the document in his hands to swirl aimlessly into the air around him. Against a lone ray of flickering yellow light, the ranger thought just for a moment that he could see the hint of something familiar.

"Rose," he tried to say, but his voice cracked and the only thing that came out was a raspy whisper. He continued to read what little he could on the heading of the document.

IN THE NAME OF THE STATE OF TEXAS

"Rose!" He finally got out.

She poked her head from around the coffin and saw what Davy was holding. It didn't take long before she was right behind him, peering over his shoulder. "Bring the torch over here, son," she called out.

"It looks real," Davy said without lifting his eyes. "Do you know what this is?"

Just as he finished asking, the torch was lifted just slightly over their head to reveal every word. Davy reached down for another page buried in dirt and picked it up, angling it just right against the flame. It read the same thing.

"They're all over the place! Look at all of them," he reacted while still trying to put all the pieces together.

"Someone was after something more than treasure here," she answered as she scanned the ground. "They were looking for something."

"Like the ancestor's album?"

Rose darted her eyes at the ranger for his suggestion. She took a few steps forward to follow the buried pages in the dirt before she noticed a small shelf stacked with papers and rolled documents, partially covered by a canvas bag with bold letters stamped across the front.

WETTERMARK BANK

"That's from an old bank in Nacogdoches." he pointed to the tattered bag to begin another tangent history lesson as he watched Rose shuffle through papers. "It was a scandal in the 1900s where a banker took off with all the money."

"Gone now," said Cannon, who was still standing to his side holding the torch.

"Yeah, gone now, and I am starting to think it might not have even been a banker who ran off with it."

Rose's search through the stacks of papers blanketed in dust carried on and on, and though her face was impossible to read, what she was holding were the revelations she'd been longing for. Rolled documents read off more than just countless land deeds to land in her family's name, there were old stocks and bonds, business shares, contracts, and even letters with addresses on them everywhere from Austin to Washington DC, this was a trove of information that she'd never heard of before.

Her heart could only sink in disappointment though.

None of it would mean anything if she couldn't prove it was theirs. She would need the ancestor's album—the original declarations from her ancestors—to do that. Her digging continued on for a minute or two until Davy and Cannon decided to join in, hurriedly looking at anything they could get their hands on without knowing exactly what they were looking for.

"Are all of these in your family's name?" Davy asked as his eyes got larger and larger with every stamped document he picked up.

Rose didn't answer.

"Rose, don't you know what this is? Someone bought all of this land and it's still in the estate," Davy explained. "It's all right here. There never was any treasure here because we've been walking on it this whole time. I don't even know where to start with how many acres there are."

"Hundreds over here," Cannon chimed in.

"Just what I have in my hand is easily in the thousands," he said without lifting his eyes.

Rose kept tossing papers to the side, nearly throwing them out of her way as she grabbed handful after handful. She still refused to say anything.

"This treasure wasn't stolen," Cannon thought out loud. "It was spent."

"Someone was using all of the gold and cash and whatever else was in here to buy up every bit of real estate in the area they could find," Davy said. "They bought up everything."

Rose was becoming frantic as she flipped through pages. She had looked over the picked-through corpse of an old west empire. One brittle page after another, each with cursive swoops across them, were only promises from long ago threatening to unravel until she could find proof it had been taken from them.

"Almost like someone was trying to—" Davy started before a shout cut him off.

"Got it!"

Rose's eager holler echoed through the vault. Her voice held a victorious ring as she held up what looked like an old leather-bound book, tied together with a worn strap. There was nothing on the cover of the book except a thinly etched symbol, almost indecipherably delicate and worn from time. With squinted eyes, Davy could just barely make out the letter "*H*" in a golden scroll, the same inscription he saw on the pistols beside the coffin.

All three huddled around as if they were fighting for heat from a dying campfire to try and see what the book held inside. It smelled of decaying leather and paper, as if it was already too old to handle before being stowed away from fresh air for more than a hundred years—yet it was perfectly preserved. Rose wasted no time in grabbing at the loose stained corner and peeling it open with trembling fingers. The first page she saw, that they all saw, lying on top as if placed there purposefully for their eyes to see before anything else, was a letter in finely crafted cursive with a few droplets of blood stains trailing off on the bottom.

Dear Hunters,

This morning the rain finally stopped as I arrived home before first light, knowing it were to be my last. What I had hoped to find upon my return had made itself real in front of my own eyes and I hope now that my children, and their children's children, can find a small piece of that. The state of Texas, the United States of America, will indeed question what I did with the money, but you will be the only to know it. Everything we have, what will come of it, where it will go, it all belongs to our next of kin until there are no more. Know that my life was found wild with adventure, but only one was incomparable. The rest never mattered.

Be sure you find the same.

H.

The three of them stared in silence, no one wanting to be the first to break it, but their minds were racing to understand what the letter was saying in those fateful final moments of a man none of them had ever met before. It didn't take long for each to realize what had happened here, how the treasure had been lost to conquest by the De Leóns, and how the land that remained now lawfully belonged to Rose. The final will and testament of her ancestors that had stayed hidden for decades through generations going back to before her grandmother was born—to when the vault had last been opened—had returned it all to her, and the rightful family it belonged in.

"Does that mean what I think it means?" Davy questioned Rose who was still staring at the book in her hands. She flipped the yellow stained letter over to the other side of the leather-bound book and shifted to give him a better view of the document that sat just behind it. The ranger stood silently and read it as best he could in the dim light of the torch crackling behind them.

THE STATE OF TEXAS
HARRISON COUNTY

BE IT KNOWN, that I, HENRY HUNTER, being

*of sound and disposing mind and memory, hereby
revoking any and all other wills heretofore by me
made, do hereby make, publish and declare this, my
last will and testament as follows, that is to say:*

"Oh shit," Davy said.

"Yeah," Rose agreed. "Everything here is what the De Leóns built their empire on. They took all of our land, and with it, our freedom. Then they used it all for themselves. My grandmother saw it happening. She tried to help, but no one listened to what she was trying to tell them."

"We waited too long," Cannon said finally. "They took too much from us. Look at this shit."

"They'll never take anything from us again," Rose told him, still holding the ancestor's album tightly to her chest before turning to the ranger behind her. "Mom used to say that Grandmother had spent her dying days rambling incoherently. No one ever believed any of it. No one until you, Davy."

"Me?"

"Back in Daingerfield, you knew our story, and you were proof of what the De Leóns could no longer control through force. You were talking about our legacy. I had already made my decision to fight against Damian long before you showed up."

"*We* made our decision," Cannon interjected.

"We," Rose confirmed. "Damian wasn't using us to find the treasure, his family had already stolen it. He was using us to find the only thing that would ever rip it from his hands like *his* family did to ours. He needed us to find the Eternal Flame that was hidden from him and use it to unlock the vault. He probably planned to bury us down here with everyone else on his way out."

"The petty bastard," Cannon cussed his memory. "The thought of someone else finding the vault and getting inside before him kept him up every night, though. He was about to lose everything his family ever built and this place was the ace up his sleeve. He believed God had given it all to them, but not being able to get to the place for himself plagued his very insides. There wasn't a single day in the last few years that man didn't begrudge our family for what was happening. He always knew he wouldn't be alone, that there would be someone else looking to take what was his."

"He was right about that. There always will be," Rose told him. "But it won't be the fuckin' De Leóns next time, that much I know for sure."

"Damn right."

Rose extended her arm and handed the old leather ancestor's album over to Davy with a slight nod of approval. He grasped it and quickly opened the old leather cover to push his nose inside and begin reading. Instead of joining him, Rose grabbed her son by the shoulder and the two walked back over to the coffin that held the remains of their embracing family. They spoke in silence closely together where Davy could not hear, but that didn't matter to him—he was lost in the historical records of an outlaw and his family that likely only a handful of people had ever seen.

He flipped past the letter from Henry Hunter and

the will he left for Angelina to pass on to every generation. First, there were only more deeds to land that
was owned by the family, just like the ones littering
the ground around them. Some granted only plots of
dozens of acres, but others held acres by the hundreds.
As he continued to turn the pages, he began to notice
letters mixed in the stack that were just barely legible.
He scanned through the words as best he could while
flipping the pages through the thickly bound book.
Suddenly stopped on one. The words seemed unreal
to see on paper, but it was the very story of the
outlaw's chimney escape from a jailhouse. The letter
had never been mailed, but instead, it made its way
back home somehow to be stored away here. Davy
fought the urge to continue reading with a huge grin
making itself known on his face. He saw the documents get newer and newer as the next generations
took hold in the family. The deeds became rarer and
the sheer number of documents he didn't even recognize were growing. Then, a headline caught his eye.

OIL, GAS, AND MINERAL RIGHTS

He flipped faster now, mineral rights documents
were attached to every new deed purchase for land
and it just kept repeating, over and over again. It
wasn't only land in Texas either. They had spread to
Louisiana, Arkansas, and Oklahoma as they grabbed
all they could. It was only here that Davy began to
piece together just how large their wealth had grown.
This was more than anything he'd ever told in his
stories; it was more than he could've ever imagined. It

was the kind of treasure that made gold and jewels look like toys and trinkets for children. Hundreds of millions that could have turned to billions through the years flowed through the pages of the ancestor's album and it became heavier by the second inside Davy's hands.

Rose and Cannon still had their heads down as they lingered solemnly over the exposed coffin resting in the middle of the vault. It was mostly shadows that filled the room, but with the light of the torch behind them, he could see among the crates there was still artwork, furniture, and even statues that were hidden among the crowded storage of a treasure that once stood great. There was no telling what truly remained within the confines, but it would seem that they had already found enough for the next several lifetimes.

Instead of carelessly breaking up the moment Rose and her son shared, the park ranger closed the book and walked back to the entrance of the vault to lean against the towering, blackened steel frame that welcomed them in. The ranger waited patiently with one leg propped up and watched the flames on Cannon's torch dance in the darkness. After a few minutes of gentle quiet that carried through the vault and into the crypt behind them, Rose and her son turned to leave, holding their embrace. Rose stuck her arm out to grab Davy on their way out, and the three of them left without saying another word. As they walked, the light of the morning sun was shining down into the crypt, illuminating it for the first time in years, guiding each step on their way out.

When they reached the ground above the crypt, the

cool of dawn had just started to give way for the familiar muggy heat of the rising sun to take over. A purple sky had burned away to billowing clouds hiding the shades of blue that remained. Bald cypress woods covered in Spanish moss and dotted with swaying pines were alive with buzzing cicadas, singing warblers, and a refreshing breeze moving swiftly through the trees. The world had carried on as it always does while they discovered the secrets locked away in the burial vault just beneath their feet. They soaked it all in together for only a few seconds before Davy handed the ancestor's album to Rose. She grabbed it without hesitation, but quickly pushed it over to Cannon after a second thought.

"It's *yours* now," she said.

He grabbed it without saying anything—or even glancing inside—and shoved it into the crook of his arm. Cannon started walking back to the home far in the distance as Rose and Davy watched until his silhouette disappeared into the woods just ahead of them.

"Your family traded the outlaw's gold for black gold; they just kept buying up all the land they could. You've got hundreds of thousands of acres and mineral rights to all of it, you know," Davy finally spoke up. "We're talking more than millions here."

"He was buying her land back," Rose corrected him. "That's what all of this was. There never was some mountain of gold. Just one man's ambition to give her back as much of the land that had been taken as possible and doing so by any means possible. His actions became their children's calling, and their children's children had no choice but to do the same, until one day, it was all taken again. It's just the way it is."

"Might be, but it's all yours now, Rose. You finally found everything you've been after. You found what had been taken from your family and you took it back. It might be some time before the state catches up to all of this, but it's coming to you one way or another."

"So, what are you gonna do now?" Rose interrupted abruptly to change the subject with a serious tone finding its way into her voice.

"I'm still a park ranger," he told her with a sense of belonging returning to his voice, unaware of where she was going with the question. "Don't see myself ever not being one, either."

"I'm sure Caddo Lake could use someone like you."

Davy paused to contemplate what she was trying to tell him, but even so, his mind drifted off to the towering pines of Daingerfield that had once occupied all of his attention not too long ago. The charm of those woods and his old ranch, however lonesome, would always feel like home to him. That would never change, but maybe some other things could.

"What will *you* do?" he asked her instead, breaking through the feelings that were coming back to him.

Rose leaned in carefully—her hands clasped behind her back with her eyes closed—and kissed Davy gently on the cheek. "Why don't you stick around and find out?"

With the words still rolling off her tongue, she turned with a quick twist and went off after her son into the woods ahead. Davy watched as Rose walked away, thinking about his life before meeting the woman who changed everything for him, and he knew right then, he never wanted to go back. The ranger took a step forward, then another, and another.

A new adventure was waiting for him through the tree line on the horizon, and it wasn't worth waiting any longer to get started.

CHAPTER 27

TEN YEARS LATER

The rhythm of hooves against the ground had settled into a steady pace down a long dirt trail. Humidity had found its way into the air again after months of dry heat that made doing anything out in it just a little bit harder. It was a ride that had been taken time and time again, one that this particular horse was all too accustomed to. Cypress trees surrounded either side of the path that led to a clearing just ahead, marking the well-trodden way home.

A calloused hand reached down to gently pat the horse's neck as they rode. "Easy girl," a calming voice followed.

Davy had a full beard, speckled with gray hair and a warm smile underneath, as they rode down the dirt path that led to the long driveway home. He had decided to stay in Caddo Lake a decade ago, but the uniform he wore now had changed with something new carefully stitched on. It was a patch handed down from the National Park Service that read *Chief Ranger* and wearing it had made Davy sit up just a little straighter ever since.

The ride home gave him some silence and time to think, but it was far from forlorn. In fact, he now struggled to remember what being lonely really felt like. That just wasn't his life anymore. When the old mare came around into the clearing, the family's long-beloved log home with a stone chimney attached to the side—alive and back in its prime—stood resilient in the distance. It was reinvigorated by the land-scaping and renovations as of late, but it held a time-less charm that would never fade.

Chief Ranger David "Davy" Patton rode his horse closer to the old home and watched as

Cannon emerged from the wood line to his right with a tall fishing pole leaned over his shoulder. He was more of a man now than ever and he carried himself as such. If not for himself, for the two much younger children who followed close behind him carrying fishing poles twice their size.

Davy allowed a slight smirk to cross his lips from under his beard as he watched the three

of them laughing together. For just a split second, Davy saw flickers of dozens of silhouettes lost in time surrounding their home, watching over the next generation with eternal hope for something greater. Just as he thought he saw an older woman who looked all too familiar lift a hand to wave at him from the front yard, they were all gone in the blink of an eye.

The ranger bounced on his horse just a bit longer down the beaten trail to the front of the

Hunter family log home that had become his own. It didn't take long until he heard the familiar sounds of a vehicle rolling up behind him. The cloud of dust swept up in its arrival covered the SUV that pulled closer and closer in a dizzying swirl. Davy watched, perched up on his saddle with his hands crossed on the horn, as the vehicle with the Nations Heritage & Culture Preservation logo on the door came to a stop a few dozen feet from him.

His eyes squinted against the dust and sun as he watched the SUV. After a few seconds,

the driver side door swung open and Rose stepped confidently out into the front yard, her gaze fixated on Davy. Her long hair reached down her back for the ground as it always had, and her eyes still went right through him every time.

A smile washed over her face, and Davy returned one right back at her.

A LOOK AT BOOK TWO
THREE BULLETS TO THE WIND

BOLD WESTERN THRILLS AND PULSE-POUNDING ACTION.

Cannon Hunter is a man who seemingly has it all. More money than he can spend, a family who would do anything for him, and a career dedicated to protecting what's left of his people. But there's one thing that eludes him—the truth about his father.

After more than a year of chasing one dead end after another, Cannon's search leads him to the Nations Heritage Culture Preservation, which claims to have the answers he's been so desperately seeking. His only lead? The Major James Out West traveling train tour, a spectacular show inspired by Buffalo Bill Cody himself. Bringing real-life gunslingers and cowboys to modern audiences, Major James dazzles crowds with grand historic reenactments. But behind the scenes, the enigmatic showman has darker ambitions—he plans to resurrect an ancient threat from the Wild West to secure his place in history.

To stop the Major's one-way ticket to disaster, Cannon gathers an unlikely team, including breakaway roper Cathay Fields and bullfighter Jim Bob, to pull off the impossible—a modern-day train robbery. As they race against time, Cannon must decide if this journey will finally reveal the truth about his heritage, or if it's just three bullets to the wind.

AVAILABLE FEBRUARY 2025

ABOUT THE AUTHOR

Nicholas Osborn is a second-generation ranch owner and storyteller from the heart of deep East Texas. With a career encompassing everything from entertainment marketing to news journalism over the last decade, he has studied the craft of authentic storytelling and honed his writing throughout the years.

Nicholas's debut series aims to mythologize the pineywoods he grew up in and welcome readers to a new chapter of modern Westerns, born of the tall tales that helped shape the genre. His writing is inspired by the history of the Lone Star State, the greater United States, and the larger-than-life heroes, gunslingers, and "black hats" that gave us the myth of the west we know and love today.

Nicholas is an owner at his family's limousin cattle ranch and first-time father with his wife of over ten years at their cottage home in Carthage, Texas. As one of multiple generations of his family working on the Red Rock Limousin Ranch, Nicholas has put his experience into words as an author with a passion to keep timeless Western culture alive and thriving for today's readers.

f 　◯ 　X